Flip Your Wig

"Masterful...A historically rich mystery with a delectable noir touch."

—*Kirkus Reviews*

"A '60s-set procedural that's both gritty and amusing... Chaney finds room in the fog for the older spirits of Philip Marlowe and Sam Spade."

—*Booklife / Publishers Weekly*

The Ragged End of Nowhere

"The novel shifts from edgy noir into history and derring-do. A wildly entertaining tale."

—*Booklist*

"A smart new take on a classic genre. If you think you've read the last word on Las Vegas, then you should check out *The Ragged End of Nowhere*."

—Don Winslow, author of City on Fire *and* Savages

"One of the most polished and assured first crime novels I've ever read."

—Jason Starr, author of Cold Caller *and* Panic Attack

"A zinger of a cliff-hanger."

—*Library Journal*

"This action-packed plot zips from beautiful but crooked antique dealers to local crime czars to tough-as-nails Foreign Legionnaires. The gritty plot, mixed with some dashes of humor, make this an entertaining read."

—*Deadly Pleasures*

"A spectacular debut. (An) intricate and intense crime thriller, detailed with gritty characterization and a fast-moving plot. Top-rate."

—*Fresh Fiction*

"A page-turning thriller that deservedly won the Tony Hillerman Prize."

—*Minneapolis Star-Tribune*

"Even as he evokes classic hardboiled novels like *The Maltese Falcon* and *I, The Jury*, Chaney makes the material his own, adding artistic flourishes and offbeat humor."

—*Mystery Scene*

Seven Times Dead

"A fast-paced novel with plenty of white-knuckle suspense and intrigue."

—*Library Journal*

"Pure noir. Readers will be reminded of Hitchcock's *North by Northwest*."

—*Booklist*

"A Kafkaesque tale."

—*Publishers Weekly*

By the same author

Seven Times Dead
The Ragged End of Nowhere

FLIP YOUR WIG

A NOVEL

ROY CHANEY

Fingerprint File

This is a work of fiction. All of the characters, organizations, and events portrayed in this novel are either products of the author's imagination or are used fictitiously.

A FINGERPRINT FILE BOOK.

FLIP YOUR WIG. Copyright © 2019, 2022 by Roy Chaney. All rights reserved. Printed in the United States of America. For information contact Fingerprint File Books at Correspondence@FingerprintFileBooks.com or FingerprintFileBooks@gmail.com.

Design: Podunk Graphics
Author photo: Janet Rider

ISBN 978-1-7375406-1-8 (hbk)
ISBN 978-1-7375406-0-1 (pbk)
ISBN 978-1-7375406-2-5 (ebook)

Library of Congress Control Number: 2021922861

For Dean Chaney

One

A BLACK VEIL of flies hung in the air. The corpse lay supine on a green vinyl sofa. Inspector Henry Nash pressed a white handkerchief to his nose.

The stench of decay burned his nostrils.

Dried blood smeared the sofa cushions. The victim—male, Caucasian—was dressed in tan chinos, a blue and brown madras shirt. A toy store Halloween mask covered his face. What was left of the victim's eyes under the plastic mask was long past recognizing a trick or a treat.

Nash's stomach churned. He sometimes wondered if he was just a garbage man, sent into dark maggoty rooms to clean out the leftovers of life and death, send it to the refuse heap. Like the garbage scows dumping trash into San Francisco Bay. It was easy to imagine sometimes, the scows loaded with the corpses the San Francisco Police Department scraped off the streets.

Six feet from Nash a row of four Halloween masks hung on

the apartment wall. Nash recognized Doctor Frankenstein's monster, and Casper the friendly ghost. Between the third and fourth masks was a bare nail where the mask on the victim's face had presumably hung.

Nash glanced at his partner, Inspector Ross Belcher. Belcher also held a wadded handkerchief to breathe through.

"The thing about death is, everybody talks about it but no one does anything," Belcher said. The crooked expression behind the handkerchief might have been a smile.

Belcher had said the same thing twenty minutes before. He and Nash, travelling southbound through the Mission District in an unmarked SFPD Ford Fairlane sedan, punching the clock. It was 1240 hours. Belcher drove. They'd just eaten lunch at the Wienie King Restaurant, on Eighth Street.

The police radio crackled. Code 10-54—*unidentified dead body*. The 100 block of Clipper Street.

Belcher and Nash had just passed Clipper.

Belcher was an imposing man with a head like a cement block. He was a full inspector, nineteen years on the force, while Nash was a newly-minted assistant inspector. Belcher had the experience on the job, in every way that counted, and his $903 monthly paycheck trumped Nash's by $72 bucks. Even so, Nash knew there was no good reason why two inspectors from the Homicide Detail should respond to a routine call for assistance from a harness bull.

Except that Belcher was bored.

At the intersection of Church and Army Streets Belcher spun the steering wheel. The sedan slid into a tight U-turn, and Belcher made his comment on death and doing something about it.

The remark had reminded Nash of a photograph he'd seen that morning, in the *Chronicle*. A ball of flame, erupting around the seated figure of a Buddhist monk in the South Vietnamese city of

Hue. The monk soaking his robes in gasoline and striking a match to protest the policies of South Vietnam's military government. The accompanying news story noted that the gasoline used was high octane, emphasizing that the monk had gone the extra mile to achieve his goal.

For whatever good it did him, or South Vietnam.

On Clipper, Belcher pulled up behind a Harley-Davidson Electra Glide motorcycle with SFPD markings. A woman wearing horn-rimmed glasses and a soiled blue house-dress met Belcher and Nash on the sidewalk. The apartment house behind her was two-tone brown. The cat she clutched to her bosom was black and white.

Nash flipped his leather ID wallet open to reveal the seven-point star—the SFPD joy buzzer.

The woman was rattled. She was the landlady at the apartment house. Fifteen minutes ago she'd gone to the fourth floor to check on a resident who owed back rent. She entered the apartment with a pass key, found a bloodied corpse on a bloodied sofa.

"I came outside for air," the woman said. "The officer"—she pointed to the motorcycle at the curb—"rode by and I flagged him down. He went upstairs and came back down. Then he used his radio and went back upstairs again. I heard a gunshot—just a minute ago."

It was apartment 406—Nash took the stairs at a run. Belcher jogged around to the back of the building to cover the rear fire escape. On the second-floor landing Nash nearly stumbled over a wicker basket full of wadded gift box ribbon. It sat in a shaft of sunlight where the apartment manager's cat no doubt slept. Nash slid the Colt .38 revolver from the holster under his sport coat and continued up the stairs.

A dead body. A gunshot.

The patrolman didn't reappear.

Nash didn't see a great many things those facts could mean. The few things that came to mind didn't look rosy.

Nash reached the fourth floor. He raised the revolver, moved forward cautiously. The silence in the building sounded like stretched nerves just before they snap. The door to apartment 406 stood ajar.

Nash kicked it open the rest of the way.

Followed the door in.

Shadows filled the room beyond. The swinging front door came into contact with something that wasn't a door stop or the wall. Nash jigged to the right, brought the revolver up higher.

"Freeze," Nash said.

The shadows moved.

A bulky figure raised one hand.

The fingers of the other hand were pinching his nostrils closed.

"Snodgrass," the figure said. "Traffic Enforcement."

It was the motorcycle cop. His voice was nasal. And muffled, understandably. The patrolman was standing behind the door when Nash kicked it open.

The acrid smell of burned gunpowder hung in the room. It was mixed with a stronger smell that was putrid and unmistakable—the smell of a stale corpse.

Nash heard a sharp noise.

He turned quickly. Raised his revolver again.

The patrolman reached for his own sidearm.

Across the room a set of thin curtains billowed in the draft from an open window. A shout, from outside: *"Police officer—freeze."*

Belcher had come up the fire escape. Now he leaned in through the open window, pistol drawn.

"Ross, it's all right," Nash said.

"Traffic," the patrolman said again, louder than he needed to.

His black leather Motor Division jacket creaked as he holstered his sidearm. Belcher pushed the billowing curtains aside, ducked his head, climbed over the window sill. When he caught the smell of death he pointed his revolver in the direction of the sofa, feeling a renewed interest in protecting himself.

Nash had just spotted the corpse too.

Nash found a switch near the front door and turned on the ceiling light.

The apartment was littered with trash, and house-hold furnishings that looked like trash. Nash removed his handkerchief from his pocket, held it to his nose. Belcher had already pulled out a handkerchief.

Belcher kneeled beside the corpse.

"Hot diggity," Belcher said, stone-faced. "Business is picking up."

Judging from the skin on the victim's hands and arms, he was not an older man. Maybe not middle-aged. Dried blood covered the victim's neck and upper torso. Blood also matted the thick black hair on the victim's head.

The Halloween mask on the victim's face was a depiction of a white male. The mask face also had a mop of black hair. Along with a bulbous nose and a dopey grin. A thin elastic band was tied to small holes on either side of the mask, but the elastic wasn't holding the mask in place. Dried blood had affixed the mask to the dead man.

Belcher lifted the victim's left arm. Moved it experimentally. The arm muscles were flaccid.

Rigor mortis had come and gone.

Belcher let the arm drop. He remarked that there was no discernible pattern to the blood smears on the sofa cushions.

"I found the victim on the couch," the patrolman said. He didn't let go of his nose. "I went downstairs to call for back up.

When I came back to secure the premises, I heard a crash."

The patrolman motioned toward a bookcase standing near a coat closet. Scattered on the floor were three photograph frames and shards of broken glass. An oblong patch of plaster was missing from the wall above the bookcase.

"I had my sidearm out when I turned," the patrolman said. "The noise could've been anything. It startled me. I discharged my weapon."

Nash slapped at flies on the back of his neck. "What happened to the pictures?"

The patrolman paused. His explanation was getting poorer by the second. "There was a cat. On the bookcase. This building is lousy with cats. I suppose I'll have to turn my weapon in."

Nash agreed. It was standard procedure within the department to perform an administrative review whenever a firearm was discharged in the line of duty. SFPD wanted to confirm that the weapon was fired, and how many times, and who did the firing, and how many grains of gunpowder had been expended. The event had to be scrutinized, dissected, notated, indexed, spindled. Maybe someone at the Hall of Justice was interested in comparing this particular gun shot to other instances of patrolmen shooting at domesticated animals of roughly ten pounds.

Belcher, breathing through his mouth, scribbled observations about the corpse and its *milieu* in his notebook. He'd stuffed his handkerchief loosely in his mouth to keep from swallowing flies. Nash was grateful for the open window. The stench in the room would have paralyzed all three of them without the draft from outdoors.

The floor of the dead man's apartment was littered with newspapers and empty beer cans, food wrappers, wadded pieces of clothing. The surface of the square Formica-topped table near the kitchenette was littered with more empty beer cans, some of which had been used as ashtrays. In Nash's estimation the one ashtray on the table had been used most recently as a bowl to eat cold cereal from, judging from the dried-out corn flakes stuck to the inside surface.

"There's not much in the bedroom except a mattress and dirty clothes," the patrolman said. His voice sounded weaker now. He gulped air, pinched his nostrils more tightly together. When the patrol-man had his queasy stomach under control again he pointed at the mask on the victim's face. "If it helps, I think it's a Beatle. Those masks were popular, last Halloween. They came with a tiny plastic guitar. My nephew had one."

Nash made no comment. He didn't know much about the English musical group that called themselves the Beatles. He'd heard of them though—it would've been difficult not to. They were all over the radio and television and in movie theaters. A few days ago he'd seen on the news that the Beatles had performed in Memphis, Tennessee, where the Klu Klux Klan burned Beatles records in the street outside the venue. The Klan was protesting a remark one of the Beatles recently made, something to the effect that the group was now more popular than Jesus Christ.

Nash recalled that the Beatles had played a concert at Candlestick Park the year before. They were returning to San Francisco to play at Candlestick again, in a few days.

Nash watched as Belcher tried to lift the Halloween mask off the dead man's face with the tip of one finger. The dried blood holding the mask in place had excellent adhesive properties. Belcher pulled the handkerchief out of his mouth, sighed. He pressed the saliva-damp handkerchief to his nose again.

"Patrolman," Belcher said, over his shoulder, "how about going downstairs and calling for the Crime Lab. We need a print man, a photographer, all the rest of the hocus-pocus." Belcher pushed his straw porkpie hat back off his forehead. "We also need a morgue wagon and a gallon of bug juice. The requesting inspector is R. Belcher, Homicide Detail."

There was no response.

Belcher and Nash both turned in time to see Patrolman Snodgrass of Traffic Enforcement bend forward and regurgitate his most recent meal onto the hardwood floor.

Nash grimaced.

The entry Belcher wrote in his notebook referenced a semicircular vomit pool, roughly 24 by 30 inches. It rested near the eastern wall of the living room, and it was assuredly not left by the victim or persons related to the crime.

Two

NASH HAD PAGED through the *Chronicle* when he arrived at the Hall of Justice on Kearny Street that morning. Chewed his fourth and fifth aspirin by the time he reached the sports page.

The aspirin did little to stop the tire iron pounding against the soft membrane inside Nash's skull.

Nash spent the previous night drinking Lucky Lager beer at the Penalty Box Tavern in the Sunset District. Then he went home to drink bourbon and watch television until the test pattern came on.

Nash was familiar with tire irons.

The front of Nash's war surplus desk abutted the front of Belcher's desk in the open bay-style room—Room 454—that housed a large number of inspectors, most of them assigned to Homicide, or Sex Crimes. Often Nash looked up from the paperwork on his desk to see Belcher sitting in exactly the same position as Nash, doing exactly the same thing. Only with a harder look, and badly discolored teeth.

Presently the pounding in Nash's head took on the characteristics of Belcher's voice.

"The old man wants to squawk at us," Belcher said.

Lieutenant Samuel Dark was the inspector-in-charge of the Homicide Detail, a wiry man with a flattop haircut. He'd lost one arm, from above the elbow, in World War II. Now he used a prosthetic limb with a metal split-hook device at the end. Lieutenant Dark didn't smile much. When he did, it wasn't a positive development.

Nash and Belcher sat in Dark's office on wooden chairs. An electric fan recirculated the cigar and cigarette smoke.

"Here's the rub," Dark said. "A citizen called in twice yesterday. Zero three-hundred hours, the first time. She sounded half sober and reported a murder she claimed to have knowledge of. She said it occurred just before midnight in an alley behind one of the topless dives on Broadway"—Dark squinted at the carbon copy of the typed phone call record—"the Kimono à Go-Go. The woman hung up without leaving her name.

"Archie Pyle talked to her the second time she called, at zero seven-fifty hours. She was stinko by then. Archie managed to get a name and address out of her. He also says she propositioned him in a semi-explicit manner. Pyle got the complainant to admit she doesn't know who got killed, or who did the killing, or what the hell any of it means.

"Pyle chalked her up as a soused crank. I think she chalks up the same way, but we've got to keep our books in order. Find out what this woman's beef is. She might be a kook or a dipso, but even a dipso kook finds an acorn once in a while."

That was the long and the short of it.

On the way back to his desk Nash paused to check the Homicide Detail bulletin board for new notices. Thumbtacked in a place of honor at the top of the board was a one-frame cartoon clipped from the pages of *Rogue* magazine.

The cartoon depicted two Edgar Poe-style ravens chatting over martinis at a swank party. One of the ravens remarking, offhand: "The thing about death is, everyone talks about it but no one ever does anything."

Droll, Nash had always thought. But not *haw-haw* funny.

THE WOMAN'S name was Pearly Spence. Spence worked as a hostess at the North Beach establishment in question—the Kimono à Go-Go. Nash studied the details carboned onto the square of card stock as he and Belcher drove out to the woman's residence on Twenty-First Avenue, in the Richmond District.

The complainant stated that she was in a storeroom at the back of the club when she heard a scream, outside. She ran out the back door, saw a man lying motionless at the far end of the alley. She also glimpsed a tan-colored delivery truck, make and model unknown, speeding out of the alley.

Miss Spence didn't approach the man lying in the alley, and she couldn't see the man well from where she stood.

Still, she felt certain he was dead, or dying.

The complainant stated that she didn't immediately report what she'd seen because she was afraid. The tan-colored delivery truck she'd seen belonged to a man named Jasper Rollo. Rollo was, according to Spence, the owner of the Kimono à Go-Go.

Because of the holes in the drunk woman's story—holes like who and why and how—Nash wondered if Spence was trying to throw police trouble at her boss to settle a score. Maybe he'd short-changed her on wages, or grabbed her rear end too often. Citizens called SFPD every day with tall stories created from anger or spite or whole cloth. It assuaged their sense of having been wronged by the world at large.

The house on Twenty-First was a death trap with pretensions. The bouquet of cracks covering the stucco facade was earthquake damage, Nash was sure.

The stairs leading up to the front door canted worryingly to the right. A portly woman in a pink muumuu answered the door bell. When Nash asked for Pearly Spence, the woman directed Nash and Belcher back down the stairs, to a plain wooden door in a wall that sealed off what had once been a garage.

"She rents from me," the woman said. "Is she in trouble again?"

"What trouble was she in before?" Belcher said.

The woman's eyes became wrinkled slits in the larger wrinkled landscape of her face. "Men come and go down there. Men of little means. There have been drinking parties, sometimes late at night. Who knows what else."

Nash didn't credit the woman's aspersions. San Francisco was a city full of shifty-looking men of little means. Some of them were genuinely destitute. The rest of them, one presumed, were poets or painters or musicians. The common assumption was that Frisco was full of artistic geniuses working as parking lot attendants, when it wasn't the other way around.

The woman who answered Nash's knock downstairs struck a surly pose in the doorway. She wore tight green corduroy pants and an oversized man's shirt, rolled once or twice at the bottom, tied in a knot above her navel.

Her blonde hair came from a bottle.

So did her puffy face and bleary eyes.

"Relax, Pops," the woman said, when Belcher explained the reason for the visit. "I had too much to drink, that's all. When that happens, I get squishy. I want attention. So I pick up the phone and call people I know. When I run out of those, I call people I don't know. I'm a candidate for a rubber room." The woman raised her chin. "Ask my shrink."

"Miss, we're not interested in where your potty training went wrong," Belcher said. "But you told a story to a police inspector yesterday that kind of makes us wonder where you got it."

Nash watched the woman's off-kilter smile turn darker. The woman confirmed that she worked at the Kimono. A man named Jasper Rollo was her boss, and he did own a tan delivery truck. "But the rest of it was hokum," she said. "From the depths of my addled soul."

Belcher asked the woman for ID. She stepped away from the doorway and Nash got a good look at the interior of the former garage. It was a studio set-up, with a breakfast counter and a bathroom toward the back. The centerpiece of the room was a long sofa with discolored flower-print cushions.

A coffee table sat in front of the sofa. A large pile of sculpting clay rested in the center of a sheet of canvas draped over the table. Fist-sized indentations had been punched into the mound of clay, from every angle.

The woman's faded California driver's license recorded a March 1935 date of birth. Thirty-one years old. The name was *Spence, Pearl Emily*. The listed address was on Tiny Street, in Milpitas.

"People call me Pearly."

Belcher nodded absently. "That's swell."

Belcher filled copious pages of his notebook with chicken scratch as he walked the woman through her story. Two nights previous, she'd gotten off work at the Kimono à Go-Go in a bad mood. She came home and poured herself a drink. One drink turned into five or six drinks. The next thing she knew she had the telephone receiver in her hand.

"I had the heebie-jeebies," the woman said. "I wanted to

scream. The voice on the phone said he was a cop. I wanted him to stay on the line, so I decided I'd better sing in the key of pig."

Belcher said, "What else do you use to get high, Miss?"

The woman gave Belcher a withering look. "Dig yourself."

THE KIMONO à Go-Go was located on Broadway, between Columbus and Kearny. Next door to a coffee shop that ran Tuesday specials on patty melts and a shoe box-sized film theater that ran foreign films about nudist colonies.

Belcher and Nash inspected the alley behind the nightclub, then walked around to the front.

A sign at the entrance promised WALL TO WALL GIRLS—GIRLS—GIRLS!

Inside the club there were no girls wall to wall, none in triplicate. There was one girl. Standing in a glassed-in booth on a raised platform, at one end of the long room where middle-aged men in business suits huddled around cocktail tables, drinking lunch from martini glasses.

A cabinet with a record turntable on top stood next to the girl in the booth. The red wall behind her was covered with oversized Japanese ideograms painted in yellow. The girl wore the lower half of a fringed bikini outfit with her white go-go boots. Where the upper half of the bikini should have been was a horizontal stripe of pale skin across bare breasts. The girl's auburn hair, stacked in a tenuous beehive arrangement, wobbled as she danced to the pop music crackling from the public address system. The dance might have been the Hully Gully or the Frug, the Watusi or the Hip-O-Crit—Nash couldn't recognize one popular dance from another. But he recognized boredom when he saw it in the girl's expression.

"What's the cover charge in this place?" Belcher said.

"Whatever it is, it's too much."

Soft green lighting gave the room an aquatic feel. Tasseled oriental lanterns hung over the wooden bar like orange moons. In the break between songs, a balding patron picked up one of the red telephones that rested in the center of each table. The dancing girl on the platform answered on a phone of her own.

A record was requested.

The stylus dropped onto a fresh 45 rpm platter.

The girl resumed her hopeless dancing.

Belcher asked the bartender where Jasper Rollo might be found. Shortly, a primped man in a tight vest and black hair combed into a pompadour appeared.

The man introduced himself as Emil Vermes. He was the club's manager.

"How can I assist you?" Vermes said. The words were coated with a foreign accent that Nash couldn't place. Belcher waved his badge while Nash asked Vermes what he knew about a fight that occurred in the alley, on Saturday night.

"I am not aware of this." Vermes poked his chin with his finger to mime deep thought. "Let me see when Mister Rollo is arriving. Please wait for only one moment." When the manager returned from the kitchen, he clasped his hands together joyfully. "Mister Rollo is not here today, but I am pleased to say that he is available to you at his home."

Vermes offered up a scrap of notepaper. An address and phone number scribbled on it.

Rollo lived in the Diamond Heights neighborhood.

Belcher and Nash had eaten lunch and were driving southbound through the Mission District when Nash said, "Where do you think that Vermes joker came from?" Belcher didn't consider the question for too long. "As near as I can tell, he crawled out of his own ass."

A moment later Belcher and Nash caught the radio call for backup on Clipper Street, where a dead man lay in a dark apartment wearing a Halloween mask pasted to his face with blood.

Three

NASH GREW UP in southern Oregon. But he was born in San Francisco, spent his earliest years there. Nash's most vivid memory from that time involved sitting at a wooden table with his father. It was a square table, in a small apartment. The sun shining through a grime-covered window.

Nash was five, six years old.

A revolver lay on the table. It had broken grips, a long barrel. Nash's father sat very still. Staring at the revolver. While shouting policemen in the hallway pounded on the locked apartment door.

They sounded angry.

That was all Nash remembered. He never learned what happened next. His father died in January 1944, somewhere on the Anzio beachhead in Italy, before he could explain the revolver episode to Nash. In later years, when Nash asked his mother about it, her only response was, "If you find yourself in Frisco, watch out for relatives."

In the five years that he'd been back in San Francisco, Nash hadn't run into any relations. But as Nash stood in the dead man's apartment on Clipper Street he was reminded of the square wooden table, the revolver with broken grips. He wasn't sure why. Maybe it was only the play of sunlight, filtered through dirty windows.

The memory didn't help Nash understand the oddball appearance of the Clipper Street pad.

The floorboards in the dead man's apartment were painted in red and green stripes. Nash saw lumps where the paint covered things that weren't part of the floor—cigarette butts, clumps of lint, a piece of shoelace. And yet, the stripes had been painted with care. The edges were straight. The paint had been applied evenly.

Nash also noted the numerous seven-inch 45 rpm and 12-inch LP records, separated from their sleeves and scattered throughout the apartment. Nash didn't see a record player. There also wasn't a tape recorder, but there were a dozen or so square boxes lying around that had once contained reels of recording tape.

In the bedroom, Nash found a battered amplifier for an electric guitar. The speaker cone had been slashed violently with a knife. Nash also found a checkerboard neatly arranged with chicken bones and bottle caps.

Belcher shouted from the living room. He'd discovered a brass candlestick holder with an oriental design. The holder weighed five or six pounds. What the tourists bought in Chinatown. No doubt, with a fair swing it could crush the back of a man's head.

The blood and hair pasted to the base of the holder settled the question. But the blow or blows to the victim's noodle hadn't put him down immediately. He'd made it to the couch.

Lay there long enough to smear blood over the cushions and himself before he died.

Unless a different pair of hands did it for him.

Technicians from the SFPD Mobile Crime Lab Unit arrived. Potential evidence was collected and bagged. Fingerprints were examined and brushed. Lifted onto cards. Everything was a piece of the puzzle, as Nash well knew. But he also knew that a crime scene didn't represent one puzzle, but two or three or several. None of the puzzles would form a complete picture, and when SFPD was through with the case there would be many puzzle pieces left over.

It was just how the game was played.

A name and phone number were found on a scrap of paper in the victim's pants pocket. As best as Nash could make out, the name was *Tina Gone*. The scribbled note was dropped into the same clear plastic bag as the victim's wallet, which had yielded an expired California driver's license and one condom in the manufacturer's wrapper.

The license bore the name *Gomez, Danilo Alonzo*. There was a Hayward address, a May 1944 birthdate.

It was a Crime Lab technician who discovered the crumpled letter dated ten days previously. Addressed to Gomez at the Clipper Street pad. It was from the President of the United States, by way of the Selective Service System. It began: "Greetings." The letter informed the murdered man that he was "ordered for induction into the Armed Forces." Gomez was directed to report to the Oakland Army Depot, the following week.

He'd been drafted.

Nash mused that at least the dead man didn't need to worry about getting zapped in Vietnam. Danilo Gomez had already earned his body bag.

The medical examiner arrived to oversee the removal of the corpse. It was the ME's opinion that, given the ambient temperature, and a scenario that assumed the victim died on the couch rather than dying elsewhere and being moved to the couch, the victim had been dead for 48 to 72 hours. Belcher and Nash weren't impressed—they'd already guessed roughly the same thing. So had the pointy-heads from the Crime Lab.

Belcher returned to the Hall of Justice. Nash stayed behind to coordinate the search for witnesses. The landlady had already confirmed that the victim was Danilo Gomez. Gomez had once told her that he played guitar in a local rock and roll act called the Subterraneans. According to other tenants at the apartment house, the victim kept to himself mostly. But he routinely played his radio at a high volume.

Nash and three patrolmen canvased the houses and apartment buildings around the 100 block of Clipper. Outside of one house, Nash encountered a young man changing the spark plugs in a Studebaker station wagon.

Inside the car a disc jockey emoted over the dashboard radio: *"Your Emperor of rock and roll is holding in his hot little hands two tickets to the big Beatles bash on Monday night at Candlestick Park. I will bestow these tickets upon the first of my loyal subjects who calls in with the answer to this hour's Beatles Mystery Question: 'How many rings does Ringo wear?'"*

The song that followed sounded lukewarm and flat. The mention of the Beatles reminded Nash of the plastic Halloween mask on the victim's face, and what Patrolman Snodgrass had said about it.

"This is a quiet street mostly," the young man working on the Studebaker told Nash. He pointed to the victim's apartment house down the street. "Someone down there plays his radio loud, but I don't have a hang-up about it."

NASH ARRIVED at the Hall of Justice just as Belcher was leaving for the day. Belcher had run the victim's ID through Records. "He picked up a Six-four-seven back in May," Belcher said. "Golden Gate Park. He gave a patrolman some lip and got cuffed. He spent the night in the Park Station tank. The address he gave was the Clipper Street location. No other incidents."

California penal code 647(f)—*public menace/ drunkenness.* The collar didn't tell Nash much. Once the morgue was finished with the corpse SFPD would, as a matter of routine, send the ID and fingerprints to the California Bureau of Criminal Identification and Information in Sacramento for a "yellow sheet." It would provide a detailed account of the victim's criminal history outside of the San Francisco Bay area, if there was one.

Belcher had one further item of note.

"The ring-in line logged two calls from a man named Pinkrose, Max W. He claims to be a business associate of the victim. Both calls came in yesterday. This Pinkrose was concerned about the victim's welfare because the victim hadn't shown up for business obligations. Pinkrose gave the victim's name as Danny Gomez, *aka* Danny O'Day. Pinkrose requested an officer visit." Belcher shrugged. He hadn't found a record of an SFPD health and safety check at the Clipper Street address. Not that it would have made a difference. Twenty-four hours ago the victim was already dead.

Belcher set the ring-in card with Pinkrose's address and phone number on Nash's desk. It was past six o'clock, Belcher had to get home and change clothes. He and Estelle, his wife, were attending a patio barbeque in Martinez. "Estelle's cousin and his family," Belcher said. "He waters down the booze to make it go farther. Last time we went there I took my own scotch and he watered that down too. Sonofabitch."

Nash had seen Belcher in action at barbeques and patio parties. Belcher plucking at his ukulele, in between glasses of scotch on the rocks and reminiscences about his Navy service in the South Pacific during the war. When Belcher began to drunkenly fumble the chords to "My Little Grass Hut in Kealakekua," Nash knew it was time to make his exit.

NASH STEPPED out and bought a roast beef with Swiss on rye at the Swing-In Coffee Shop down the block. He brought it back to the Hall of Justice, ate the sandwich at his desk, with a can of Cragmont soda pop he stabbed holes into with a letter opener because he couldn't find a church key.

Nash studied a month-old *Newsweek* magazine while he ate. He read an article about how dogs pick up vibrations in the air that communicate good feelings. And another one, about a World War II-era Japanese soldier who was discovered recently on an island in Indonesia.

The soldier had been a lieutenant in Emperor Hirohito's Imperial Army. He was stationed on Morotai Island, in the Moluccas, when American and Australian forces stormed ashore there in September 1944.

The lieutenant and five of his men were pushed back, deep into the jungle. But they continued to fight. Soon the lieutenant found himself alone, with only his Arisaka rifle, a captured US Army-issue machete, and a dagger that his father had once given him.

For twenty-two years the lieutenant led a primitive existence in the hills of Morotai. He was apprehended by visiting US Army and Navy personnel in June, but not before killing an Army military policeman with the dagger.

Nash studied the photograph that accompanied the article. The lieutenant looked rail thin and bone weary as he was escorted by two Army MPs to a tribunal in Honolulu. Nash saw pride and defiance too, in the old soldier's eyes.

It was an odd story, but not unheard of, Nash knew. The South Pacific was full of remote islands where Japanese soldiers were left behind when the Japanese Imperial Army retreated. A fair number of those soldiers had surrendered by the mid-1950s, but every so often another one turned up.

The *Newsweek* article reminded Nash of a story Belcher had told him once.

From Belcher's time in the Solomon Islands, during the war.

A Navy pilot crash-landed on an uninhabited island northeast of Bougainville. The island was covered in dense foliage, and the wreckage of the flier's plane couldn't be located. Belcher and others had flown over the island in a US Navy Catalina seaplane, pouring baskets of tennis balls out the door.

Written on each ball was the message: WAVE A PIECE OF CLOTHING.

The Navy pilot was never found. The story, in the telling, amused and saddened Belcher in equal proportions. Nash tried to imagine what the Japanese soldier in the *Newsweek* article would have made of tennis balls falling in torrents from the sky.

Nash finished his sandwich and consulted his notebook.

He'd written down two telephone numbers earlier. One number was transcribed from the note found in the deceased Danilo Gomez's shirt pocket. The other came from Emil Vermes at the Kimono à Go-Go. To these two numbers he added the phone number left by Max Pinkrose, the "business associate."

Nash picked up the telephone and dialed.

There was no answer at Pinkrose's number.

Nash dialed the second number, got a young woman who

worked for the Janus Answering Service. Miss Tina Gone was a subscriber to the service, and Nash duly left a message for her.

Nash dialed the third number.

A young woman answered that telephone too.

She told Nash in a thin flat voice that Jasper Rollo was floating face down in the swimming pool. He'd been doing it for quite some time.

Four

NASH STOOD ON the sky-blue tiles at the edge of the swimming pool. A man was indeed floating face down on the calm surface of the pool. Just as the young woman Nash spoke to earlier on the telephone had said.

The man's chest rested on an inflatable cushion that kept him afloat. His arms and legs hung submerged in the water. The back of the head and the rubber strap of the diving mask and the yellow tube of the snorkel didn't move. The sun-reddened skin on the man's shoulders and back nearly matched the red stripes on his swimming trunks.

Nash couldn't imagine what was so interesting about the bottom of the pool.

Twenty yards away, beyond a row of Japanese maple trees, stood Jasper Rollo's ranch-style house. A hi-fi setup in the basement room beyond the open sliding glass doors played East Indian music. It buzzed in Nash's ears like coppery honeybees.

A sudden breeze sent a multi-colored beach ball scudding across the surface of the pool. The ball came to rest at the edge. Nash plucked it from the water. Took aim. Threw the ball.

It bounced off the floating man's back.

Startled arms and legs beat the water.

The man rolled. Got his legs under him, his feet on the bottom of the pool. He stood with his shoulders and head above water. Pulled off the mask and snorkel apparatus. He pushed wet hair off his forehead. A heavy moustache hung over his upper lip.

A sunburned walrus.

"What are you doing on my patio?" the man said.

Nash introduced himself, raised the SFPD joy buzzer. The seven-point lawman's star didn't shine when it caught the light, continued looking dull and scratched. Nash hadn't spoken directly to Jasper Rollo when he'd called earlier. Apparently, the girl who answered the telephone hadn't relayed Nash's message accurately.

"The young lady inside the house said I'd find you out here," Nash said.

"She didn't mention a policeman."

Nash shrugged. He assumed that the teenage girl in tight-fitting white shorts who answered the doorbell when Nash rang had gone back to painting her toenails and watching *The Dating Game* on television. She was buxom and tanned. Her eyes looked drowsy and red-rimmed.

A small child, maybe two years old, dressed in green, had waved its arms at Nash from inside a playpen made of white cord crosshatched on a metal frame. The child might have belonged to the teenage girl, but Nash doubted it. The girl's eyes might have been red from crying or lack of sleep, but Nash doubted that too. In an ashtray on an end table, Nash had noticed clumps of ash and half burned bits of paper that he was sure hadn't come from a tobacco cigarette.

Nash took a seat on the end of a poolside chaise lounge. "What's taking place at the bottom of the pool?"

Rollo pushed through the water to the edge of the pool. He tossed the mask and snorkel onto the tiles.

"Nothing is taking place at the bottom of the pool," Rollo said. "That's the point. Depriving oneself of sensory input from the eyes and ears and nose, and the senses of touch and taste, frees the mind of all of the useless clutter of everyday life. Car horns and commercial jingles and synthetic food and synthetic tax men. All the rest of the plastic world.

"If you can block out that clutter, it frees a person to think clearly. And clear thinking is the path to self-awareness, and higher knowledge. So, it's not about the pool. Not about the snorkel. It's about my experience as a human being."

Nash remained silent for a beat. Then, "You don't say." Self-awareness? Nash was aware of himself enough to know that he was a poorly paid cop with sore feet. And that he spent a fair amount of his time listening to blustery citizens who existed on the cusp of fatheadedness.

Nash watched Rollo turn his head, cup his hand over his nose. Rollo blew hard through his nostrils, to rid them of mucous and chlorinated pool water. For a moment Rollo studied with interest what had collected in the palm of his hand. As though reading his future. Then he gave Nash a dubious look.

Maybe the mucous signs weren't good.

"Why are you here, Inspector?" Rollo said.

Without divulging Pearly Spence's name or going into great detail, Nash explained there had been a report of a fight in the alley behind the Kimono à Go-Go, the previous Monday night. Rollo's delivery truck was spotted at the scene.

Rollo raised his face to the sky, maybe asking a deity for

patience. "I do own a delivery truck—a 'Forty-nine GMC. Bought it from a butcher shop in Pinole, it still has the name of the shop on the panels. Right now it's on loan to a friend who needs wheels to move house. As for a fight at my club, I was there that night. There was no funny business in the alley, or anywhere else. Who reported this fairy story to you?"

Nash ignored the question. "Who did you loan the truck to, Mister Rollo, and when did you loan it?"

"Inspector, I haven't broken the law. And I try not to involve myself in the petty squabbles of life. So you'll excuse me if I don't answer your questions. As a Sufi wise man once said: 'Voices make up the winds of time, but the winds of time listen to none of them.'"

Nash leaned forward on the chaise lounge. Rested his elbows on his knees. "I don't know about the winds of time, Mister Rollo, but I'm guessing you neighbors are getting tired of listening to your hi-fi."

"My neighbors don't hear much, Inspector. But music, since you've raised the topic, is also a path to enlightenment. It helps to expand the collective consciousness. It brings us closer to the divine unity of the universe that we call love." Rollo fixed Nash with a crafty smile.

"So we should all turn up our hi-fi's and buy snorkels and splash around in your pool?"

"You could do worse."

"It's going to be a crowded pool."

Rollo hoisted a leg onto the tiles. Climbed out of the pool. His wide torso and large stomach were supported on spindle legs. Rollo picked up a white towel from the lounge chair next to where Nash sat, wiped his face and hair.

Nash got to his feet slowly, meeting Rollo's gaze on a level plane. "By the way, I met your young friend in the living room on the way in. Who did you say she was?"

Rollo draped the towel around his neck. "I didn't say."

"Have a talk with her. If she's smoking grass in the house, you're in a spot too. This is your house."

"I have no idea what you mean, Inspector."

"If she's underage, that's a whole other can of worms."

Rollo gripped the ends of the towel more tightly.

"All right, Inspector. I loaned the delivery truck to one of my employees. Her name is Pearly Spence."

Nash was surprised to hear that name, but he didn't let on. "Why did she need the truck?"

"To move furniture—as I've said. She's pulling up stakes and moving north. Up to Marin, or Sonoma County. I loaned her the truck last week. I haven't seen it, or her, since. I expect that she'll be returning the truck tomorrow, but I'm not worried about it. I don't often use the truck anymore."

Pearly Spence reported a violent crime involving a tan-colored truck that she was in possession of, but she kept the possession part under wraps when she spoke to Belcher and Nash? Nash wondered if the truck had been banged up or stolen, and Spence was trying to cover up that fact by reporting a cockamamie story to SFPD.

Rollo said that Spence worked for him, on and off. She'd only just returned from a long stay in Los Angeles. She called herself an artist, had a pad in the Richmond neighborhood for the last few months. Rollo often loaned his truck out, he said. To whomever needed it.

"If that's all there is to it, Mister Rollo, why didn't you want to give me her name?"

"I don't wish to get caught up in the tentacles of government intrusion."

"I'll need the license plate number of the truck, and a piece of identification." Nash smiled. "To keep the government octopus fed."

Nash followed Rollo across the lawn. In the basement room Rollo went to the hi-fi console, plucked the tone arm off the LP record on the turntable to stop the music. Cardboard LP covers lay scattered around the hi-fi.

One cover caught Nash's eye.

The picture showed four skeletons standing in a row. They wore tuxedo coats. They held black top hats above their heads in their skeleton hands. Fashionable walking sticks in their other hands. A row of boney Fred Astaires, caught in the middle of a song and dance routine.

The picture was rendered in black and white, like a sketch. But in place of skulls, someone had superimposed photographs of the heads of four smiling young men.

The name of the combo appeared in block letters above the skeletons: THE BEATLES. The name of the LP appeared below the dancing skeleton feet: EIGHT ARMS TO HOLD YOU.

Nash wondered if the cover was supposed to be avant-garde. It looked cheap and comical to him.

Nash recorded the details of Rollo's California driver's license and the tan Chevrolet truck in his notebook. Rollo assured Nash that the name of the truck's previous owner, the Finest Kind Meat and Sausage Company, was painted on the sides of the truck. Hard to miss.

Nash left the house the same way he'd come in. In the living room the young woman in the tight shorts was still perched on the couch, painting her toenails. The small child continued to chirp and burble in its playpen.

Nash wasn't sure, but it seemed to him that the girl was studiously painting the same toenail she'd been working on when he arrived.

Five

CHESTER AURELIUS BOGGS stood in the dusty light of his room at the Sir Francis Drake Hotel on Powell Street, next to Union Square. He adjusted the hang of his new green sport coat and studied his reflection in the mirror.

Boggs was having second thoughts.

Boggs had read in *Playboy* magazine that bold colors were part of the new "Mod" look. The salesman at the Roos-Atkins shop down the street assured him that the coat would look eminently fashionable, combined with the other finery Boggs had purchased. The gray Dacron Sansabelt slacks. The dark brown Florsheim wingtips with buckles. The Arrow shirt with the button-down collar. The extra-wide paisley-pattern neck tie in yellow and Chinese indigo.

But the sport coat troubled Boggs now.

Boggs had been in Brownsville, Texas visiting family when the Old Men called. They wanted him in San Francisco. Right now, or sooner. Boggs left Brownsville so fast he'd hardly had time to shave. Arriving at San Francisco International, Boggs found that TWA had lost his luggage en route.

Boggs had never met the Old Men in person. He wanted to make a good impression. He couldn't turn up in a polo shirt and deck shoes.

Boggs studied his reflection some more. Thirty-six years old. The receding hairline made his prominent forehead look out of proportion to the rest of his face. The diet pills he consumed hadn't stopped the growth of the spare tire that was his gut.

Boggs raised his large fists. Dropped into a fighting stance, like he used to do, for the newspaper pictures when he was a young boxer in El Paso. Boggs knew he still had the fighting instinct. The Old Men knew it too. Boggs could hit the ground running, get the job done, before the other Joes could sort their assholes from their elbows.

Boggs straightened up.

Adjusted the hang of the sport coat again.

He found himself thinking of a Malaysian man he'd caught up with in Bangkok, Thailand.

Lahto.

Boggs tracked Lahto to a nightclub on Surawongse Road. When Lahto left the club shortly after midnight, Boggs followed. Boggs recalled vividly the way the Brylcream made the Malaysian man's black hair look like patent leather.

Boggs approached Lahto quietly, from behind.

Wrapped the garrote wire around Lahto's throat. Pulled it tight.

Blood spurted onto Lahto's green silk shirt. The wire had cut into Lahto's windpipe when the man had managed a loud high-pitched scream.

Boggs had puzzled over the scream later. Boggs would've

thought that even a partially-sliced windpipe would prevent a loud scream. And yet the Malaysian man with his tiny arm bones and his silk shirt and his hair cream had somehow cried out mightily.

The cry had startled Boggs. Enough to make Boggs run from the scene, when he knew it was good tradecraft to calmly walk.

But that was it, Boggs saw now. The color of the sport coat was the same shade of green as Lahto's silk shirt. The color had reminded Boggs, subconsciously, of the puzzling *grand mal* cry that had unsettled Boggs that night in Bangkok.

Boggs pondered that obscure linkage as he fitted the automatic pistol into the flat shoulder holster he wore underneath the new coat. He tucked the brass knuckles into his pants pocket. Slid the knife into the sheath strapped to his right ankle.

Boggs pulled his wallet out to make sure the driver's license he carried belonged to his current alias—William Donald Slocum of Shreveport, Louisiana—while he hummed a few bars of a slinky song he'd heard in Brownsville. The one about boots made for walking.

As Boggs stood in the hallway waiting for the hotel elevator, he reconsidered. Now that he thought of it, Lahto's shirt hadn't been green. It had been white. And Lahto had worn a dark vest with it. Gray, or black.

The elevator arrived.

Boggs shot his cuffs, stepped inside.

Maybe it was just an ugly sport coat.

Six

NASH STOPPED TO use a pay phone outside a liquor store on his way out of Diamond Heights. The sergeant on the Homicide Detail watch desk had a message for him, as Nash thought he might. A caller—female—had said only that someone named Gone would be available between eight and ten o'clock that night. The address belonged to an apartment house on Broderick Street, at the edge of the Marina District.

The apartment house was a brilliantly white four-story building with curving Art Deco lines. Like a sleek yacht, or an intrusive medical instrument. Beside the front door a row of metal mailboxes and buzzer buttons stretched across the stucco.

Nash pressed the button for *Gone, T.*

The shadow of a palm tree swayed across the cement walkway while Nash waited for someone to answer the buzzer. The air seemed too warm. It was the kind of evening that produced too many street corner loiterers and too many street corner weapons.

That morning, the television news on KPIX Channel 5 reported that Negro residents predicted race riots, as large and uncontrollable as the Watts riots in LA, would erupt soon in San Francisco. It would be, the pundits said, the Negro community's response to poverty, unemployment, and police harassment.

It was a news story, but only just. Everyone in the city expected trouble—not just the Negro community. There was a general belief that, as the students in Berkeley said, *the shit was coming down*. No one knew exactly what shit it was, but it was most assuredly on its way.

A soft female voice answered on the intercom speaker.

Nash identified himself.

The woman named Tina Gone stood in the open doorway of her fourth-floor apartment in her bare feet. Her soft features matched her soft voice. A suntanned face, high cheekbones framed by shoulder-length brown hair. The sharp blue eyes looked tired. Pop music from inside the apartment wafted into the hallway.

Nash flipped open his credential wallet. "Miss, I believe you left a message for me."

The woman glanced at the identification card and the SFPD badge. Then she looked back at Nash, comparing the ID picture to the genuine article. A young woman who worked in Records at the Hall had once told Nash that the picture on his ID card resembled the French movie actor Jean-Paul Belmondo, but with less nose, while in real life he looked like Hoagy Carmichael, nose and all. This was news to Nash. He thought he resembled a slightly less despondent Joey Bishop.

Inside the apartment, the woman apologized if she sounded foggy. She'd just woken from a nap. "You want something to drink?" she said. "I have Tab and beer—Old Milwaukee or Hamm's. Or I could make coffee."

Nash declined a beverage. Tina Gone motioned toward three tall chairs pushed around a breakfast counter as she padded across the carpeted living room floor to the curtained window. She wasn't much older than twenty-five, Nash guessed. Her shapely figure was enclosed in tight black dungarees. Her black shirt had the Breton-style collar that was popular with the North Beach beatnik crowd.

Tina Gone worked the curtain cord. The curtains slid back to reveal a segmented window that seemed to stretch from one end of the apartment's north wall to the other. In the distance Nash could see a net of tiny bright lights. Boat and pier lights, in the marina.

Nash also noticed the two brown Samsonite suitcases set side by side, against the far wall.

"Nice view," Nash said.

His eyes drifted back to Tina Gone.

"Don't be impressed," Tina Gone said. "The walls have no insulation and the plumbing is old." She turned down the phonograph volume a bit more. Then she took a seat across from Nash at the counter. "The neighbors—well, don't ask. I washed a load of clothes in the laundry room last month. When I pulled it out of the dryer all my underclothes had disappeared. Crazy."

Tina Gone paused. Then, "I didn't know Danny O'Day's real name was Gomez. I heard it on the radio. The murder. It wigged me out. What happened?"

Nash gave the woman a bare summary. He didn't add any information to the little that was released to the press. For one thing, there was the issue of protecting the polygraph keys. An individual, for example, who confessed to the crime but didn't know that the victim was found with a Halloween mask stuck to his bloody face would find his or her confession viewed with a degree of skepticism.

Nash opened his notebook. "Were you a close friend?"

"I wasn't any kind of friend." The woman slid a Belair menthol cigarette out of a pack on the counter. She ran the tips of her thumb and index finger along the length of the gasper, further straightening what was already perfectly straight. "I interviewed Danny once. For a bit I wrote about his group—the Subterraneans. He was a musician, and I earn my crust of bread by writing about cats of that stripe. I intended to write another piece, about Danny alone, before he went into the Army. He'd recently gotten his draft notice. It troubled him, deeply."

"They have that effect."

Tina Gone lit the Belair. Nash tapped the eraser end of his pencil on the notebook page. Unaccountably, Nash felt nervous. He posed hard questions to citizens every day, but right now he felt he was the one being scrutinized, for truth and lies.

"I went to his place," Tina Gone said. "To interview him about his songwriting. It was last Sunday. Evening, kind of late. He was polluted on cheap wine, could hardly talk. I left, quickly."

Tina Gone nodded toward the sink counter. Next to the remains of an avocado and tomato sandwich sat a loose pile of five-inch by seven-inch black and white snapshots. The photographic paper had curled at the corners. "Those photos were taken at Golden Gate Park on Tuesday. At the free concert—I've got to write a few hundred words about it. Danny said he might drop by that day. He wanted to play his songs on his guitar. Just him, alone. Real folkie, like Bob Dylan used to do. Dylan's real name is 'Zimmerman,' so I don't see why a 'Gomez' can't be an 'O'Day.' Danny didn't show up though."

"What kind of trouble was Gomez in?" Nash said. A leading question, steering the discussion elsewhere. Nash didn't see a use for Bob Dylan, or his folkie songs. Unless Dylan had written a song about clubbing Danilo Gomez to death.

"Danny was in trouble with booze. Beyond that, I don't know. But I had an uneasy feeling, at his pad on Sunday. It was dark inside. Just a lot of shadows. I thought someone else was in there too. Hiding. They didn't want me to know they were there."

"What gave you that idea?"

"A feeling. Like I said. A chill."

"Your phone number was in his pocket when he was killed."

Tina Gone nodded to herself. "That's why you called. I wondered. I must've given it to him. I don't recall."

Gone stated that she was twenty-six years old. She'd resided in the San Francisco Bay area since 1959, when she arrived from Chicago to study at Stanford University. She wound up studying San Francisco coffeehouse life instead, dropped out of Stanford to write what she called a "two-tiered hipster-folk-beatnik novel that pushed toward the Kerouac end of the dharma spectrum, with a nod to Lord Buckley and Ralph Gleason."

The novel hadn't panned out. After a stint writing for a weekly newspaper in Orinda, Tina Gone believed she was now making a small name for herself writing a twice-weekly column on popular music for the San Francisco *Chronicle*.

"It's called 'The Gone Scene,'" she said.

When Nash didn't immediately react, she gave him a complicit smile. "As in, you know, something very 'cool,' very 'way out.' 'Happening.'"

Nash nodded. He understood the vernacular. Nash also knew of Lord Buckley's hipster gibberish. But the only famous Gleason he'd heard of was Jackie. And Nash couldn't begin to guess what Miss Gone's desire to inhabit Jack Kerouac's end of the "dharma spectrum" might entail. These days even Kerouac wrote like a cheap imitation of Kerouac.

Nash did recall though that Kerouac had written a novel titled

The Subterraneans, a few years back.

"I saw the Subterraneans play exactly once," Tina Gone said. "At a pizza parlor, in Sausalito. The audience consisted of twenty people who sat at tables eating pizza and ignoring the band. So the band sat down onstage and ate pizza too. Then they threw ice cubes at the audience."

Tina Gone tapped her half-smoked Belair against the lip of the ashtray speculatively. "Danny was a gifted songwriter. When the Subterraneans got onto the bill with the Beatles at Candlestick, I immediately wanted to write a think piece on Danny and the band. I wanted to blow the horn for an up-and-coming local act."

Nash paused in his note-taking. Outside, the roofs of nearby buildings had grown darker. Dusk had turned to night. Nash had assumed that Gomez was a no-account musician who died a no-account death. Now the dead man with the Beatle mask had a more formidable connection to that popular British act.

"Did Gomez know the Beatles?" Nash said.

"No one knows the Beatles. Not in this town. But the promoter wanted to use a San Francisco act to open the concert, and the Subterraneans were a good choice. Danny's songs are clever and catchy. Top of the heap stuff."

Tina Gone nodded in the direction of the record player. "Not unlike what's playing right now."

Nash listened. The music playing at low volume came from a box-style record player resting on a credenza in the living room. The song sounded light and airy, driven by the slow strum of a guitar. The male singer had a small sharp voice, almost pointedly so.

It reminded Nash of nothing much.

"It's called *Revolver,*" Miss Gone said. "The new Beatles LP."

Nash had to admit he didn't know much about the Beatles

other than the obvious—"They've found a new way to print money." Nash recalled the newspaper photographs, the piles of burning Beatles records in cities across the Bible Belt. "And they've offended the church people."

"I used to be real jazzbo," Tina Gone said. "Monk, Mingus. Cannonball Adderley. But the Beatles twisted my conk. They've become so famous they have to live inside the cage of their own success."

Tina Gone got up, stepped over to a shelf above the kitchen sink.

"Don't take my word for it, Inspector. See for yourself." She reached into a tin can that had once contained saltine crackers. Returned to the table, holding two tickets.

She dropped them onto the Formica breakfast counter.

Nash studied the tickets.

They were priced at $6.50 each and featured a plug for a local radio station—KYA RADIO 1260 WELCOMES THE BEATLES. A photo of the four smiling Englishmen appeared on the face of the ticket. The show would begin punctually at eight o'clock in the evening, with no refunds for unused tickets.

Tina Gone winked. "It's one of the perks of working for the *Chronicle*—free tickets from promoters. It's the only perk, come to think of it."

"You're not going?"

"I may be out of town."

"I noticed the suitcases."

"I'm going to Ecuador. Next week, hopefully. I tell people it's a writing assignment. Which it is, but mostly I just want to spend a few weeks on an exotic beach. I hope I don't get dysentery."

"You don't know when you're leaving?"

"I'm on a standby ticket. Pan Am. It's cheaper."

Nash glanced again at the two suitcases in the living room. He couldn't help but wonder if there were other reasons why Miss Gone wanted to leave town soon. Reasons related to Gomez's murder, perhaps. It was his job to wonder such things, he didn't necessarily pride himself on it.

Nash's eyes drifted to the record player, the credenza it rested on, the LPs scattered around. One of the LP covers stood out. He'd seen the same curious skeleton image at Jasper Rollo's house, an hour ago.

"I bought it yesterday on Haight Street," Tina Gone said when Nash asked her about the LP. "It's the Beatles concert last month in New York City, recorded on the 'que-tee.' Someone out here pressed it, cheap and fast and illegal—like bootleg liquor. Mostly it's a recording of young girls screaming. Every now and then you catch a few snatches of a song, like a choir singing through a jet engine. People will buy anything if it has 'Beatles' stamped on it. People like me, evidently."

Nash was fully aware that a large number of illegal things could be bought in Haight-Ashbury. Two years ago, that neighborhood had still looked blue collar, full of Negro families and immigrants. But Haight-Ashbury grew more eccentric by the day. The long-haired students from San Francisco State College and the assorted hangers-on had taken over the old Victorian homes and used them for drug parties and "love-ins."

Within SFPD, the Haight-Ashbury district was now referred to as "Hippieville"—"hippie" being the diminutive form of the word "hipster." From what Nash heard on the street, the pseudo-intellectual hipster Beats, or beatniks, looked down on the uncouth young hippies looking for cheap and easy kicks. The Beats viewed hippies as a decidedly inferior grade of hipster. Maybe the hippies felt the same way about the beatniks.

Tina Gone started to say something but paused. She grasped for the right words. "Do you know what's sad, Inspector? Danny

O'Day was a Mexican boy who wanted to be just like the white boys whose pictures he saw on record sleeves. He learned how to sing and comb his hair and play the guitar, just like them. He even threw away his own name. He didn't want to be who he was. That seems sad to me."

Gone was raising a fresh gasper to her lips when Nash heard a sound that hadn't come from the record player.

A sound like shoes kicking gravel.

Tina Gone looked up at the ceiling, a gentle frown on her face. Not sure what the sound was, but not worried. Then Nash saw the hole in the center of a web of cracks in the plate glass of the picture window in the living room.

Before Nash could move, a second gravelly sound reached him. A can of coffee resting on the drain board next to the kitchen sink suddenly hopped across the countertop, before falling to the floor.

It was gunfire.

Seven

NASH HADN'T SET out to be a policeman. But the prospect of spending his life chasing a profit margin in the business world didn't interest him much. When Nash finished college and needed a job the San Francisco Police Department was hiring, so he applied. Being a policeman was useful and honorable, he told himself. It was a living that didn't require him to sell his soul for a handful of coins.

It didn't become obvious to Nash until much later that being a policeman was like painting a target on his back. In the figurative sense and, on occasion, the literal one.

After the first two shots tore through the front window, Nash grabbed Tina Gone and pulled her down behind the breakfast counter. Nash was reaching into his blazer for the .38 revolver in the shoulder holster when he realized it was useless.

Night had fallen. Except for the lights of windows in nearby buildings, and the more distant glow of the marina, Nash could see nothing out of the apartment's window.

There was nothing to shoot at.

And Nash was too far away for a revolver to be of any use, even if he could find a target. A sniper with a good rifle, shooting from an upper-floor window or a rooftop, wouldn't have much to fear from a fly speck waving a police revolver in a distant and well-lit room.

A third shot ricocheted off a kitchen appliance with a dull crack. Tina Gone cried out. She pulled her legs up under her, the side of her face pressed against the wooden cabinet door. Nash peered out from behind the counter.

The fourth shot exploded a ceramic flower vase.

Nash could see the cracks radiating out from the ragged holes in the picture window. The switch that controlled the overhead lights in the kitchenette was positioned on the wall six feet away.

Nash glanced again at Miss Gone. Her eyes were shut tight, body hunched up. A shipwreck survivor, clinging to wreckage.

"Stay put until I say otherwise," Nash said. He wished he felt as confident as he tried to sound.

Nash opened the other of the two cabinet doors at the back of the breakfast counter. He found a cooking pot. He counted to three in his head, tossed the cooking pot over the top of the counter.

It was, hopefully, a diversion.

The pot was still in the air when Nash scrambled for the light switch on the wall. He had just hit the switch with the edge of his hand when he heard the crash and clatter of the pot hitting the credenza. Followed by a shrieking sound.

The impact of the flying pot had knocked the tone arm of the record player askew. The needle skidded and scratched across the grooved surface of the record.

Nash dove for the floor.

He landed face down on the carpet, behind the sofa. Nash had concealment but he didn't have cover—the thick cushions of the sofa weren't going to stop a round from a high-powered rifle.

At least the lights in the kitchenette were out.

The needle of the record player had come to rest in a new record groove, but the groove was scratched. The singer sang three words over a buzzing drone, then the needle skipped back and the same three words were repeated, again and again. Over the same buzzing drone.

Nash heard Tina Gone shifting position behind the breakfast counter. He raised himself up, elbows and knees.

The distance to the light switch beside the front door was roughly fifteen feet. For twelve of those feet Nash would be out in the open.

Nash brought his feet forward until he was sitting on his heels. His hands flat on the carpet.

Like a sprinter, waiting for the report of a starting pistol.

Then Nash cannoned forward.

He hit the far wall. The edge of his hand came down on the three plastic light switches. He missed one of the switches with the first pass, had to try again before the floor lamps and the table lamp and the ceiling light over the credenza were extinguished.

The apartment was filled with shadows now.

Nash slid down the wall into a seated position on the carpet. He directed Tina Gone to run toward the front door. Nash had the door open when she barreled into him from behind.

They ran hell-bent down the hallway while behind them the needle on the scratched LP record in the now empty apartment continued its circular journey: *"—and float downstream...—and float downstream...—and float downstream"*...

CITIZENS RUBBERNECKED from sidewalks and porches while police radios crackled and red roof lights revolved. Four SFPD patrol cars from Northern Station stood at odd angles in the street outside the Tahitian Breeze Apartments.

Nash and six patrolmen had just completed a cursory search of nearby buildings with enough height to provide a line of fire into Tina Gone's apartment. A patrolman had identified a jimmied lock on a wooden door leading onto the roof of an apartment building northeast of the Tahitian Breeze. A position at the south end of the tarred rooftop would have given a sniper a roughly one hundred-yard shot into Miss Gone's apartment.

An initial search of the rooftop yielded cigarette butts, a coffee can full of dirt. One well-scuffed women's pump shoe in mauve. A seagull, recently deceased.

When Inspector Lou Crandall of the Homicide Detail arrived forty minutes later, Patrolman E. Dobbs of Northern Station had just completed a second search of the rooftop. He'd discovered a single brass cartridge case, partly hidden under the metal flange of a ventilation duct.

Crandall was a quiet middle-aged man. Rounded shoulders, a bristly moustache. Like Belcher, Crandall was a Navy veteran from the Pacific Theater in World War II. Belcher had once told Nash that Crandall survived three years in a Japanese prisoner of war camp. Nash found it hard to credit, the generally placid and comfortably overweight Crandall toting that kind of heavy freight.

Crandall took control of the crime scene. It was quite evident that the cartridge case Patrolman Dobbs had found came from a 30.06 cartridge, a standard cartridge for high-powered rifles. Nash believed the total number of shots fired was four. The other casings had either been collected up by the shooter or sailed off the roof when they were ejected from the rifle. Or they were still on the roof, well-hidden.

As dictated by SFPD regulations, Crandall was required to put the casing in an evidence bag, but no one wanted to go down to the patrol cars to get one. Crandall toyed with the casing, letting it roll out of the palm of one hand into the other hand and back again, while Nash recounted the sequence of events.

"Where did you stash the woman?" Crandall said, when Nash finished.

"A prowl car."

"Does she know any reason why a fellow citizen wants to do her grievous harm?"

Nash had asked her that question himself, of course. Tina Gone could think of no one who wanted to do her harm, in any capacity. Crandall dropped the cartridge casing into his pocket. Wiped the end of his nose with the back of his hand.

"It's late," Crandall said. "Get her settled in somewhere. Nash, has it occurred to you that you might be the target? If everyone who hated SFPD took a shot, we'd be Custer's last stand."

Nash didn't credit the idea. Granted, the presence of a police inspector at the business end of an unexplained shooting was a curious fact. But no one had known where Nash would be at that time.

Even Miss Gone hadn't known when Nash would show up.

He couldn't have been the intended target.

Nash shrugged it off. Or tried to.

Down on the street, Nash walked to the patrol car where Tina Gone sat. The adrenaline that had run through Nash a short time before left him feeling wrung out and off balance. A patrolman had just finished taking a preliminary statement from Miss Gone.

The revolving roof light on a nearby patrol car created a lurid halo around Tina Gone's head as Nash explained that it wasn't advisable for her to stay at her apartment that night, for reasons that should be obvious.

"I'll need some things," Tina Gone said. "Or is that *verboten*?"

Nash accompanied Miss Gone upstairs. Nothing had changed inside the apartment. Except that one of the patrolmen had mercifully taken the needle off the scratched Beatles record.

Tina Gone tossed a few clothes and other items into a beach bag. Nash carried her portable typewriter case as they walked to his car.

"It doesn't look like a police car," Tina Gone said as she got in.

Nash set the typewriter case on the back seat, climbed behind the wheel. "It's my own vehicle. Your apartment was my last stop on the way home. I didn't expect it to turn into a crime scene or I would've brought my police horse."

Tina Gone ran her fingers on the raised lettering that appeared on a chrome strip on the dashboard. "You drive a Plymouth Fury. It sounds violent."

"Safe as houses."

"Not my house."

Tina Gone asked to be taken to her brother's residence on Hayes, a block north of the Golden Gate Park panhandle. Her brother Timothy taught social science courses at the San Francisco College for Women, she said. As part of a sociology experiment, he'd recently set up a charity kitchen on Haight Street that handed out hot food on paper plates to the needful. As Tina Gone pointed out, the needful population of Haight-Ashbury was growing at a mad rate.

Tina Gone helped out at the free kitchen herself on occasion.

"Timothy came to Frisco in 'Sixty-two or 'Sixty-three," she

said. "My older sister was the first one to come out here. Nine, ten years ago. Then she went to LA. Elsewhere, I don't know where. She's kind of the black sheep. Not so good about keeping in touch."

Nash turned left onto Lombard Street, then right on Scott. Tina Gone gazed out the window. At Scott and California, two men in white t-shirts shouted at each other across a trash can. One of the men flicked a lit cigarette at the other, who threw his arms up and stormed off.

"Are you going to do soup kitchen work in Ecuador?" Nash said.

"I'm going there to write. A new manuscript idea." Tina Gone spoke haltingly. Like she was talking about a daydream she'd once had, and didn't clearly recollect. "It's a fiction piece. With non-fiction overtones, and an inner poetry. I don't know if that makes sense. William Burroughs went to South America looking for inspiration. I'll go there too."

"I thought he went there looking for narcotics."

Tina Gone gave Nash a half smile. "Burroughs wrote *Naked Lunch* by typing the story out, then cutting the pages into squares. Then he rearranged the squares until they fitted together in off-kilter ways. Once, I tore the pages out of a copy of *Naked Lunch*. I cut them into squares and tried to rearrange them back to ordinary prose."

Tina Gone's thoughts returned to Ecuador. "I wanted to leave last month. I keep changing my mind. I go to Coit Tower and stare at the city. I try to reach a decision, but all I see are clouds. But gunfire at night might convince me to leave sooner rather than later. I always feel out of step. Wherever I'm at. I might as well feel out of step in Ecuador."

Nash understood, or thought he did. When he'd first moved to San Francisco his marriage had already begun to unravel. He spent many evenings alone at North Beach coffeehouses, the Café Trieste in particular. Nash listened to the coffeehouse poets, and poets *manqués*. He sympathized to a degree with the beatniks and their search for experience in the "right now." The atom bomb gave anyone who was paying attention a distrust of any future beyond the next ten seconds.

But Nash also began to realize that the beatniks had their own biases that were no different than the biases of the so-called squares. So, a game of make-believe, this push and pull of being in step or out of step, and with whom or what?

At a stop light on Divisadero, Nash noticed Tina Gone studying the patrons of an all-night diner through the diner's front window. Mouths moved silently, heads nodded. Bodies shifted in chairs, hands gesticulated. From a distance it looked absurd. Lost puppets in a meaningless pantomime.

The traffic light changed.

Nash drove on.

"Inspector, I didn't tell you the entire truth earlier," Tina Gone said. "A man named Max Pinkrose manages the Subterraneans. Or managed them—past tense now, I suppose. He also owns Hi-Tone Records, in North Beach. Present tense."

Shadows and colored light slid across Tina Gone's face as the Plymouth slipped past bright storefront signs. Her voice grew colder. "What I should have told you is, I've let Max Pinkrose pay me to write good things about his acts in my column. I've taken his bread because I need it. When I dropped in on Danny at his place the other night, it was because Pinkrose paid me to interview Danny for an in-depth piece. I'll appreciate it if you can keep that to yourself. I don't need the *Chronicle* giving me their tired old ethics. Chasing the middle-class conformist nightmare is not something I'm proud of. The very idea gives me the ickies. But I have to earn bread, like every good stooge."

Nash didn't know what the ethical standards were for newspaper columnists. He didn't much care. But Max Pinkrose was the citizen who had called in to request a health and safety check on Danilo Gomez.

"Tell me about Pinkrose."

Tina Gone started to, but her character study was interrupted by their arrival at her brother's house, on Hayes Street. Nash parked on the street, behind a late model sports car that Tina Gone said was her own. She'd let her brother use it while his station wagon was in the shop for repairs.

The sports car was a yellow Sunbeam Tiger. Black convertible top, 260 cubic inch V-8 engine. Ford two-barrel carburetor. The 1964 model had sold for $3,450, before tax and license. Nash knew these facts because he'd once considered buying a Sunbeam Tiger himself. But on his SFPD salary he settled for the '62 Plymouth, which he'd bought used from a U-drive outfit in Santa Clara. The Plymouth had a cranky push-button transmission and cigarette burns in the upholstery that weren't Nash's fault, but he didn't have to take out a loan to pay for it.

The Tiger was parked in front of a tall Victorian house on a street full of tall Victorian houses. A dense red light filtered out from around the edges of the closed window curtains, and through the lunette window above the front door. Nash carried the beach bag and Tina Gone carried the typewriter case up the concrete steps, along the front walkway.

Nash had just started up the front porch steps when a sharp scream came from inside the house.

It was the scream of a terror-stricken man.

Eight

TINA GONE STOOD frozen on the porch. Nash dropped the beach bag and grabbed the door knob.

Pushed the front door open, hard.

The red glow in the lunette window came from an unshaded floor lamp standing near the front door. The bulb screwed into the lamp was a photographer's red safety light.

Nash was more concerned with the shadowy figure standing in the center of the room.

The figure wore a long dark robe. It stood with one arm raised, as though hailing Nash, or placing a curse on him. The sound of sleepy saxophones drifted out of a phonograph speaker. Thin strands of sandalwood-scented smoke from burning joss sticks curled in the air. The room smelled like a Chinatown opium den after a coupon sale.

Behind Nash, Tina Gone found the switch and turned the ceiling lights on.

The light from the standard General Electric soft white bulbs pushed the dull red of the safety light back.

The figure in the robe lowered his arm.

He was a thin young man. His curly black hair hung in thick clumps to his shoulders. Nash could see now that his robe was a brown terrycloth bathrobe. The garment appeared to bear the name and crest of the St. Francis Hotel on its chest pocket.

The robed man wasn't alone. An overweight pale man with hair cut close to his scalp sat on a pile of dark-colored pillows at the far end of the living room.

The fat man sat Indian style, legs folded together. His eyes closed. He also wore some type of robe, green and gold. At the moment the fat man was engaged in making burrowing motions with his hands above his head. As though trying to scrape away the air above him. The fat man hummed to himself, a low-pitched congested noise that didn't mix well with the soft honk of the saxophone from the phonograph.

The robed man in the center of the room smiled.

"I didn't expect you, Tina," he said.

Tina Gone looked sheepish as she introduced the man in the bathrobe as her brother, Timothy. Nash introduced himself to Timothy as an SFPD inspector. He flashed his badge.

"We heard a scream," Nash said.

"The Emperor," Timothy Gone said. He motioned toward the seated fat man. "You're wondering, what is this about?"

"The question crosses my mind."

The fat man continue his rabbit ritual while Timothy Gone spoke in academic tones. "The Emperor has taken three hundred micrograms of lysergic acid dythalimide twenty-five. Right now, he's exploring his mind, the part that exists beyond the doors of perception. The scream you heard was, I firmly believe, a scream of discovery."

"He discovered he's a rabbit, evidently." Nash winced as he watched a stream of saliva slip from the corner of the fat man's mouth. "Why do you call him 'Emperor?'"

"He's Riley Bardell," Tina Gone said. Nash heard the tang of sarcasm in her voice. "'The Emperor'—on KYA radio. A disc jockey."

"He's known as the fifth Beatle," Timothy Gone said.

Tina Gone half-closed one eye, took aim at Timothy with the other. "I have it on good authority that the Emperor has never met Beatles one through four."

KYA—the radio station hosting the Beatles concert at Candlestick Park. Nash didn't know much about disc jockeys, what they called themselves, but in the back of his mind he recalled a high-speed voice rattling: *"This is your Emperor speaking."* Where had he heard that?

Timothy Gone said the Emperor had taken the sugar cubes containing LSD-25 at precisely eight o'clock. "I told him to eat light today, make sure he was prepared for the journey. Just scrambled eggs and toast. Water to drink. No alcohol. No cigarettes. No caffeine. His body needs to be at peace with itself. Only then can his mind attain that same peace."

Half an hour later the Emperor began to feel a numbness that he likened to the Novocain administered by a dentist. By 2145 hours, according to Timothy Gone, the Emperor reported that his body was dripping viscously onto the floor, like honey from a spoon. Gone had then advised the Emperor to situate himself comfortably on the cushions. "It's my responsibility to keep his mind from tipping over into a bum trip. I'm his guide."

At 2200 hours Timothy Gone began to apply music—first a series of Schubert string quartets, then the warm tones of Pacific Coast jazz that played now. "The Emperor had the usual light flashes, and for ten minutes he repeated the lyrics to the song

'Puff the Magic Dragon' in a Porky Pig voice. The only words he's spoken in the last hour was the exclamatory phrase 'armadillo women.' It was followed by the scream you heard."

Tina Gone gave Nash a wry smile. Nash could only shake his head. Timothy Gone moved across the room carefully. As though his movement through the room could, itself, disrupt the fat man's LSD experience.

Speaking softly, Timothy Gone directed the fat man to open his eyes. Gone repeated this request three times before the fat man seemed to understand.

Slowly the heavy eyelids rose.

The Emperor blinked several times. He took in the sight of three people watching him closely. His gaze darted quickly around the room while noises seeped out of him. Some of the noises were guttural and some of them sounded melodic and some of them were just noises.

Affixed to the adjacent wall was a poster-sized black and white image of the film comedian W.C. Fields. The comedian's eyes had been painted over with spiraling orange circles. A speech balloon cut out of white construction paper was glued above the comedian's head. It contained the message: TURN ON. Nash surmised that a cartoon speech balloon for the fat man on the pillows would be filled with gurgles and burps.

Nash retrieved Tina Gone's beach bag from the porch, where he'd left it in the rush to enter the house, while Tina Gone explained to her brother the events that had led to her turning up on his doorstep.

Timothy Gone's expression went through several shades of astonished as the details sunk in.

"Was it a prank, Inspector?" Timothy Gone said.

Nash didn't know many pranksters who got their chuckles with high-powered rifles. "There was something else behind it.

We're investigating. We'll know more shortly."

The fat man across the room suddenly cried out. His eyes were tightly shut again.

"He's out of his gourd," Nash said.

"It's a controlled ritual," Timothy Gone said.

"Can you shut him up?"

"He's searching for peace."

"He's disturbing the peace."

Tina Gone picked-up the beach bag and typewriter case, carried them into another room while Nash and her brother continued to study the emotive fat man.

"The Emperor is a speech-oriented personality," Timothy Gone said. "Verbalizing in new ways is part of the LSD sacrament. I'll keep a close eye on him, Inspector, but that's all I have to promise. LSD isn't illegal yet."

"What do you get out of it, Mister Gone?"

"I owe the Emperor, a favor or two. He's helped me with fundraising, so I agreed to help him discover the inner regions of his psyche."

Fundraising? Nash wondered if that was the new slang for selling natural or synthetic hallucinogens on the streets of Haight-Ashbury. "What kind of fundraising?"

"I run a charitable organization. It helps feed the downtrodden of this city." Timothy Gone seemed to straighten up and stand taller as he explained himself. "Maybe you'd like to help, Inspector? A personal check or money order, fifty dollars? Make it out to the Greater San Francisco Co-Prosperity Sphere, Seventeen-thirty-three Haight. It's tax deductible."

Nash said he'd have to forego the donation for the moment. But Gone was right about one thing: LSD-25 would be illegal soon. The California legislature had voted to prohibit the manufacture, sale, or use of lysergic acid diethylamide-25.

The statute would take effect in October. There was talk that a nation-wide ban on the drug would be set in place soon.

In the meantime, use of the drug had escalated. The curious wanted to experience LSD right now, rather than risk police trouble down the road. It was an odd turn of events. Nash could recall, only a few years previous, the Veteran's Hospital in Menlo Park running LSD experiments on volunteers from the local Rotary Club.

"That's quite a get-up," Nash said about the Emperor's clothes. "I think he beats you in the robe stakes."

"The Emperor is wearing a kaftan," Timothy Gone said. "They originated on the Indian subcontinent, although his hasn't been any closer to India than Sonoma County. There's a group of middle-aged women living on a chicken ranch in Petaluma, they make them out of old drapes."

Just then the Emperor raised his head and bellowed. "*Sheila?*"

Timothy Gone explained that Sheila was the Emperor's chick. She and a young assistant from the radio station named Bart had arrived with the Emperor. They'd grown bored watching their colleague navigate his inner cosmos, and disappeared a short while ago.

Tina Gone returned to the living room just as the fat man let out another cry for Sheila. The Emperor now looked resolutely angry. He puffed and labored and got to his feet unsteadily. The fabric of the kaftan clung tightly to the formidable stomach.

The Emperor huffed and shuffled off. He stepped through the doorway into the kitchen. Timothy Gone crossed the room quickly to follow him.

Before Gone reached the doorway there was a loud crash from the kitchen. Followed by a scream and the sound of things rolling across the floor.

Nash followed Timothy Gone and his sister into the kitchen.

Lying on the floor in front of an open pantry door was a young bespectacled man and a blowsy blonde woman. They were half dressed and drunkenly tangled up together amidst an ironing board, three or four coats still on hangers, a collection of empty Pepsi-Cola bottles spilling out of an overturned wooden crate. The woman pushed her red skirt down while the young man pulled his blue pants up.

The Emperor bleated, shook his head.

"Careful," Tina Gone said as she reached down to help the blonde woman button her blouse.

Nash had seen enough. He reminded Tina Gone to stop by the Hall of Justice in the morning so that Nash could get her signature on a formal statement. Then he departed. Outside, the cool night air and the silence felt welcoming. Nash climbed into the Plymouth and turned the key in the ignition. It had been a thirsty evening. He wondered if it was too late for a beer at the Penalty Box Tavern. He decided it wasn't, just as he always decided.

Nine

CHESTER BOGGS SAT on a vinyl-cushioned stool at the end of the restaurant counter. A well-worn breakfast menu lay open in front of him.

At seven o'clock in the morning the Gold Spike Diner on Fillmore Street smelled of fried potatoes, bacon grease, industrial dishwashing detergent. Boggs smiled at the waitress who brought the coffee pot over, refilling his cup.

She was a young woman. A pallid complexion, a weary look. Her name was Bernice, if the nametag pinned to her chest could be believed.

Bernice walked with a limp. She wore one white shoe with a thick sole and one white shoe with a thin sole.

Boggs supposed that a gimpy leg was one good reason why a young woman might be weary beyond her years. But Boggs thought he could see the outline of a nice figure underneath the sagging pink and white waitress uniform. He supposed that her dirty blonde hair looked all right too, when it wasn't hemmed in by a hair net.

"Don't I know you?" Boggs said as Bernice poured the coffee.

"If I ever met you, mister, I'd remember," Bernice said. "You look a little bit like trouble."

Bernice finished refilling the cup. She gave Boggs a closer look. Then she turned, walked down the counter. Refilled another customer's coffee cup before returning the glass pot to the warming burner.

Boggs had no doubt, Bernice was the waitress he was looking for.

The Old Men had feelers out. One of the feelers went by the name of Handy. Earlier that morning Handy thought he spotted the target walking along Post Street. Near the Geary Expressway. Handy had followed the target to Fillmore.

The target entered the Gold Spike.

Handy walked past the diner slowly. He spotted the target sitting down at the serving counter at the back of the diner. Underneath a clock on the wall that advertised Calumet Baking Soda on its round face. A waitress behind the counter handed the target a menu.

Handy concluded that the man would be in the diner long enough to eat breakfast. Handy found a telephone booth nearby on Turk Street, called Boggs. The phone call had gotten Boggs out of bed at the Drake Hotel.

While Boggs was getting dressed, Handy returned to the diner to find the target gone.

Handy had only been absent from the street outside the diner for fifteen minutes, but the target had disappeared again.

Handy had dropped the ball.

When Boggs arrived, Handy brought him up to speed. Then Boggs sent Handy on his way. Now Boggs sat at the end of the counter. Right where the target sat sixty minutes before.

Boggs sipped his second cup of coffee.

He motioned to Bernice for his check.

Boggs laid three ten-dollar bills on the counter.

Fanned them out.

Boggs hadn't ordered breakfast.

Bernice came over, an order pad in one hand and a pencil in the other. She saw the three ten-dollar bills. Boggs could see her adding up the situation. One bottomless cup of coffee was twenty-five cents. With three ten-dollar bills, Boggs could pay for every breakfast being eaten at the counter, still get a healthy dose of change back.

Bernice leaned tentatively against the counter. She asked Boggs what he'd had.

Like she couldn't quite remember.

"Coffee," Boggs said. "Without a bottom."

Bernice scribbled out the check and tore it off the pad. She set the square of paper on the counter. Boggs pushed the ten-dollar bills toward her. Bernice cocked her head to one side, what she must've believed was a thoughtful look. She opened her mouth. Not finding anything to say, she closed it again.

"My treat," Boggs said. He wasn't sure what that remark meant in this context but it was the first thing that popped into his head.

Boggs continued. "I want to buy a little help. I'm looking for a friend of mine. He eats here, now and then."

Boggs gave the waitress the description of the target, the one Handy had given him.

Bernice frowned. A Negro cook called to her through the serving window. Bernice moved off to deliver a pair of fried eggs to a pot-bellied man in a blue and white seersucker suit.

"The foreign gentleman," Bernice said when she returned.

She'd recognized the description. "He doesn't speak much English." Bernice nodded her head. She saw now. What the score was, part of it. "Why are you looking for him, mister? Are you fuzz?"

Boggs caught the scent of Bernice's perfume. It was syrupy and pungent. He shook his head. He wasn't a cop. Boggs pushed the three ten-dollar bills further across the counter. The edges of the bills rubbed up against the dry cracking skin on Bernice's hand.

"He comes here, for breakfast," Boggs said. "I've got some things he needs, but I've got to find him first."

Bernice studied the fanned bills.

She glanced down the counter.

She picked the bills up quickly, tucked them into her apron pocket. She squared her shoulders. Looked down her nose at Boggs.

She wanted Boggs to know that she wasn't a woman who could be bought, even though he'd just paid her.

"I've only seen him twice," Bernice said. She spoke quietly. "Once this morning"—she glanced over her shoulder at the clock on the wall—"about an hour, hour and a half ago. He was here yesterday too, about the same time. I never saw him before that and I might not ever see him again. All I know about him, he doesn't speak English real well, and he was wearing the same clothes this morning that he wore yesterday, near as I could tell. I hope that's worth thirty bucks to you. It's no skin off my nose if it isn't."

Boggs stopped Bernice before she could walk off. Boggs pulled out his wallet. He removed a business card for the Drake Hotel, used Bernice's pencil to write the name Ed Barker on the back.

Boggs handed the card to Bernice. "If you happen to see my friend, give me a call? It'll be worth another thirty, at least. Don't tell him I'm looking for him. I want it to be a surprise."

Ten

NASH POURED MILK into his cup of coffee. It was 0840 hours. He hadn't gotten much sleep. One thought had run loose in Nash's mind. Kept him awake until dawn.

The remark Lou Crandall had made.

About Nash being the target.

It was absurd, of course. Maybe even a symptom of—what was the hip psychological jargon that *Time* magazine tossed around? *Paranoia?*

Nash supposed that a sniper could have followed him from the Hall of Justice to Diamond Heights, then to the Marina District.

Not impossible.

But a sniper couldn't have scouted a firing position and gone to work in the time between Nash's arrival at Miss Gone's apartment and the first gunshot.

No, Nash couldn't buy that theory.

Miss Gone said that she thought someone else was inside Gomez's apartment the night she was there. Hiding. If so, maybe that individual believed Gone had seen more than she had, knew more than she knew. Decided to do something about it.

Something permanent.

As Nash stood drinking his coffee, he ran a finger lightly across the postcard taped to the refrigerator door.

The card depicted a tree, leaning seaward on a rocky cliff over the Pacific Ocean: VIEW OF THE SCENIC OREGON COAST.

Irene sent him the card after she'd left San Francisco. Six months ago. It arrived after the string of hours-long phone calls, but before the silence. Nash knew that eventually the erosion of the earth underneath the tree would reach a point where the roots could no longer hold it in place.

The tree would topple, right off the edge of the cliff.

It was inevitable. Death and taxes. Nash had come to identify with the tree. Caught between the way things would never be again, and a precipitous drop into a highly doubtful future. Maybe it was all part and parcel of *the shit coming down*.

NASH GLANCED at the handbills taped to the front window of the Winchell's Donut House on Market. One advertised a three-hour boat cruise hosted by a group of single adults who called themselves the San Francisco Swingers. The boat sailed from Pier 43½ on Saturday night, $3.75 a ticket.

Another handbill advertised a "Beatles Go Home" dance concert at the Fillmore Auditorium on Monday evening—the same night the Beatles themselves would appear at Candlestick Park. Nash couldn't imagine what an anti-Beatles dance was. But he also couldn't imagine calling ORdway 3-5579 to make a reservation for a swinging boat ride.

Nash wondered idly if he liked people enough.

AT THE Hall of Justice, Belcher sat at his desk with the pieces of his Smith & Wesson revolver lying on a white handkerchief in front of him. A bottle of cleaning oil and a pile of small cloth swabs pinned two corners of the handkerchief down. Nash saw that the Gomez murder had been added to the Homicide Detail assignment board, with Nash and Belcher's names attached.

Belcher took a doughnut from the box Nash had brought. He handed Nash two photostats in return.

"Take a gander," Belcher said.

Nash studied the photostatted copies of a handwritten letter and the envelope it arrived in.

The letter read:

i give you fair warning there is sickness coming it is called BEATLES they pervert our nationality and give children mental disturbance i don't have to prove this it is proven we kill the SICKNESS or we suffer and die and i will kill it in frisco don't you wish you knew don't look for me i can SEE YOU EVERYwhere

The letter bore an illegible signature and not a single full stop. The envelope was addressed simply to "Police Chief, San Frisco, Calif, Please Rush." Nash noticed there were three more five-cent stamps on the envelope than the post office required, but nut cases had always been the post office's best customers. They wanted an audience, badly, and paid extra to ensure that their pronouncements weren't returned to them for insufficient postage.

Nash didn't make too much of the letter. There was no shortage of kooks. On the other hand, Nash had watched the assassination of Kennedy and the murder of Oswald on television in November 1963, like everyone else in the country. All it takes is one kook with a rifle and fifty cents worth of cartridges to hotwire history.

For a moment Nash thought of the sniper in the Marina District. But he couldn't see a possible connection, that kook and this letter. Absurd. Unless the letter writer had resolved to take pot shots at anyone playing a Beatles record.

Belcher wiped powdered sugar from his mouth, took another doughnut. He said the letter had been mailed from San Rafael, two days previously. The Marin County Sheriff's Office was following up. "They think it's the same bum who wrote last year to tell us that J. Edgar Hoover would be smitten with a flaming sword, to cleanse him of the devil's forked tongue. Not everyone here disagreed with that one."

Belcher took a bite of the maple-frosted, then set the doughnut down on a napkin carefully, as though practicing infant care on a tiny plastic doll. He picked up a pencil and a page torn from a telephone message pad.

The square of paper included the standard heading WHILE YOU WERE OUT. Belcher added the words FUCKING AROUND, then handed the note and three sheets of single-spaced typing to Nash.

"A citizen of the female type was here to see you, eight o'clock sharp," Belcher said. "Said she knew you and she needed to make a statement. Dempsey helped her out because he had time to kill and she smelled nice."

Tina Gone had left the note. She'd written in an energetic scrawl that she was sorry she'd missed him. She'd be available that evening, if he wanted to continue their conversation.

That was all.

Belcher had already read Tina Gone's statement, but now Nash recounted the rifle fire at Tina Gone's place the night before, and the situation he found at her brother's pad later. It didn't make a great deal of sense any way Nash explained it, and Belcher wasn't any help.

Nash asked about the patio party.

Belcher brushed his paws together to rid himself of doughnut crumbs. He lit a gasper, sat back in his chair. "My sister-in-law did a hula dance to show off her new bikini. She slipped on a martini olive." Belcher exhaled cigarette smoke from his nostrils in a bullish stream. "Her fat caboose landed on my ukulele, I'd left it on a chair. The uke got smashed. I did too."

NASH WORKED on his report of the events of the previous evening. When he finished, he attached Tina Gone's statement and dropped the report into the wire basket for the Homicide Detail's file clerks. Nash was making notes on an unrelated case when Belcher announced that an autopsy on decedent *Gomez, Danilo Alonzo* was scheduled for the next afternoon.

Word of a Beatles angle to the Clipper Street homicide got around fast. Nash was coming out of the second-floor men's room after visiting Records when he ran into June Moon, from Permits and Registration. She told him, in a confidential tone, that she had it on good authority—that is, her teenage daughter, Vicki—that the Beatles had run their course. "Herman's Hermits are the 'happening' bunch now. Especially the one named Peter—Vicki says his voice is dreamy." June Moon gave Nash a playful wink as she walked off.

It was Lieutenant Dark who had the last word.

"Jellicoe just gave me an earful," Dark said, when Belcher

and Nash stepped into his office. Dark had just come from the upstairs office of Chief of Inspectors Gus Jellicoe. "Between this San Rafael nut and your Clipper Street murder, he doesn't like the Beatle complications. He smells bad press. He wants you two jokers to get Clipper Street into the tubs and closed, most ricky-tick."

Nash and Belcher left the Hall thirty minutes later. On the way to North Beach, they stopped at an Esso station for gas. The kid in coveralls working the pumps was listening to a transistor radio tucked into his pocket. The soft pop song coming from the radio reminded Nash of the Pacific Coast jazz playing inside Tina Gone's brother's house the night before. Coy saxophones, drum brushes. Breathy woodwinds. Nash recalled the jazz music as many different shades of blue. All swirling together softly, in a dusky kettle.

It was the kind of recollection Nash kept to himself.

Eleven

THE INTERIOR OF the Hi-Tone Records office and studio—"The Golden Sound of the Golden Gate"—on Water Street was painted a shade of yellow like dried-out hot dog mustard.

The property was a re-zoned house. A middle-aged secretary with sharp eyes sat behind a desk in what was once a living room. One corner of the desk was propped up with telephone books. The secretary was propped on her elbows, a cigarette dangling from her lips. Heavy mascara gave her a used-car lot Cleopatra look.

Belcher waved his SFPD badge under her nose.

"So what," she said.

"So where's your boss?"

While the secretary worked the buttons on the intercom, Nash stepped over to the framed black and white publicity stills hanging on the wall. A photo of Danilo Gomez, in his Danny O'Day persona, caught the young Mexican man with a phony smile and a long spit curl. The photograph looked wildly out of date to Nash. Like a twenty-year-old supper club advertisement, from Baltimore, or Piscataway.

Nash glanced into an adjoining room, the former kitchen. An aging FrostQueen icebox still stood in one corner, near a small window boarded over with wood. On the other side of the room, a long console desk covered with knobs and switches and sound meters. A wide window had been fitted into the wall above the console desk. Beyond the window was the live room, where the microphone stands, guitar amplifiers, and drum kit seemed too small and close together for serious musicianship. Two reel-to-reel tape recording units stood to one side of the console desk, and Nash noted the several boxes of recording tape lying around. The boxes looked identical to the tape boxes found in Gomez's pad.

"The studio used to be the garage," said a male voice, behind Nash.

Nash turned.

A tall man carrying a plastic flyswatter had appeared. His voice was flat and deep. The words he spoke tumbled out slowly.

Max Pinkrose gestured with the flyswatter. "We took out the wall and added that window. We dumped the mixing desk where the kitchen table used to be. There you have it—'Hitsville USA.' Except the wiring is hinky. We blow more fuses than Krushchev."

Pinkrose wore a green shirt with a frilly collar. A multi-colored scarf was tied around his neck, in the manner of the young pop music stars with bright toothy smiles who appeared on TV. But Pinkrose had the lean hard face of a veteran dirt farmer. His hair was cut in feed store bangs that traversed his forehead like plate armor. Pinkrose looked as musical as a ten-pound shovel blade scooping twenty pounds of manure.

Nash and Belcher flashed their SFPD credentials.

Pinkrose's secretary was busily gathering her things into a white purse. She headed for the front door, reminding Pinkrose that she was on her way to the Texaco station on Bay Street for cigarettes, gasoline, and Green Stamps. "Sixty more stamps, I'll have enough for steak knives," she said. She gave Belcher a hard look, a use for steak knives already suggesting itself.

Belcher and Nash followed Pinkrose into a backroom office. A Smith-Corona manual typewriter rested on a typing table next to Pinkrose's desk. The sheet of typing paper rolled onto the platen look liked it had yellowed in place and died of boredom.

Belcher took a seat on a wooden chair. Nash stood. Framed 45 rpm records hung on the wall. One disc was "Garden in My Head," as performed by the Subterraneans. A tune called "Lonesome Town" on the flip side. The misshapen and multi-colored lettering of the Hi-Tone logo on the record label looked like the opening credits to a Bugs Bunny cartoon.

In the same picture frame, beside the seven-inch black disc, was the paper picture sleeve that went with it. It showed four young men in clothes covered with plaids and stripes. Wide belts with large round buckles. The band jumping in place, caught midleap, all moppish hair and smiles, marionettes bouncing on wires.

The listed songwriting credit for "Garden in My Head" was O'DAY—PINKROSE. Nash saw Pinkrose's co-writing credit on the other Hi-Tone records framed on the wall.

"'Lonesome Town' is a Ricky Nelson number," Pinkrose said. "It was a funny choice, because Danny wasn't lonely. His head was full of voices. All of them whispering bad things."

Pinkrose wasn't done. "Danny O'Day was a prick. From what he said, even his mother didn't like him. But he was a prick with a small piece of talent. A pebble of talent, in the larger rock of his head, but it was enough. It tears me up inside, thinking of the serious jack I could've made on that walking pustule."

"You two had differences?" Belcher said, deadpan.

Pinkrose found what he wanted on the desk—a pack of Kool menthols. He shook a gasper out. Belcher followed suit with an unfiltered Camel, and a Chesterfield king size appeared in Nash's hand. Pinkrose reached out, his stainless steel Zippo lighting Belcher's gasper, then Nash's, then his own. Pinkrose had the curious habit of closing the lid of the Zippo quickly to extinguish the flame after lighting each cigarette. Then raising the lid, working the flint wheel again, to light the next one.

There was a general reshuffling as the three men looked around for ashtrays. An engraved emblem on Pinkrose's Zippo caught Belcher's interest.

"Marines?" Belcher said.

Pinkrose nodded.

Belcher said, "I won't hold it against you."

Pinkrose said, "Navy?"

"Seabees."

Pinkrose studied the hot ash of his cigarette as though pondering the science of fire. "That's too bad."

"I cry about it every night."

"You ought to."

"Tell us about O'Day."

"His name wasn't 'O'Day.'"

"We heard."

"It was 'Gomez.'"

"We heard that too."

"'Gomez' in Spanish means 'asshole.'"

"I'll be damned."

The small room filled with a cloud of bluish smoke. Pinkrose kept his hand cupped around his cigarette when he puffed on it, as though shielding it from a brisk wind. Pinkrose said he'd known Gomez for roughly ten weeks. He'd spotted Gomez in Alameda, playing in a dance band called the Sombreros. At the time, Gomez was being dumped by his girlfriend. She was also the singer in the band.

Pinkrose offered to book some gigs for Gomez, even give him important studio time. But Gomez had to agree to front a group that Pinkrose already managed, a Castro Valley outfit called the Cave Dwellers.

Gomez agreed, but he hated the name. In early July the Cave Dwellers became the Subterraneans.

Belcher's stub of pencil hovered over the page of his open notebook. "Was Gomez a juicer? Did he smoke reefer, pop pills? Chase underage skirt?"

Pinkrose nodded along. "Whichever one you want."

"Where was he from?" Nash said.

"New Mexico."

"What part?"

"Didn't care enough to ask. As an entrepreneur"—Pinkrose's slow diction made the word sound like a ballet movement—"I wanted the Subterraneans to record, right off the bat, a little tune of mine. A tragedy song, like 'Tell Laura I Love Her.' But the gimmick in my song is, instead of the boy professing his immortal love for his girl while he's dying in a car wreck, he's attacked by a shark while he's surfing, and professes his immortal love after he's chewed up and spit out and washes up on the beach. Like a Beach Boys tune. Except with blood, and sharp teeth.

"But then I heard Danny's 'Garden in My Head.'

"It was pretty good.

"I recorded 'Garden' lickety-split. Why not? I rolled tape, mixed it, pressed forty-fives. Had that song on the street in, what, three days? Four? 'Garden' got the Subterraneans on the Candlestick bill with the Beatles. The promoter wanted a hot new local act. He heard 'Garden' on the radio and told me, 'I want them.' I said, 'You've got them.'"

Pinkrose pointed a crooked finger over his shoulder. On the wall behind his desk was a poster advertising the upcoming Beatles show at Candlestick Park. As a last-minute addition, the name "The Subterraneans" appeared on a white sticker pasted onto the finished poster. Underneath the names of the other supporting acts—the Remains, the Cyrkle, the Ronettes.

In the center of the poster was a picture of the four young men who made up the Beatles rock group. Their faces surrounded by the American Stars and Stripes and the British Union Jack, as though a Beatles show in San Francisco was the result of high-level diplomatic wangling.

"Which brings me to something else," Pinkrose said. He winced, shifted in his chair, like his bones had gotten twisted. "On Monday a young fellow walked in here, out of the blue. Didn't know him from Shinola.

"He looked rough, like he'd been sleeping under a car. He was all jerky-twitchy. Doped up. He told me his name was Frank Barcelona, and that he used to play saxophone in the Beatles. Then he told me he wanted to play saxophone in the Beatles again. I laughed in his face. The Beatles don't use a saxophone player. Never have."

Belcher flicked cigarette ash into an empty soda pop can. "Keep going. When you get to a good part I'll let you know."

"This Barcelona wanted me to put him in touch with the Beatles," Pinkrose said. "He figured that if I managed the Subterraneans, I must be in thick with the Beatles crowd too. That didn't bother me. I get a lot of crazies here. They all want me to do things for them. Everybody thinks they're the next Herman's Hermits.

"Barcelona's American, I guess, but he said he lived in

Germany, a few years back. In the Army, like Elvis. He said he played with the Beatles at a strip joint in Hamburg. He wrote songs for them, and they took his songs back to England and turned them into hits and left him high and dry. Now he wants his share of the song royalties. He said if he didn't get it, the Beatle named Ringo would find himself in *mucho* hot water."

Pinkrose picked a piece of tobacco off the tip of his tongue with two fingers. "I told him to get lost. So he reaches into this paper sack he brought with him. Pulls out a photograph and lays it on my desk. Then he pulls out a roll of half-inch recording tape and a long-barreled revolver. I said, 'Whoa, partner.' He waved the dingus around and told me that he wanted to settle his business with the Beatles pee-dee-que." Pinkrose nodded at Belcher. "You need me to spell that?"

Twelve

PINKROSE TAPPED THE end of an unlit cigarette on the surface of his desk to pack the tobacco down. The tapping had the cadence of a gavel bringing the room to order.

"It's clear to me that Barcelona intends to do harm if he doesn't get the money. 'Don't make Ringo suffer,' that's what he said." Pinkrose repeated the phrase slowly, as though speaking to the dull-witted. "Why he's picking on that Beatle, not the others, I couldn't say."

Nash rolled the words around in his mind. They probably meant nothing. An empty threat from an addled braincase. The sound of Belcher's pencil lead scraping across paper continued. Belcher was dogged about taking notes. Nash assumed that it had to do with the chaos of his combat experiences in the war. Keeping extensive notes on every little thing was one way to keep the world in order. So that it didn't sneak up behind you, all of a sudden. With a grenade.

Pinkrose wasn't finished.

He said the man named Barcelona had left the photograph behind, so Pinkrose could use it to establish Barcelona's *bona fides* with the Beatles.

Pinkrose removed the photo from a drawer, set it on the desk. A three-by-five inch black and white photo. Scalloped edges. It showed six young men at a table littered with drinking glasses, dark beer bottles, full ashtrays. The men pressed in close to fit into the picture, smiling hugely. They wore dark-colored shirts and displayed well-greased hair combed back tight, the ducktail style.

The snapshot looked softly out of focus.

Like a photograph of a photograph.

Pinkrose leaned across his desk, a number two pencil in hand. He pointed with the eraser end at one of the young men in the photo. "This boy is Stuart Sutcliffe. He died in Hamburg a while back." Pinkrose moved the eraser end down the line. "George Harrison. Paul McCartney. Pete Best—he was the first drummer. He was replaced by Ringo Starr. These are all facts you can get from the fan magazines."

"You'll have to fill us in," Belcher said, stone-faced. "The Chief cancelled our subscriptions."

Pinkrose's eraser moved on. The next young man displayed a sly smile and lively eyes. "This one is John Lennon. Most people believe he's the Beatle leader. He made that crack about the Beatles being more popular than Our Lord Jesus Christ."

The last of the six young men seated at the dirty table had light-colored hair and crooked teeth. He held a half-smoked cigarette level with his ear, his other hand gripping a nearly empty pint glass of beer. Dark eyes lurked under heavy eyebrows.

"Barcelona," Pinkrose said. "He told me this picture was proof he was a Beatle. Of course, there is no record of a Beatle named Barcelona. It is my considered opinion that he's batshit crazy."

Pinkrose turned the photograph over. Block letters, scribbled in ink on the back: TOP TEN CLUB, HAMBURG, JUNE 61.

"This snapshot wasn't his only proof, according to him," Pinkrose said, still not done. "He had the reel of tape. He said it was a recording of him playing with the Beatles in Hamburg. About the same time this picture was taken.

"I loaded the tape onto the playback in the studio, just for a laugh. It's about twenty-five minutes. Mostly it sounded like an English rugby team duking it out inside a musical instrument store. But there were one or two songs I recognized. Crude, but Beatles songs I've heard."

"I understand about the picture," Nash said. "Why did he leave the tape with you?"

Pinkrose set his forearms on the desk. He hunched his shoulders, expecting a sudden hard wind. "I wouldn't say he left it. I got so fed up, I chased him out the door, dingus or no dingus. He left behind the picture and the tape. Then he came back, in the middle of the night. Smashed the window in the studio and climbed in, stole a stack of tapes. One of them was the tape he'd left. And one of them was full of songs I just recorded with the Subterraneans."

Belcher said, "Did you report the break in?"

"I'll handle it myself."

"Figure yourself for a tough guy?"

"Nuts to you, Seabee."

The photograph on the desk wasn't proof of anything. A picture had once been taken of these six men together, that was all. Barcelona might have been a tourist, a waiter, a passing drunk. But Nash recalled in vivid detail how Danilo Gomez had looked, on the vinyl sofa, a Halloween Beatle mask stuck to his dead bloody face. The newspapers didn't have that detail. A detail that made Pinkrose's story more interesting than it might otherwise have been.

Belcher said, "What you're trying to sell us, Pinkrose, is that this fellow showed up with this picture and a tape and a revolver, then he ran off and murdered Gomez. Because you declined to put him in touch with the Beatles."

"I didn't say that."

"Pull my other leg, it's got bells on."

"I'm telling you what I know."

"What else can you tell us about Barcelona?" Nash said.

"Nothing. Talk to my secretary, Miss Amador. I showed her the picture. She thought she'd seen Barcelona before, around town."

"When did you see Gomez last?" Belcher said.

"Friday, and every day before that. When the Subterraneans rehearsed. After Friday, he was a no-show."

"It was odd that he didn't show?"

"He'd done it before."

"Often?"

"Too many times."

"But you didn't call SFPD those other times," Nash said.

"Usually he was sleeping off a drunk. He always turned up again, after a day or two. This time he didn't. I wanted someone to check on him. I never heard back from you folks"— A look of disgust crossed Pinkrose's face, like he'd picked up the slack for goldbricking police officers before—"so I did it myself, twice. I didn't get an answer when I knocked on his door, either time. I talked to his landlady. She thought she'd seen him go out earlier, so I let it drop. What else could I do?"

"When was this?" Nash said.

"Day before yesterday."

Nash asked Pinkrose if he was aware that Danny Gomez had received a draft notice. Pinkrose laughed, slapped the desk top. "The Army got off lucky." As for his arrangement with Tina Gone, Pinkrose didn't look surprised to hear the name. "She's a reporter. If she happens to mention one of my acts or one of my records, I slip her a gratuity. It's just good business."

Pinkrose had no idea why Gomez might have a number of empty half-inch recording tape boxes at his apartment, but the question gave him pause. "Maybe it has to do with the topless joint."

Belcher looked up from his notepad. "The topless joint?"

"That one on Broadway. He used to play there on his own, time to time. I can't imagine why. It's a tit bar. People go to tit bars to see tits. They don't go to see crazy Mexicans plunking on guitars."

Nash took a guess. "The Kimono à Go-Go?"

Pinkrose shrugged. "Is that a tit bar on Broadway?"

It was one of them.

"It might be the one," Pinkrose said. "I don't recall. I never went to see him there. As I think I've already made clear, my interest in tit bars begins and ends with tits."

There was a brief silence, Belcher and Nash considering this development. Nash thought of the woman named Pearly Spence. Her story about a murder in the alley behind the nightclub. It was a phony report made while she was drunk and feeling blue, or so she'd said. Nash couldn't begin to imagine how it might connect to the murder of Danilo Gomez, even if the report had a basis in fact, which it didn't. Gomez killed in an alley, then transported across town, to his apartment couch?

Ridiculous, of course.

But the name of that club coming up, right then. It was an odd coincidence, at the least.

At Belcher's request, Pinkrose wrote down names, addresses, phone numbers for the three surviving Subterraneans. The three musicians would be at the studio that afternoon to rehearse. "I'll be down in San Jose," Pinkrose said. "There's a boy down there I might hire. The Subterraneans will appear with the Beatles at Candlestick, if I have to sing for them myself."

Pinkrose was pushing the sheet of notepaper across the desk toward Belcher when the sounds of Miss Amador returning from the Texaco station reached the back office.

Pinkrose called out to her. A moment later, she appeared in the doorway. Pinkrose asked about the nut who said he once played in the Beatles.

Raylene Amador raised a finger to wipe at the frosted white lipstick that had congealed at the corner of her mouth. She frowned. "It was at a record shop, on Haight. Once or twice, when I was delivering posters and promo discs. This guy, he wears a leather jacket with a patch on the back. Like a motorcycle club patch. I didn't talk to him."

"Can you describe the patch?" Nash said.

"Kind of round."

After Amador left the room, Pinkrose said, "She's a good egg. She sings, weekends at the Round Table Restaurant. She was one half of the first act I ever recorded—'Chuck and Mookie.'"

Belcher said, "Which half?"

ON THEIR way across town Belcher and Nash stopped for coffee and a slice of pie at the Three Gals Café on Fern. Next door to the Rite Aid drugstore. While they ate, Nash thought again about Pinkrose's stunt with the Zippo—striking a new flame for each light, pausing for a second in-between flames. Cupping his hand over his lit cigarette.

Nash recognized the quirks now.

Pinkrose was practicing light discipline. The way a soldier in combat learns to. Pinkrose the Marine was still, twenty-one years after the end of the war, trying to keep from being shot by the enemy at night. Not consciously, but somewhere in the dark corners of his mind, where the raw animal fear lives.

Pinkrose's business arrangement with the Subterraneans also gave Nash cause to wonder. Pinkrose managed the act, but he also recorded and released their records. Which meant, in theory at least, Pinkrose the manager negotiated recording contracts with himself. Suddenly the M. PINKROSE songwriting credit on the framed records hanging in the Hi-Tone office made more sense. Maybe handing over part of the songwriting royalties to Pinkrose was part of the price of hitting the big time, or the bread line, with Hi-Tone Records.

But did that shed light on the Barcelona story?

As Nash ate pie he noticed an advertisement taped to the wall behind the counter. It was an ad for ice cream bars bearing the sketched faces of the four smiling Beatles on the wrapper. They were Beatles "krunch-coated" ice cream bars. Manufactured by the Creamy Boy Dairy of Gilroy, California.

"Man, I wouldn't buy ice cream from anybody named Creamy Boy," the waitress said, when Nash asked about the bars. "And the Beatles, I heard they're pinkos. I have no inclination to learn Russian, myself."

Nash mulled over that remark. Like a lot of people, the waitress was afraid.

But afraid of what?

Nash was reminded of an advertising postcard he'd gotten in the mail several weeks back, by mistake.

The card featured purple letters on a green background, the word THEM positioned at the top in stylized "Pop Art" lettering.

An advertisement for a dance concert at the Fillmore Auditorium. THEM was the name of the featured musical act.

What had piqued Nash's interest was simply the word: THEM. It represented nothing, and yet everything, that people feared. Some citizens feared Russian submarines off the coast, listening devices in Ma Bell's telephones, an atom bomb in the Radiation Lab at Berkeley. Free love was a communist conspiracy, and LBJ did whatever the military-industrial complex ordered him to do over the CIA transmitter implanted in his brain.

All the daily evils and depravities could be tied back to THEM.

As Nash figured it, THEM was just another angle on the *shit coming down* theory. Every Joe Public and Lee Harvey in the city and maybe the entire country had become a paranoiac. And Nash feared the people who were afraid. Fearful people do desperate things. Often it was the Homicide Detail that had to poke and prod the bloody results.

The rhubarb pie tasted lousy.

"Let's shake the trees," Belcher said.

He stuck Nash with the check.

AT THE Celestial Eyeball record store on Haight, wind chimes caught the opening shop door, colliding in delicate tones. The music playing on the record player behind the front counter was loud. It seemed to Nash to be full of sharp red tones, like bloody splinters. Nash felt the high-pitched guitar noise as it crawled up the back of his neck.

Nash tried to shake the feeling off.

The front counter was deserted. The back room was hidden from view by a curtain of colored beads strung on fishing line. The only customers were two teenage girls standing beside a rack of LP records, at the back of the shop.

Nash noticed a copy of the illegal *Eight Arms to Hold You* LP. Displayed on a shelf behind the cash register.

Belcher rang the service bell. Not that anyone could hear it.

The din from the record player speaker became sharper and more brilliantly red. The pummeling drums and punchy bass guitar notes pushed an echoing metallic wail to the front of the song. The pinpricks Nash felt on his neck travelled down his arms, to his fingertips. He wanted to pound his fist on the glass top of the counter, on the wall, on the mook who ran this joint. Just to relieve the tension.

Nash was moving toward the far side of the counter with a view to taking the 45 rpm record off the turntable forcibly when the song ended of its own accord. The tone arm lifted off the record automatically, returned to its stand.

At that same moment a young man emerged from the back room. He wore wrinkled cast-off clothes and wire-framed glasses with square lenses. His Adam's apple protruded markedly from his neck, a malignant growth. The pile of curly red hair on his head looked like shrubbery.

He stepped behind the counter.

"Can I help you, gentlemen?"

"We're not 'gentlemen.'" Belcher opened his leather credentials wallet and held it up. Shrub tilted his head to one side, squinted. Studying the identity card and the badge like they were rendered in classical Sanskrit.

Belcher played it heavy-handed. He fixed the young man with a hard stare while he pulled out his notebook.

"What's your name, sir?" Belcher said.

Shrub moved up and down on the balls of his feet as he answered. Nash glanced at the two girls in back. They spoke quietly to each other. Didn't look too interested in flipping through the racks of LP records.

Belcher set the three-by-five photograph that Pinkrose had given them on the counter. "Take a look."

Shrub's face was screwed into a sour expression. Shrub said he didn't recognize anyone in the picture. Nash glanced around. Pictures of the Beatles were pasted on LP sleeves and posters throughout the store, but the clerk was determined not to identify anyone in the photograph. Because then the two police inspectors would be here longer.

Shrub wanted them out, right now.

When Shrub glanced toward the back of the shop, Nash followed his glance. Nash studied the two teenage girls, their two worried looks, more closely.

"Those faces don't mean anything," Shrub said, about the photo. He shook his head. The curly hair wobbled. His face grew redder. "I got nothing to say. This city is a gas chamber. Your consumer society death factories fill the air with poison. The poison in the air poisons the soil, which poisons the crops and the farm animals, which poisons the food we eat, which poisons us, if you can dig your own scene. You're killing the earth, man, with your plastic nine-to-five conformist mindfuck. But all you want to talk about is some faces, in some picture."

Belcher looked angry. "Don't talk bebop to me, shitbird."

Nash smiled. He caught Shrub glancing again toward the back of the shop. The two girls seemed to catch his glance. One of them looked quickly at the beaded curtain leading to the back room.

Nash wondered if maybe Shrub's explosion of social criticism was a ploy to distract his and Belcher's attention.

Belcher tried more forcefully to get Shrub to study the picture as Nash began walking slowly toward the rear of the shop. The two teenage girls saw him approach.

They shuffled further along the record bins.

Then one of them turned, abruptly.

Walked briskly toward the front of the shop, on her way out.

The other one quickly followed.

Nash didn't stop them.

Nash entered the central aisle between the record bins. He walked toward the beaded curtain at the back. Mixed in with the wooden beads were small round plastic ones that sparkled.

Nash was ten feet from the curtain of beads when Shrub called to him from the counter.

"What do you need, officer?" Shrub said. "The back room is a storeroom."

Nash glanced over his shoulder.

Belcher was giving him a questioning look.

Shrub looked ready to jump out of his shoes.

Nash reached the curtain. Pushed the strands of beads aside. He reached under his sport coat. Placed his hand on the butt of his revolver.

He wasn't sure what to expect.

On his right, a tall wicker screen. Nash stepped past the screen and found himself at the end of a long narrow room. The room was lit by a single naked low-wattage bulb. The walls were lined with industrial-weight metal shelves loaded with brown shipping boxes.

Along the back wall, in a nook created by a break in the shelving, was a table. Nash saw several small white cylinders, like short cigarettes, on the table. Then he saw the pile of loose marijuana.

The cylinders were marijuana joints.

Tea sticks.

Herbal jazz cigarettes.

Maybe to sell to the girls who had lost their cool, precipitously exiting the shop before the fuzz grabbed them by the collar.

Nash generally looked the other way, when it came to grass. Busting citizens for small-time infractions wasn't worth it. The paperwork, the custodial hassle.

But this kind of stunt wasn't anything Nash could ignore.

Nash emerged from the back room to see Belcher tussling with Shrub, who apparently had made his own dash for the front door.

Belcher pushed Shrub against the wall, face first. Jacked one of Shrub's arms up between his shoulder blades, to keep the young man's attention focused on pain. Shrub shouting, in-between gulps of air.

A thin trail of blood ran from the corner of Shrub's mouth.

"Pig." Shrub spit the word out.

"Oink-oink," Belcher said.

Thirteen

NASH HAD EXPERIENCED sound as colors or as other aberrations of the senses, such as pinpricks on skin or tastes on his tongue, for as long as he could remember.

Nash was in the Air Force when he learned what his condition was called.

Synesthesia.

Nash found the word in a correspondence course textbook. From what Nash gathered, he wasn't the only one. Many people saw bursts of color or experienced tactile sensations or distinct tastes or smells when they listened to music or heard other sounds. Even voices. Some people had these experiences just reciting the letters of the alphabet, or reading a newspaper.

Nash had gone through periods when the synesthesia was very active, other periods when he didn't notice it at all. He'd never discussed the condition with the Air Force doctors or, for that matter, the SFPD medical staff he'd seen. Nash didn't consider his synesthesia to be any more dangerous than tone deafness or a persistent numbness in a finger or toe. But if he talked to a doctor about it, it would be noted in a medical file. Nash could never erase it, once it was written down. People who hadn't experienced synesthesia would view it negatively.

Nash didn't need a skull plumber from the police department's health unit poking around inside his cranium.

But the music inside the Celestial Eyeball had set off Nash's bells. He was grateful now for the comparative silence, as he retrieved a set of handcuffs from the SFPD sedan so Belcher could cuff Shrub. Then Belcher dumped Shrub on a wooden bench near the front window, while Nash returned to the car to radio Park Station.

Shrub stared intently. At the toes of his suede boots, at Belcher, at the ceiling. Nash's haul from the back room included the loose marijuana, several thin packets of Bugle brand cigarette papers, a shoe box half full of marijuana cigarettes. The cigarettes were identical in diameter. Nash was forced to admit that, whatever else he might be guilty of, Shrub was not a sloppy worker.

Shrub's driver's license gave his age as twenty. Dayton Philip Millard, his full name.

"What's your hang-up with grass?" Shrub said.

"I don't have a hang-up with grass," Nash said.

"He has hang-ups with the California Penal Code," Belcher said.

Nash said, "It speaks to me, in tongues."

"Shit," Shrub said to himself, shaking his head. Not quite believing how his afternoon had suddenly jumped from a high floor, a swan dive onto the pavement.

But Shrub was not without hope. He decided to change tack and perform his duty, an upstanding citizen. He asked to see Belcher's snapshot again. This time he identified three of the five pictured Beatles. Shrub's memory had cleared up remarkably.

Shrub sailed to a finish when he identified the sixth man in the photograph as "Frankie." Shrub didn't recall a surname, but Frankie had been to the shop two or three times in recent months. Frankie wore a black leather motorcycle jacket. The patch on the back identified him as a member the Coffin Cheaters Motorcycle Club. On one occasion Frankie had stopped by with another Coffin Cheater, a man named Magoo. The Cheaters hung out at a tavern called the Mole Hole, on Cole Street.

Shrub also thought he'd seen Frankie at the free concert. Tuesday, at the Panhandle. Barcelona and an older man shared a goatskin bag there, filled presumably with wine. Standing together at the back of the crowd, taking it all in.

That was all Shrub recalled.

Shrub flashed his pearly whites.

An SFPD patrol unit from Park Station arrived and Shrub took a seat in the back of the prowl car. Snitching to the pigs hadn't helped him. Belcher and Nash gave the patrolmen the rundown on Shrub's backroom hobbies. Rather than a simple *possession* charge, the two harness bulls might put together a felony 606, *possession of marijuana for sale,* or even a 608, *sale to minors,* but it would take work, and luck. The two girls who ran out of the shop were probably still running.

BELCHER AND Nash drove west on Haight. Clouds had rolled in, a light rain fell. Nash studied the young dropouts from the so-called "plastic nine-to-five conformist mindfuck" as they loitered on the sidewalks.

Nash didn't care if a person decided to drop out of one rat race or another. But in Haight-Ashbury they often dropped right onto the sidewalk. They had to be carried off in police trucks and ambulances. Most of them weren't old enough to have ever had a nine-to-five job, plastic or otherwise.

The beatniks had once referred to San Francisco as 49 square miles of zen clarity surrounded by the offensive murk of western civilization. But the spiritual muscles of the Haight-Ashbury neighborhood were open to dispute. Only a few weeks previous, a half dozen chemically-altered members of the Now Generation had sat Indian-style in the street at the intersection of Haight and Ashbury. They closed their eyes, held hands, chanted solemnly, trying to levitate the street, everything in it, through sheer force of will. What they got for their trouble was a delivery truck from the Grubnitz Brothers Furniture Store that took the street corner too fast, plowed right into them.

Four of the six grooveniks survived, but they were now getting their chemicals in their hospital beds, mostly through tubes. The other two were pushing up daisies. The furniture truck might not have been zen but it packed a good wallop.

At a stop light at the intersection of Haight and Cole, Nash watched a man in a buckskin jacket shake and rattle across the street.

ADMIRAL LOVE was written in black laundry marker on the back of the jacket. The sprinkle of rain caused dirt and grime to run in dark rivulets down the man's face and neck as his feet jittered forward and his index finger waggled in the air. It looked like a case of the amphetamine yips. Lately the word on the street and in police cells was that amphetamine, in its various forms, had taken over in Haight-Ashbury. The space travelers had moved beyond groovy colors and melting scenery. Now they'd taken up the existential question of how long they could keep their arms and legs flopping around before they slipped into a bug-crawling psychotic state.

"Next time it rains, we'll bring tiny hotel soaps and pass them out," Belcher said. "Free showers, to go with free love and free VD."

A radio call came in. The dispatcher read a shorthand message from Records: "*Barcelona, Francis Wainright. Male Caucasian. DOB Seven-fourteen-'Forty. May 'Sixty-four, arrest, Pinole, Contra Costa County Sheriff. Assault related to bar fight. Six-month sentence, Contra Costa County Jail. January 'Sixty-five, arrest, Turlock, Stanislaus County Sheriff. Public drunkenness, one night in the drunk tank, Modesto. Address of record: Twenty-seven-ten Sereno Drive, Vallejo. Nothing further...*"

"I expected more," Belcher said.

"Be patient," Nash said.

"Patience doesn't pay the rent."

"What rent?"

The street outside the Mole Hole on the 900 block of Cole was littered with cigarette butts and spit and modified Harley-Davidson and BSA motorcycles. The building had one scarred wooden door, no windows. Inside, a light shone down the length of the bar, a jailbreak searchlight, while stubble-faced men with lopsided haircuts drank canned beer.

Belcher and Nash pushed through the cigarette smoke and sweaty funk that filled the room. Most of the men inside the dark bar at this time of day were older, the anger and frustration carved into their faces.

A bike gang was a young man's game. The men still playing it past forty or even thirty were men who realized they had no options. They were out of luck and down for the count, ever since they were born, just as their tattoos claimed. Nash considered it ironic in the extreme that the iron horse disciples of the open highway seemed to wind up in later years confined in dark box-like rooms like the Mole Hole. Conversing with the dust motes, and themselves. When they weren't grinding out hard time, San Quentin or Folsom.

The bartender didn't know Frank Barcelona. Or so he claimed. In response to Belcher's second question, the bartender nodded toward the rear of the tavern.

Female legs and arms cut from department store mannequins hung from the back wall, exotic antler trophies. At a table underneath the assemblage sat a broad-shouldered man, greasy black hair, black beard that flowed off the crags of his face like hanging moss. The Ray-Ban wraparound sunglasses that hid his eyes were of a type favored by wan young women in monochromatic French films. The man wore a beat-up leather vest. He clutched an open can of Schlitz beer in each hand.

Belcher and Nash flashed their SFPD buzzers.

The man said his name was Magoo.

"Magoo what?" Nash said. "What's your driver's license say?"

The man removed his wallet, opened it, a labored grunt marking the occasion. Belcher and Nash took seats across the table. The man flipped the license out.

Nash examined it.

Magoo had started life in December 1933 as Teeter, Hiram. The faded photograph on the well-worn California license showed a clean-shaven man with neatly cropped hair. The man in the photograph looked like the captain of a college football squad, or a member of the Young Republicans Club.

"I was a square, back then," Magoo said. "But my mind expanded."

"How big?" Belcher said.

"It encompasses multitudes."

"You're a fathead."

"We're looking for Frank Barcelona," Nash said.

"You want me to squeal."

"I wouldn't say that," Nash said.

"I'm not a rat fink."

"Sure you are," Belcher said.

Magoo ran an oil-smudged thumb thoughtfully along the metal lip at the top of a beer can. Nash noticed that the backs of Magoo's hands were tattooed with sequential directives: "fail" on the right, "fail better" on the left.

After a long moment Magoo seemed to reach a decision. He'd chosen the path of least resistance. "Frankie is a Cheater, but he doesn't ride with us much," Magoo said. "He lays low. He has an old lady who lives around here. Her name is 'Cherub' or 'Chippie', I don't know. I haven't seen Frankie in a couple of days."

"Where is he?" Nash said.

"He likes to ride up north, into the redwoods, alone. He rides up, turns around at Eureka, rides back. He says the trees help him get his head together. Maybe he's up there now, I don't know. He doesn't answer to me. He's free. Freer than you are."

"Keep talking," Belcher said.

Magoo let out a wheeze. He swallowed more beer and set one can aside. "Last time I saw him was at the Panhandle. It was Tuesday. Or Monday, one of those. There was an out of sight jam scene going, all day. Electric cats, folkie cats. Me and Frankie, we got together here. I delivered a present up the street, for Frankie, then we hit the Panhandle. Last I saw Frankie, he was grooving. Heavy sounds."

"What kind of 'present?'" Belcher said.

Magoo motioned indistinctly with his hands. "About that size. Brown paper. He asked me to deliver it for him, and pick up a different present. Like an exchange, of presents."

"What was in it, the one you delivered?"

"Frankie didn't say."

"What do you think it was?"

"Nothing Frankie was worried about."

"And you picked up a different package?"

"He said it was a present too."

"You must have an idea about it."

"It felt like a wadded dish towel."

"Why didn't Frankie deliver his own package?"

"I was going there. Frankie wasn't. Simple. The other guy runs a restaurant on Haight. Frankie told me to slide by, drop off a present, pick one up. No big deal."

"Which restaurant on Haight?"

"Where the Greek joint was."

Nash said the name, but Magoo wasn't clear on what the actual name was.

But the name of the man there was Timothy Gone.

Magoo knew Gone because Magoo had done plumbing work on the building when Gone took it over. "I put in an extra sink, some floor drains. Real nice."

Belcher raised his chin and looked down his nose at Magoo. "What did you get out of it, delivering these presents?"

"This and that."

"What kind of 'this and that?'"

"Both kinds."

The exchange of packages couldn't have sounded fishier. Magoo was hedging his bets. If he'd known for sure what was in the packages, he would know whether the contents were dangerous or not. But he truly didn't know, and he was a little worried. So he broached the subject himself. To cover his ass, in case Belcher and Nash already knew about the packages, what was in them. Maybe Magoo thought it would give him some good citizen leverage, down the road.

If real trouble started.

Belcher pressed Magoo for more, but Magoo had said all he was going to say on that subject. "I helped a friend. That's not illegal, is it?" Nash wondered what Timothy Gone had to say about the packages. Nash was sure the answer would be interesting.

Nash tossed out a different question. "What does Barcelona tell you about the Beatles?"

Magoo's thick paw of a hand came up to wipe at the black hair hanging under his nose. Magoo said, "He jokes about the Beatles, or those other guys, what do you call them—the Hermits? We were passing a jug of wine back and forth one night. Frankie said, 'I used to be a Beatle. Me and them are *sympatico*.' He says stuff like that. Crazy shit. He gets ideas stuck in his head, they crash around. He told me once, he likes to lay on the grass in Golden Gate Park when it rains, so he can listen to the screams of every single raindrop just before it hits the ground."

"What does he say about the Beatle named Ringo?"

Magoo shook his head. "I don't know. Frankie knows a lot of shit. He has nine Chinese mojo dragons tattooed on his back. He says they're spokes in his 'wheel of becoming.' I can't explain it. He's got troubles too. His girlfriend fights all the time with some other guy, over custody of a kid. When Frankie talks about it his head explodes."

Magoo didn't know exactly where in the Haight-Ashbury neighborhood Barcelona's girlfriend lived. As for employment, Magoo was inclined to believe Barcelona was unfit for steady work.

"Man, his head is in a different space," Magoo said. "Maybe try that club he plays at, what's it called—the Go-Go Club? In North Beach."

Magoo hiked a thumb over his shoulder, as though North Beach was located just inside the tavern's toilet facilities.

Nash heard the penny drop. "The Kimono à Go-Go?"

Magoo froze while he processed this new information. Then slowly he nodded his head. "He told me he gigs there, but I don't know."

"What do you mean you 'don't know?'" Belcher said.

"It's not my scene."

Frank Barcelona appeared at the Kimono à Go-Go, where Danny Gomez also appeared?

Nash and Belcher couldn't get anything further out of Magoo on that subject either. It looked like they'd be making another visit to the club on Broadway, very soon.

Nash and Belcher got up to leave. Magoo reached into his vest pocket. His hand came out holding a business card that he handed to Nash. One side contained only the name MAGOO and a replica of the club's jacket patch—a skeleton hand holding a monkey wrench.

Printed on the back of the card, in *sans serif* script, was the message:

YOU HAVE BEEN ASSISTED BY A MEMBER OF
THE COFFIN CHEATERS MOTORCYCLE CLUB
SAN FRANCISCO CHAPTER

"I help people with busted cars on the highway," Magoo said. "I give them a card. Good public relations."

Nash wrote Magoo's current address on the card, tucked the card away.

"One last thing," Belcher said.

Belcher reached across the table and yanked the sunglasses with the black insectoid lenses off Magoo's hairy face.

Magoo blinked. His eyes looked too small, too close together.

They also looked bloodshot, to a degree that Nash had never seen. The bright red eyes of a jungle predator, waiting in the night to pounce.

On the way out, Nash heard a high-speed disc jockey voice on the radio behind the bar: "*This is your Emperor speaking. For two tickets to Monday night's boss Beatles bash beside the Bay, be the first of my loyal subjects to call in and tell me the name of the Beatle music Ringo listens to on the train in the movie* 'A Hard Day's Night.' *The Beatle music. Ringo. The train...*"

That name again.

Ringo.

Fourteen

CHET BOGGS LAY supine on the bed. He studied the ceiling. The plaster underneath the white paint had been troweled on in swirling uneven strokes, ripples on a pond. Boggs imagined throwing a rock at the ceiling. A splash. Then cool water, showering down on him.

Boggs smiled.

It was a funny kind of thought.

Boggs was a little stoned.

After a while Boggs became distracted by the shape and overall paleness of Bernice the waitress' bare bottom. Bernice lay on her stomach, her head resting on her crooked arm. The threadbare bed sheet covered her feet and ankles and thighs, but her buttocks remained exposed to the late afternoon light, filtered through thin dull curtains.

Bernice's bottom was gibbous. Like the moon.

Boggs laughed softly, to himself.

Then Boggs stopped laughing, sat straight up on the mattress. Head swiveling, eyes searching the dusty shadows in the room. A gut-wrenching panic hit him, a cannonball.

His pistol and shoulder holster were gone.

The knife in its sheath was missing from his ankle.

It came to him slowly. In a fog that rolled into the back of his mind like an unfurling sigh.

He'd tucked the pistol and the knife under the seat of the car. The rented Ford Galaxie 500 he'd been sitting in, outside of the Gold Spike Diner on Fillmore. Waiting for Bernice's shift to end.

Boggs laughed to himself again.

Even quieter than before.

He lay back on the mattress.

Sitting in the Ford, he'd studied Bernice's mismatched legs, the involuntary wobble in her hips as she exited the diner and walked along the sidewalk. Boggs wondered why a woman with a gimpy leg would choose to work as a waitress. Maybe it wasn't a choice. Maybe she worked as a waitress because it was the best deal she could get.

Boggs got out of the car.

He approached Bernice. Said hello.

Asked her if there was a place they could go. Just to talk.

The girl's apartment was on Telegraph Hill, but Bernice directed him to a neighborhood market first. She needed groceries. At the cash register, she pretended she'd forgotten her coin purse.

Boggs didn't argue about paying.

Bernice's digs had a narrow living room. A shadowy bedroom and a bathroom lay beyond. An ice box and a tiny range top in one corner, near a window that looked out on an alley. Looking across the alley, Boggs saw an identical-looking window in an identical-looking building.

Bernice put away the groceries. She found two water glasses and filled them, Red Mountain jug wine, $1.45 for the half gallon. She carried her glass to a lumpy davenport.

Sat down.

Sighed.

Loose pages from sketchpads lay scattered around the living room. The sketches were done in the soft grays of pencil, or the dark slashes of charcoal. Boggs saw city scenes, figure studies. Three or four sketches that depicted horses stumbling, their necks arching dramatically as they fell.

Some of the sketches were signed SUMMER '66.

Boggs sipped his wine and studied the sketches. Bernice lifted the lid of a ceramic jar and removed a flat package of cigarette papers. She took one paper between her fingers, reached back into the jar for a pinch of marijuana. She distributed the pot meticulously in the cradle her fingers made in the rolling paper. She added another pinch, then a third.

Boggs hadn't smoked marijuana much.

But he wasn't afraid to swing.

"Turn on the radio, will you," Bernice said.

A Silvertone solid state portable radio with a long antenna sat on the floor. Boggs turned it on. The flurry of static receded as Boggs worked the antenna around. The pop music on the radio had a fast tempo. The guitar playing sounded chaotic, a guitarist with his fingers on backwards.

Boggs and Bernice smoked the marijuana joint. When the joint was gone Boggs refilled their glasses with wine. He inspected the drawings and sketches more closely.

One of them caught his eye.

A drawing done in pencil. Four skeletons, standing in a row. The lines were thick and dark. The skeletons dressed in tuxedo coats. Long coat tails, bow ties. They stood with their right arms raised over their heads, boney hands clutching black top hats, a cornball vaudeville song and dance act, breaking a sweat.

The drawing was signed AUTUMN '66.

"Sometimes I feel like an Autumn," Bernice said. She was rolling another joint. "Sometimes I feel like a Summer, or a Spring. Not a Winter though. Not yet."

Bernice lit the second joint. Inhaled deeply. Let the smoke drift slowly out of her mouth.

She nodded toward the skeleton drawing.

"A fellow paid me, to make a copy of that." A ponderous look fell over her features. "But he wanted the skeletons to look like Beatles. You know? Paul, Ringo, Johnny"—Bernice paused. "The other one. So I sketched out a copy, and I bought a teeny-bopper magazine and tore out pictures of the Beatles, just the faces. Then I glued them over the skulls."

The ponderous look on Bernice's face deepened. "The fellow who paid me, he said it was a statement. The vacuous spoon-fed society we live in, something like that. Does my voice sound all right, it sounds squeaky to me."

They smoked the second joint down to a nub while Boggs studied the skeleton sketch. He wasn't sure he knew what the Beatles looked like, but the picture of the skeletons made him laugh. When he looked at Bernice she seemed to move farther and farther away, even as she continued to sit on the couch next to him.

Boggs said the first thing that came to mind.

"This is heavy, baby."

Bernice looked up. "What?"

Boggs poured more wine.

"You're kind of a square, Ed," Bernice said, matter of fact. "You try to go with the flow, but you don't really get it. Right?"

Boggs was confused. Who was Ed? What seemed like an hour

passed before he remembered that he had told Bernice in the diner that his name was Ed.

After a third marijuana cigarette Bernice stood up and took off her waitress uniform. The dress unbuttoned down the front. Bernice wore white underpants and a white brassiere. Boggs studied how the elastic bands of her underpants and the tight edges of the bra seemed to impress themselves deeply on Bernice's skin. It suddenly occurred to him, the underwear was squeezing her body out of it.

The bedroom was empty.

A mattress on the floor.

Boggs peeled off his new clothes.

They balled on the thin mattress for ten minutes. Boggs knew that it was ten minutes because he looked at his wristwatch when he sat down on the bed, looked at it again when they were done.

Bernice got up and padded, naked and lopsided, into the living room. Her right leg was the short one. Boggs had seen the knob-like protrusion and two patches of scar tissue, just below the right knee, on the outside of her leg. He hadn't noticed anything unusual in balling a girl with mismatched legs. But she'd been lying down. Maybe if they balled standing up—against the icebox, perhaps—that might be different.

Bernice limped back in, lit a store-bought cigarette. She stood naked at the end of the mattress, smoking.

She nodded in the direction of his feet.

"Do you always ball with your socks on?" she said.

Bernice got back on the mattress. They went at it again for five or ten minutes—Boggs wasn't sure about the duration of this second effort. They both lost interest at about the same time.

Bernice rolled off him.

Shortly she fell asleep.

After the patterns in the ceiling plaster, and the contours of

Bernice's bottom, Boggs got out of bed. Pulled his shorts on. He walked into the living room and sat down on the couch.

Picked up the phone.

He called the Drake Hotel. Asked for his messages. The hotel clerk read a phone number back to him. Boggs took a drawing pencil from a box on the coffee table, writing the number down on a corner of sketch paper.

When he called the number, he found himself talking to Emmett. One of Boggs's contacts.

Emmett gave Boggs a name and an address.

The name was an oddball one.

The address was on Haight Street. Not far from the panhandle of Golden Gate Park, according to Emmett.

Boggs wrote the address down.

Emmett had tracked the target to that address an hour ago. Emmett believed the target was still there, right now.

Boggs hung up the telephone, quietly.

He returned to the bedroom and picked up his clothes.

Boggs dressed in the bathroom. He didn't want to wake Bernice. But when he came back out he found Bernice sitting on the couch. She'd put on underpants and her corrective shoes. She sat forward, the edge of the sofa cushions. One hand holding another store-bought cigarette close to her mouth. She was studying the address Boggs had written on the corner of sketch paper.

"What do you want to go there for, Ed?" Bernice said. "Have you found a calling?" Bernice considered it an amusing remark.

Boggs didn't laugh.

She saw the cold expression on his face.

Silently, Bernice got up and returned to the bedroom.

She closed the bedroom door behind her.

Boggs's thoughts were suddenly clear. There was no more Mexican dirtweed funny business in his head.

Bernice had seen the address he'd written down. She knew the location. She'd remember it. That wasn't good.

Not good at all.

Boggs tore the note off the sheet of sketch paper, tucked it into his pocket. Bernice might be a problem he'd need to come back and fix.

Fifteen

ON HAIGHT STREET, Nash and Belcher dropped by Timothy Gone's charity kitchen. The dining room with the low ceiling where Greek men had once played bouzoukis and served *halva*, *ful medames*, anari cheese, and *dolmades* was now littered with wooden picnic tables of uncertain origin.

The faded mural on the wall, a Greek fishing village at sunset, was largely obscured by posters advertising VD treatment at the University of California Medical Center, on Parnassus Avenue. The only patron in the dining room was a slack-jawed young man who bounced a red rubber ball on the floor with the close attention of a tightrope walker splitting the atom. A round Mexican woman named Eunesta who worked in the kitchen said the establishment was in-between meals right now. Timothy Gone wasn't there.

Nash used the avocado green princess telephone mounted on the kitchen wall, dialed Gone's home telephone number.

No answer.

An hour later, at the Hall of Justice, Belcher and Nash had a powwow with Lieutenant Dark. The suggestion that Frank Barcelona had threatened grievous bodily harm to one of the Beatles had Dark concerned. Chief Jellicoe had already ordered Dark to make sure that threats to the health and welfare of the visiting Englishmen and their entourage were dealt with swiftly, and quietly.

When it came to the Beatles, Jellicoe wanted nothing but sweetness and light in the local press. Even if SFPD had to bust some heads.

At his desk, Nash drank coffee and puzzled over the contents of his in-tray. In the background he could hear the tap-tap of Hank Stain typing with two fingers, hunt and peck style. Nash read an internal bulletin, about a soft-spoken man who'd called SFPD's Potrero Station at 2143 hours the previous evening. The man suggested that the internal organs of the four Beatles should be collected for scientific research immediately, along with the organs of San Francisco Giant's coach Chub Feeney. What the connection between the English pop group and the baseball team manager was, Nash couldn't imagine. Unless it was that neither of them had managed to sell out Candlestick Park that year.

Meanwhile, television crews in Walnut Creek, Benicia, and Pinole had filmed citizens burning Beatles records, protesting the pop group's "Jesus" remark. In Sutro Heights and Daly City, teenagers gathered to have their Beatles haircuts clipped into more orderly styles, in demonstrations of mass barbering.

There was no news on the letter writer from San Rafael. It was possible the Marin County Sheriff's Office had filed SFPD's request for follow up in their round file, and returned to their bar stools.

After lunch, Nash and Belcher rode the elevator down to the

Crime Lab offices to talk to Alva Tombes.

Tombes's office looked like a pawn shop where nothing ever departed. Tombes didn't know what the status of the fingerprint work was—Leon Upchurch was in the field right now, another case. The blood sample evidence, so far, reflected only Gomez's Type O positive blood, and the blood distribution patterns noted in the room all supported the theory that the victim was hit near the table, probably from behind, then staggered to the couch. Whether or not the victim stretched out on the couch under his own power or was placed in that position by the assailant, or assailants, was open to conjecture.

All in all, Tombes felt reasonably sure the known facts weren't the shattering breakthrough the two inspectors hoped for.

Belcher and Nash collected more less-than-helpful information when they returned to the Hi-Tone Records studio on Water Street, an hour later.

Max Pinkrose was out searching for a singer, and Raylene Amador led Belcher and Nash into the studio's soundproof live room. Inside were two of the three extant Subterraneans—Dick Grogan and Bob Hickey.

Grogan played the drums, which he called "skins." Hickey wore eyeglasses with thick black frames that he pushed back on his nose with his finger, every two or three heartbeats. Both musicians wore madras shirts, white denim pants with stovepipe legs hemmed two or three inches too short.

Belcher sat down on a metal folding chair. Rested his pork pie hat on his knee.

Nash remained standing.

Grogan said he'd recently completed a bachelor's degree in chemistry at San Francisco State College. He saw himself as just killing time in a rock group, until he found a real job.

Grogan shot Hickey an uncomfortable look when he realized

he'd used the word "killing."

The one missing Subterranean was Eddie Euclid, who played the guitar. Euclid hadn't turned up for rehearsal that day, or the day before. Hickey thought Euclid may have quit, with Danny Gomez dead.

"Eddie is kind of wild," Hickey said. He studied his fingernails like they'd grown faces. "He's into that scene around Golden Gate Park, he's got a girlfriend who has a kid. They drink a bunch. But hey, I'm not throwing stones. I don't walk in Eddie's shoes."

"They're big and they stink," Grogan said.

"Is Euclid a hippie?" Belcher said.

Grogan shrugged. "He's a no-goodnik."

Nash opened his notebook. Not much to notate. Danny Gomez joined the group in June. It was Max Pinkrose who invited him to join. Prior to that, the group was called the Cave Dwellers. The Dwellers had been an instrumental combo, played surf tunes and movie theme songs at high school dances in Alameda County, and points south.

"We had matching purple velour suits," said Grogan.

"'Prune' suits," said Hickey.

Grogan and Hickey hadn't socialized with Gomez, before or after he joined the band. Neither had Eddie Euclid, as far as Grogan and Hickey recalled.

"Danny had his own thing," Grogan said.

"He smoked grass," Hickey said.

"He popped pills," Grogan said. "Uppers, downers. Floaters, fastballs. Shriekers."

"It doesn't matter if we say that, right?" Hickey said.

Grogan said, "He had that pad in the Mission District. I saw it once. It was a firetrap. Danny was a pig."

When Belcher asked about the Kimono à Go-Go, the two

musicians said they'd never gone there. Neither of them had heard of Frank Barcelona either. They agreed that Gomez was hard to get along with, but couldn't think of a reason why anyone would murder him.

Hickey said, "Just lately Danny and Eddie started experimenting with feedback from the amplifiers. Just funny electrical noises."

Grogan said, "If you turn the amplifier up to the top, the sound folds back on itself and screams."

"I'm not sure it was real musical," Hickey said.

"We're musical primitives," Grogan said.

"It's a drag," Hickey said. "We've got a single on KFRC and KYA, we're booked to open for the Beatles, but Danny is dead. Even if Mister Pinkrose can find another singer there's no time to rehearse. We'll get our doors blown off at Candlestick. What do we do now?"

Grogan snorted. "'Star'—it's just a plastic label."

"We recorded about thirty of Danny's songs in the last two weeks," Hickey said. "Now we're recording them all again. Something went bad with the recording heads and it wiped the tapes. We're playing from memory, there's nothing written down. It's hard to remember all that shit."

Nash recalled what Pinkrose said, the poor electrical wiring in the Hi-Tone studio. Nash felt certain that blank recording tape wasn't a sinister development.

Nash nodded toward the guitar resting against the wall. A folk-style guitar, with a black neck strap attached to it and the words THIS MACHINE KILLS MACHINES written under the sound hole, in block letters.

"That's one of Danny's guitars," Hickey said. He pushed his hair out of his eyes and off his forehead. When he let it go, the hair fell right back into his eyes. "It's a play on what Woody

Guthrie wrote on his guitar—'This machine kills fascists.' Danny said that people go through life like machines, just punching the clock. He believed a good song kills the robot part of your mind and frees it so that it can feel, and love."

Neither of the two former Cave Dwellers knew that Danny Gomez had received his draft notice. When Belcher posed the question, the two musicians looked worried that a wrong answer might get them drafted too.

On the way out, Nash got the address of the absent Subterranean from Raylene Amador. She puffed on a Pall Mall cigarette, clicked her tongue, consulted an address book. Nash was fairly certain Miss Amador was too ornery and hardscrabble to have ever sung pop melodies as "Mookie."

Sixteen

BELCHER AND NASH arrived at the Kimono à Go-Go at 1450 hours. The rumpled suit-and-tie businessmen turning a boozy lunch into a smashed afternoon were engrossed in the matinee show.

A woman in high heels and a silver bikini bottom gyrated on a small round stage, while a flamenco tune crackled over the PA system. At the moment the topless dancer was engaged in the complicated work of swinging one fully rounded breast in a clockwise motion while the other breast swung conversely.

Belcher leaned back, arms akimbo. Studying the trick while sozzled businessmen at shadowy tables clapped along. Nash pulled his sunglasses off as he too followed the dancer's progress. They didn't book acts like this on the Red Skelton show.

When the act wound down, a reedy male voice announced over the public address system: "Gentlemen and ladies, Miss Ineda Mann will take a short break."

Belcher said, offhand, "There's no 'ladies' here."

The murky green and orange hues of the bar were now augmented by baby spotlights, the beams reflecting off the moving parts of mobiles hung from the ceiling. The tinted squares sent prisms of yellow, red, and ocean blue floating softly across the walls and the clientele.

Belcher flashed his joy buzzer at a skittish waitress. Shortly a thin woman wearing a tight red skirt appeared. The skirt seemed designed primarily to keep the woman's hips and legs from moving more than an inch or two, in any direction.

The woman's name was Dorla Foote.

She was an assistant manager.

"Let's talk privately," the woman said.

Nash and Belcher followed the woman to an office where three identical black telephones sat on an otherwise empty desk. The calendar on the wall had been issued by the E-Z Cab Company of Sausalito, for the 1963 calendar year.

Nash unwrapped a stick of Blackjack chewing gum, folded it into his mouth. He wondered why Mrs. Foote's hair looked like a well-coiffed Brillo pad. The crow's feet at the corners of her eyes became vulture toes when she smiled.

"Mister Rollo took some musician friends up to Humboldt County, to record drum sounds," Foote said. She rested her tightly wrapped posterior against the edge of the desk. Folded her arms casually. Gave Belcher a smoky up-from-under look. "Mister Rollo likes to record music outdoors. He says redwood trees enhance resonance. Isn't that a scream?" Then, more quietly, "He's an innovator."

Dorla Foote said she'd started working at the club only a few weeks before. She liked the job fine. Belcher asked about Frank Barcelona.

"Frankie?" the woman said, not surprised to hear the name. "He plays here, now and then. Usually a saxophone. Tuesday and Wednesday nights we let musicians come in, play in-between the girlie acts. Strictly 'amateur hour'—we don't pay them."

"Where can I find him?"

Foote chewed on a red fingernail. When she spoke there was a flutter in her voice, like a vocal cord breaking loose. "There's a cocktail waitress who worked here—she and Frankie are kind of an item. Her name is"—the woman paused for a quick chew on a different nail. Then, "Her name is Pearly."

"Pearly Spence," Nash said. The conversation had taken an unforeseen turn. Pearly Spence was mixed up in this? Nash was surprised, but maybe not too surprised.

Dorla Foote had never met Pearly Spence but she'd heard about the woman. Word at the club was, Miss Spence and Mister Rollo went at it hammer and tongs.

"She's worked here before, three or four times in the last couple years," Foote said. "Mister Rollo fires her, hires her back, fires her again. That's what I've heard." A coy look appeared on Foote's leathery face. "I hear she and Frankie play house, if you catch my drift."

On a hunch Nash said, "There was a fight out back in the alley, Monday night. What was it about?"

Dorla Foote looked at Nash like he suddenly interested her in impure ways. "I wouldn't call it a fight," Foote said. "What I heard was, Frankie took something from the club that didn't belong to him. Mister Rollo and George—he's a bouncer—told Frank to bring it back. Whatever it was. 'Nuff said."

Foote didn't recall Barcelona ever talking to her about the Beatles, but she knew that he had the snarling heads of nine Chinese dragons tattooed in an arc across his back. The Chinese women working in the club's kitchen called him "Kowloon."

Foote had heard about Danilo Gomez's death on the radio. She had only met him once, her second or third night on the job.

"He and Frankie played that night. Some kind of jazzy honk-honk music. It seemed to bug people. When I heard that his real name wasn't 'O'Day,' it didn't surprise me. Danny looked as Irish as a refried bean."

Belcher paused in his note-taking. Nash almost swallowed his gum. Barcelona knew Pearly Spence biblically. Now he and Gomez are pals. And the alleged murder that Spence called SFPD about might've been a simple exchange of views, and fists, between Rollo and Barcelona. With someone leaving afterward in the delivery truck Rollo loaned to Spence.

Nash shifted his position against the wall. The room seemed too warm.

Dorla Foote snapped her fingers.

She had an idea.

"There's a gentleman who comes here, he's in the music business. He talked to Danny for a while." Foote slid her backside off the desk, stepped around behind, opened a desk drawer. Came up with a stack of business cards and removed the rubber band holding them together.

She found the one she wanted, handed it to Belcher.

Belcher glanced at the card and handed it to Nash. Underneath the name, JERRY TURNER, were the words ARTISTS AND REPERTOIRE. The job title meant exactly nothing to Nash. Printed in the bottom left corner was LOS ANGELES and a phone number. In the bottom right corner was SAN FRANCISCO, and another phone number. Across the top of the card, handwritten:

Stanley Hotchkiss.

"They both come in," Foote said. "They use the same phone numbers, I don't know. It was Mister Hotchkiss who talked to Danny. I don't know if he works for a record company or a TV show or the Knights of Columbus, but you can keep the card, if you want it."

Nash refigured the facts.

Danilo Gomez played his songs at the Kimono with Frank Barcelona. Barcelona tried to sell a recording of the Beatles to the man who managed Gomez's musical career. When Barcelona got the bum's rush from that same man, Barcelona turned around, broke into the Hi-Tone studio. With his purported *inamorata* making drunken phone calls to SFPD about a murder that didn't happen, behind the Kimono. Except that something did take place in the alley that night, and it had involved Frank Barcelona and Jasper Rollo.

The threads of the case were starting to knot.

Nash wondered who would get strangled.

Outside in the Ford, Belcher and Nash lit gaspers and smoked. "How about this—Gomez and Barcelona wanted to put a fast one over on Pinkrose," Belcher said. "So they record some songs that sort of sound like the Beatles, then try to pass them off as the real thing, make a quick buck."

There was a long silence before Nash said, "What if Pinkrose is lying? Maybe it wasn't a recording that Barcelona had to sell. It was something else. Something that Pinkrose wants to keep under wraps."

Belcher walked the idea around the block. "Gomez had something on Pinkrose, but he couldn't approach Pinkrose himself. He had to get Barcelona to do it. Then Gomez gets himself killed and Barcelona falls off the edge of the earth."

"Barcelona is dead?"

"I don't know. Gomez is dead."

"I think we can agree on that."

Belcher scratched his chin with the thumb of the hand that held his cigarette. "If the two of them worked a blackmail angle, and that's what we're talking about here, and with Gomez out of the picture, Barcelona gets all the spinach. And maybe it's a lot of spinach. Enough to make it worthwhile to kill your friend and disappear yourself."

Belcher exhaled cigarette smoke. The smoke cloud flattened out against the inside of the windshield like a bad idea hitting the horse it rode in on.

But another talk with Pinkrose was indicated.

EDDIE EUCLID'S listed address was a Victorian on Grove, two blocks off Ashbury. Inside the house the electric wail of a guitar attached to a strong amplifier sliced down from upstairs. The house had been converted into apartments. Mailboxes bolted to the wall in the entryway told Belcher and Nash that Eddie Euclid lived on the third floor.

Another burst of amplified guitar strings reached them.

Belcher set his jaw. "Let's go see the maestro."

On the first-floor landing Nash and Belcher stepped around the bare frame of a motorbike leaning against the wall. The frame was covered with scratches, as though the missing components of the bike had been chewed off by feral beasts. Two floors further up, a photograph of Ho Chi Minh was thumbtacked to the door Belcher and Nash were looking for. Sound vibrations rattled the door knob as a further volley of amplified guitar noise cascaded out from behind the door.

Belcher pounded on the door with his fist. The amplified guitar fell silent. After a long pause a man inside the apartment said: "What do you want?"

Belcher said, "Sir, open the door."

"*No hablo Ingles.*"

"Sir, are you in distress?"

"*Largo de aqui!*"

Nash knew the back and forth could go on all day before

Belcher mentioned SFPD. More than one widow was collecting on a life insurance policy left behind by a cop who took a bullet through a closed door. But the 'occupant in distress' angle smoothed over the rough edges. It was a law enforcement officer's duty to aid citizens in distress. If a door had to be kicked open first, well, it's all part of serving John Q. Public, and all the little Publics.

From inside the apartment, a further electric squeal was closely followed by a dull thud-like noise as something that wasn't a finger or a plectrum hit the guitar strings.

Belcher turned to Nash. He held one finger up, looking like he wanted to recite the properties of *pi* for Nash's edification.

Then Belcher stepped back.

Sized up the distance to the door. Glanced to the left and right. Took one heavy step toward the door.

Belcher jumped with one foot, kicked with the other.

The sole of Belcher's left shoe hit the door, the space just above the door knob.

Wood splintered. The door wobbled. Swung open.

Not fast but not slow.

Belcher hopped forward, trying to regain his balance. Stumbling into the apartment. Nash caught the door as it swung back toward him.

Nash followed Belcher inside.

A shirtless man, wearing a colorful Indian-style headband to hold his shoulder-length hair back, had just gotten to his feet. The man stood in the center of a bare off-white mattress, on bare off-white feet. Nash, wondering about the Speedy Gonzales voice they'd heard through the door, looked around for a Mex. If the shirtless man had ever been Mex, he wasn't now.

A teenage girl sat on the mattress behind the man. Her legs folded under her, an army surplus wool blanket wadded in her lap. The man's hands gripped the neck of a white electric guitar attached by a black cord to an amplifier. Electric squeals from the amplifier filled the room.

Belcher was reaching into his jacket for his SFPD badge when the shirtless man lunged, swinging the guitar at Belcher's head.

Belcher tried to deflect the blow. The electric squeals became a piercing shriek as the guitar came into contact with Belcher's arm. Belcher grabbed the young man, handily tossed him onto the mattress. Pulled the guitar from the man's hands.

The metallic screams from the amplifier continued.

While Nash patiently watched, Belcher took hold of the guitar neck with both hands, swung the guitar at the amplifier, like chopping wood with an axe. Pieces of guitar flew across the room.

The electric screams abruptly stopped.

Belcher tossed the mangled guitar aside.

Pulled the amplifier's electrical cord from the wall socket.

Silence.

Belcher waved his SFPD joy buzzer.

"Police," Belcher said.

"No shit," the shirtless man said.

"Are you Edward Euclid?"

The shirtless man sat up on the mattress. Folded his arms tight. He resolutely stared past Belcher's legs at the far wall. The girl seated on the mattress clung harder to the wadded blanket.

Nash saw the legs of a second girl, through the open window across the room.

The second girl wore a knee-length dress. She stood on an iron fire escape platform outside the window.

Dancing. Slowly. Softly.

Nash shouted to the girl, telling her to come inside. She didn't respond.

"Man, I haven't done anything," the shirtless man said.

Belcher stepped onto the mattress. He kicked the shirtless man's leg for no reason, then kicked it a second time, for the hell of it. Belcher raised his thumb, motioned over his shoulder, Nash's direction. "I've got a witness, he'll swear in court that you reached for something, he thought it was a weapon. Which necessitated the pushing of your head through that wall. So answer my questions. First question: Are you Edward Euclid?"

Outside the window, the pair of skinny legs extending below the hem of the knee-length dress continued to dance, sleepily, on the fire escape.

Nash stepped over to the window.

The girl outside was no older than the girl on the mattress. Her thin cotton dress covered with embroidered butterflies, her eyes far off. A crown of woven dandelions circled her head. The iron fire escape platform she stood on was just big enough to allow her to shuffle her bare feet a few inches, side to side. Swing boney hips, in slow motion. Tread the air, with matchstick schoolgirl arms. Humming softly to herself.

What interested Nash more, when he poked his head out the window, was the truck parked on the patch of grass behind the house.

It was a GMC delivery truck. Late Forties model. Painted a light shade of brown. Except for the lettering along the side, which was bright green: FINEST KIND MEATS & SAUSAGES. It was clear from where Nash stood, looking out of the third-floor window, that the truck was missing its tires and hood, and most of the engine.

Seventeen

NASH ARRIVED BACK at his apartment shortly after 1700.

He found a stack of paperback books on his kitchen table.

Nash's landlord, Mrs. Fish, lived in the house above Nash's basement apartment. On occasion she left him books that she'd finished with. Last time around, it was *The Valley of the Dolls*. Nash had lasted twenty pages, then used the book as a coaster for a bottle of fair to middling bourbon. Mrs. Fish had liked the tale well enough, but then Mrs. Fish's pastime of choice was sitting in the lounge at SFO, watching the shiny airplanes take off and land.

Nash was supposed to meet Tina Gone that evening at a restaurant called Steve's Broiler, in San Bruno. When Nash called her that afternoon from the Hall, she offered to put him in touch with Danilo Gomez's old girlfriend. But Nash would have to buy Tina a drink at Steve's, for her trouble.

Nash readily agreed.

Nash showered. In the kitchen he opened a can of Lucky Lager beer with a church key.

His thoughts returned to the dancing girl on the fire escape, at Eddie Euclid's hangout.

Nash had brought the girl inside, sat her down next to the other girl, on the mattress. The two girls were underage, and under the influence of illicit chemicals. Euclid denied it, even after Belcher tossed him around the room. The dilated pupils and sleepily distracted movements of the girls told a different story.

"I don't know anybody named Barcelona," Euclid said, right after his head hit the wall the second time. "The truck just appeared. Like, out of nowhere. The kids who crash here, they borrowed a few pieces. That's all I know, boss man."

Belcher and Nash dragged Euclid downstairs and outside.

In addition to four tires and a hood, the truck was missing a front bumper, a grill, headlights. Most of the engine components, down to but not including the block.

A plastic hose hanging from the rear panel indicated that gasoline had been siphoned from the tank. Nash noticed car parts that didn't belong to the truck scattered in the tall grass. Stripping cars was apparently a favored social outlet among the house's tenants.

Euclid thought that the truck appeared in the backyard the same day the folk music festival in Golden Gate Park went down. Euclid first saw the truck that night. Was that Tuesday? Euclid couldn't recall.

While Belcher questioned Euclid, Nash searched the truck.

The truck's license plates, front and back, were gone. So was the registration slip holder from around the steering column. Nash discovered a receipt in the glove box from a repair shop on Alvarez Street that contained the truck's license plate number. He'd run the number through Motor Vehicles, but it was a formality. Nash had no doubt the truck belonged to Jasper Rollo.

Nash also found a tiny triangle of paper under one of the truck's windshield wipers. It was the shade of green the Traffic Bureau used for citations. Nash made a note to run the plate number for recent traffic violations.

Euclid denied knowing Rollo.

And, like the other surviving members of the Subterraneans, Euclid claimed he hadn't associated with Gomez, outside of the band.

"Danny had his own trip. We didn't hang. I saw him Friday, at the studio." Euclid snorted sharply, clearing his porcine nostrils. "We were going to rehearse but he was zonked. I left. I didn't see him again. *Nada*. I didn't like him. He was a punk. Frisco is a punk town."

Nash looked up to see the second girl from Euclid's apartment stepping back onto the fire escape to resume dancing. Maybe the music inside her head never ended. A soft breeze blew her long straight hair across her face as she shuffled her feet, treaded air, turned toward the sunlight.

A FLATBED truck with a winch carried the carcass of Jasper Rollo's truck to the city impound lot. Not much point, at the moment, in pursuing a Grand Theft Auto charge against Euclid. No one, including the owner of record, Jasper Rollo, had reported the truck stolen.

But Barcelona was now a known acquaintance of Danilo Gomez. Maybe the discovery of the truck in Eddie Euclid's yard wasn't such a mystery. Euclid admitted that Gomez had been to Euclid's pad on at least one occasion. And the pad was close to Golden Gate Park, where Barcelona was seen on Tuesday. Had

Barcelona and Gomez taken the truck? Were they forced to ditch it, fast?

Nash was still asking himself those questions three hours later, when he walked into Steve's Broiler. The dinner rush at Steve's had thinned out. Tina Gone sat alone at the nearly deserted bar, her vodka martini half finished. The vibraphone jazz music playing in the background sounded warm enough to melt the ice in the ice machine behind the bar.

"This place is anonymous," Tina Gone said, when Nash sat down. "It's nice, not to have to be anyone. Have you found the man who shot out my window?"

Nash smiled. "Was it a man?"

"It was a woman?"

"More reasonable to assume it was a man."

A barman in a white tunic appeared. The dry vodka martini Nash ordered came with three olives and too much vermouth. "To make a dry vodka martini, one pours the vodka into a shaker of ice and shakes it," Nash said to Tina Gone in an affected voice, the barman out of ear shot. "Then one pours it from the shaker into a chilled glass. Then, being careful not to spill any, one fills an atomizer with vermouth, spritzes a cloud if it under the nose of the customer."

"You come from an affluent background, with your 'ones' and your 'atomizers.'" Tina Gone gave Nash an amused look that curved toward him fast, a speeding baseball.

"Not too affluent. When TV dinners first appeared, my mother broke down and bought one. She pried the turkey and mashed potatoes and peas out of the compartments in the tray, set the frozen chunks together in a skillet, and heated it all up on the stove. She thought that was how it worked."

Tina Gone raised her martini glass in mock salute. "Here's to the modern world. Soon everything will be frozen squares, maybe us too." Tina Gone frowned comically. She shook her hair. She prodded a green olive in her drink with a frill toothpick.

Gone had agreed to put Nash in touch with Carol Demko, who was appearing that night at the San Bruno National Guard Armory. She sang with a rock and roll outfit, the Medicine Hat Blues Band. According to Tina Gone, Demko was twenty-two years old. Came to San Francisco from Lodi, California, in the Central Valley. Demko liked to sing onstage in her bare feet.

Tina Gone didn't know how long Demko was Danilo Gomez's squeeze. She did know that the Medicine Hat Blues Band was one of the acts signed up for the hastily assembled "Beatles Go Home" concert, at the Fillmore Auditorium. It was scheduled for the same night the Beatles were performing at Candlestick Park.

"It's not only the 'Jesus Christ' remark," Tina Gone said. "People are just tired of the whole commercial bag the Beatles and the other English acts are into. The local bands want to showcase music with integrity. I don't agree that the Beatles have no integrity, but I dig what Carol and her band are saying. Pop music isn't bad. It's what people do with it that's bad."

"What does the name of her band signify?" Nash said.

"One of them comes from Canada. Medicine Hat—that's a town in Canada?"

"I thought it was a reference to narcotics."

"Everyone likes their medicine. Even a vodka martini. I'll probably have my Beat credentials revoked for imbibing square cocktail party drinks."

"I thought beatniks were *passé*."

"What makes you think so?"

"Or don't you read Herb Caen?"

"I don't need to. I see Herb Caen every time I go to the *Chronicle* office. He likes us young *passé* things. He chased me around the water cooler once, just to make a *passé*."

Nash watched Tina Gone shield her lips behind her fingers as she laughed. Nash found it an endearing quirk. At the moment, Danilo Gomez and Frank Barcelona were two shadows that might even be the same shadow in two disguises, but Tina Gone was real. The yellow stripes on her black sweater, her white go-go boots, the Jackie Kennedy sunglasses pushed back on her head, the look of willful carelessness in her eyes, all said so.

Ethical questions flashed in Nash's mind. He dismissed them. But he knew that if this meeting was entirely official, he would have approached it more officially.

THE V-8 engine growled. Tina Gone drove the Sunbeam Tiger fast. The Armory in San Bruno was only a short distance from the restaurant. With the convertible top down Nash sat back, let the cool wind rush past. They sped along the stretch of El Camino Real that cut across San Bruno. The shadows on the street grew longer as the sports car passed by.

A crowd milled on the sidewalk in front of the San Bruno Armory. Nash saw a lot of desert boots and chinos and tidy haircuts on the young men. Capri pants and plastic hair bands and sensible shoes on the young women. The strict dress code of the free and easy "hippie" counterculture in Haight-Ashbury hadn't yet reached San Bruno.

Tina Gone parked. They walked across the lot to the rear of the Armory building. A wide man in a sweatshirt stood on a loading dock, watching over the back door. Nash started to reach for his badge but Tina Gone spoke to the man quietly. The man opened the door, poked his head inside, shouted.

A minute later a beanpole with thick black hair stepped outside.

"Tina," the thin man said, opening his arms wide. "Groovy to see you." The man held a black cane in one hand. The kind of cane that went with the black cape with red lining that he wore over his white t-shirt.

The man introduced himself to Nash as Oates. Oates raised his arms again to further display the cape. Oates didn't ask who Nash was, and Nash didn't tell him.

"Come inside," Oates said to Tina Gone. "Dig the scene." Oates crossed his arms, the cape covering him, almost a priest's cassock. Nash wondered what Oates would say if Nash asked him to turn into a bat and fly away. The caped Bela Lugosi could do it, in the movies.

"I'm looking for Carol," Tina Gone said.

Oates raised his eyes to the night sky, maybe searching for signs of his fellow creatures. "It's cool." The expression on Oates's face suggested it wasn't cool at all. Oates unfolded his arms, tapped the surface of the loading dock with the tip of his cane. The maneuver reminded Nash of the four skeleton Beatles on the LP covers.

Oates turned quickly, got a good departing flutter out of the cape. Disappeared back into the building.

Soon the sound of amplified guitars and crashing drums reached Nash and Tina Gone on the loading dock. Even muffled by the closed back door, the band playing inside sounded extremely loud to Nash. The door opened again, the roar of the amplified instruments growing to a crescendo. A short woman with shoulder length blonde hair fashioned into large flip curls at the bottom, an upside-down ocean wave, stepped outside.

The woman's face was round. Her lips were small.

Her buckskin shirt was heavily fringed.

Tina Gone stepped up to hug her. When Tina Gone introduced Nash as a police inspector in San Francisco, the young woman looked taken aback.

"I don't talk to fuzz much," Carol Demko said.

Tina Gone and Nash followed Carol Demko to a '50 Chevrolet station wagon parked at the edge of the lot. The vehicle was painted in red, white, and blue stripes. Whoever had done the painting had used a large-bristled paint brush—Nash could see the brush marks in the paint.

Carol Demko unlocked the car door, reached inside, retrieved a pint bottle of Southern Comfort whiskey. She unscrewed the cap and took a long snort.

Demko said, "Danny and me got together last year, over the summer. When I put together my first band, the Sombreros. We were together until June. Then it was splitsville. I had to get out. Get some air. I didn't see him again after that, except for one time, a couple of weeks ago."

Demko offered the bottle of Southern Comfort around. There were no takers. She shrugged. "When the Sombreros broke up, Danny joined the Cave Dwellers, who changed their name to the Subterraneans. I joined Medicine Hat. We play Howlin' Wolf and Big Bill Broonzy songs. Except that we use heavy chords and tremolo bars. We make Howlin' Wolf really howl. No disrespect to the man, of course."

"You saw Gomez, two weeks ago?" Nash said.

There was a long pause. Tina Gone placed a sympathetic hand on Carol Demko's shoulder while the woman studied the label on the liquor bottle, as though she just now realized what she was imbibing. Finally Carol Demko nodded, more to herself than in answer to Nash's question.

Demko chose her words carefully.

"I went to his place, just to talk," she said. "I'd heard about his new band and I wanted him to know about mine. But he got angry. Danny was born mad. Mad at the world. It was a real negative scene, so I split. That was the last time I saw him. I'm not sure what day that was, exactly."

After another belt of Southern Comfort, Carol Demko reached down the front of her fringed shirt, removed a flattened green and white pack of menthol cigarettes from inside her brassiere.

Nash gave her a light.

"Where does his family live?" Nash said.

"His mother lives in New Mexico," Carol Demko said. "He never mentioned anyone else. He was kind of on his own, like from day one. You know? I never saw him do anything other than play a guitar and fight and get loaded. I shouldn't talk about him like that because he's dead, but it's the truth."

"The truth won't hurt him now," Tina Gone said.

Demko said, "It won't set him free either."

"Did he sell narcotics?" Nash said.

"He sold whatever he could get his hands on. He tried to sell me once or twice." The woman paused to give Nash a tight-lipped stare. But Demko hadn't heard of Frank Barcelona. As far as she knew, Danilo Gomez didn't have friends, in any of the usual senses.

"When we were together, he didn't hang with anyone but me," Demko said. "Nobody else would put up with it. His temper, his bullshit. He could be sweet too, but you never knew which Danny you were going to get. We used to fight a lot—with fists. He didn't always win. He was not a together person.

"But Danny could write a song. He wrote songs about things that songs are supposed to be written about. 'Who am I?' 'Why am I here?' 'Who are these rubes around me?' He wrote songs for angels to sing."

Across the dark parking lot, someone on the loading dock, calling the woman's name. Demko flicked the half-smoked cigarette onto the pavement. Time to go to work. Nash saw tears in her eyes. Nash tried to imagine tiny Carol Demko throwing punches at a hot-blooded Mexican man hopped up on grass and pills and booze. It was a stretch, but who knew?

INSIDE THE Armory, Nash stood beside Tina Gone as they watched Carol Demko and her band step onto the stage. The four young men with Demko looked like they'd just finished their shift at a machine shop. Demko stepped up to the microphone. She said to the crowd, "Tell you what, people. If we play some tunes, you've got to dance and party. That's the deal. Is that okay with you?"

Nash didn't think the songs Demko's band played sounded like blues songs. They didn't sound like anything else either, but the group performed them like they meant it.

The Medicine Hat Blues Band played for forty minutes, then hustled off the stage. Tina Gone went to find refreshments and returned with three cans of Hamm's beer. She and Nash worked on the beer while another band prepared to play. Tina Gone wanted to stay and watch them. She handed Nash the third can of beer to clinch the deal.

The next act called themselves the 13th Floor Elevators. It seemed to Nash like a silly kind of name.

The hall went dark. The band began to play. The only light came from the colored lights that lit the stage, and the red electric exit signs over the hall doors. The band included a wild-haired man holding a ceramic whiskey jug up to a microphone, puckered lips blowing over the top of the jug, a moonshine flute. Nash wasn't sure this music was the blues either, but the first song seemed to grow louder and unfold and bloom, in the manner of a flower.

Nash started to feel, tangibly, the layers of the music as it crisscrossed the dark room. He also felt the onset of a headache. His synesthesia was playing tricks. Nash saw splashes of red and yellow at the edges of his vision. Then the two colors coalesced into a soft orange sun that seemed to hang over the crowd. The first song segued into the second song. The third song came huffing and puffing behind the second, a Southern Pacific locomotive, while the crowd danced. Not in any particular style. The dancers moved every which way.

Tina Gone tugged on Nash's arm. She smiled. Nash thought her smile looked like all the colors of the rainbow that he'd never paid attention to, and now wished he had.

Tina Gone began to dance too.

Nash looked up to see if the benevolent orange sun was still there. He found instead that he was standing inside some sort of architecture that existed within the larger architecture of the Armory building.

He saw white pillars rising up, curving, cathedral-like. Nash's headache grew stronger. He watched Tina Gone wade into the sea of dancers. She began swaying with the movement of the waves. Nash lit a gasper. He wondered if he might succeed in taking Tina Gone home with him tonight.

The band onstage reached a boiling point. The drums pounded. The slashing guitars careened and ricocheted. Nash saw a warm yellow light appear at the back of the stage. It rested on top of a pyramid shape painted on the back wall. The light blinked, a large yellow eye. Nash was almost certain that all of this was the work of the synesthesia. He dropped the half-smoked gasper, crushed it under his shoe. The music collapsed into a cacophony of broken sounds. Nash watched, dumbfounded, as the guitarists onstage pulled on their guitar strings until the strings broke. Now the guitarists simply stood there, holding their broken useless instruments, staring mutely back at the audience, while the yellow light at the top of the pyramid continued to blink and the drummer behind his kit tossed off paradiddles and the electric amplifiers hummed and rumbled.

Nash decided that fresh air was called for.

TINA GONE drove Nash back to the restaurant where he'd left the Plymouth. Nash tried to make light conversation that might work itself around to an invitation back to his place, but the headache that had begun at the Armory had left his thoughts scrambled and numb.

But something somehow was decided. Tina Gone dropped Nash beside his car in the parking lot at Steve's Broiler. She waited while he climbed into the Plymouth.

He pulled out of the parking lot, onto the street.

She followed.

Through his partly rolled down window Nash heard the Sunbeam's engine chewing up the road behind him. In the rearview mirror Nash saw that the Tiger kept to the designated safe distance—one car length for every ten miles an hour. For reasons that he couldn't pinpoint, the thought of Tina Gone practicing sound traffic skills made him smile.

The night air helped clear Nash's head. The spectacle at the Armory receded. The Sunbeam's headlights stayed in his rearview mirror back into San Francisco. Down Nineteenth Avenue to Sloat. Sloat to Sunset to Pacheco.

On the front stoop outside of Nash's basement pad Tina Gone wrapped her arms around his neck, pressed her lips hard against his. His hands searched for a handhold somewhere along the smooth curve of her back. He failed to find one, searched lower.

"Nice digs," Tina Gone said when they were inside. Her face was buried in his neck and her hair brushed his cheek. Tina Gone pulled her sweater off, shook her hair free of the garment. The black and yellow sweater landed on the television. In her brassiere now, she stepped back, shook her hair some more, just to do it.

Then she pushed into him. As near as Nash could tell, Tina Gone wanted to climb onto his lap while he was still standing. Nash was trying to find a way to make it work when the phone rang.

"Don't answer it," Tina Gone said.

"You either."

The telephone bell rang six times.

Then it stopped.

Tina Gone kissed him hard.

They fumbled toward the sofa. Nash noticed that Tina Gone's hair smelled like the incense her brother burned in his house to mask the musky odor of reefer. The telephone started ringing again. Nash counted six rings.

Then a seventh ring. And an eighth.

Ma Bell sounded angry tonight.

A heavy sigh.

Nash got up and answered the telephone.

It was a sergeant at the Hall of Justice. He'd been instructed to ring Nash all night until Nash answered. The sergeant directed Nash to stand by for a call from Inspector Ross Belcher.

Nash hung up while the sergeant tried to reach Belcher. Tina Gone sat upright on the sofa now. She lit a gasper, motioned to Nash. He nodded. She lit a second gasper and held it out for him to take.

Two minutes later Belcher called.

"A little something in Hippieville has gone bump in the night," Belcher said. "You'll never guess. I seem to recall you told me about your new playmate, and that she has a brother who runs some kind of hinky soup kitchen on Haight? Right at the moment there's a dead man inside that kitchen. He's missing his head. You interested?"

Eighteen

INSPECTOR LOU CRANDALL stood silently beside an open window in a back room of the former Greek restaurant at 1733 Haight Street. The window looked out on an alley that was, right now, bathed in the whirling red of an SFPD prowl car roof light. The features on Crandall's pale round face were obscured by the smoke from his howitzer cigar.

Nash stepped further into the room. He'd found three more prowl cars and two unmarked SFPD vehicles parked out front when he arrived. Belcher told Nash to see Crandall, inside the charity kitchen.

Belcher didn't say much else.

Nash stepped over to where the corpse lay. The bare hands of the deceased male Caucasian were tied behind the victim's back with electrical cord. The dead man's torso had fallen forward, but it was clear that he had been on his knees, possibly with his head bowed, when he was killed.

What remained of the man's neck was a bloody mass of torn tissue and exposed vertebral bone.

The man's head had left a dark red trail on the floor after being kicked aside, presumably by the murderer. The head now rested under a wooden chair next to a metal cabinet that held large boxes of powdered milk, instant rice, Malt-O-Meal. The severed head faced outward from the shadows under the chair, stealthily watching the room from a hiding place. Except that the eyes in the head had no spark of life in them.

Nash had grudgingly left the warm embrace of Tina Gone to show up here. He'd helped her find the clothing she'd vacated, promised to call her as soon as he could. He told Tina only that he was needed at a crime scene, he didn't mention where. She'd left the apartment with him and climbed into her sports car.

Nash watched her drive off.

He wasn't happy about it.

Pre-*coitus interruptus* was never agreeable.

It was Crandall who broke the silence. "What do you think, Nash?"

Nash didn't have to think too hard. "It looks like an execution."

Nash listened to Crandall clear his throat. The sound had a loose wet edge. Crandall removed a black leather billfold from his jacket pocket, tossed it to Nash.

The victim's wallet. It contained two hundred dollars, mostly in tens and twenties. The victim hadn't been killed for his money, but Nash hadn't been in much doubt on that point. A common stickup isn't normally concluded with the forcible removal of the victim's head.

There was also a driver's license, issued by the state of Louisiana to William Donald Slocum. Oddly, the washed-out photograph of Slocum looked very much like the dead face under the wooden chair across the room. As everyone knew, photographs taken at the Department of Motor Vehicles never looked true to life. It had never occurred to Nash that they might look true to death.

Slocum had resided on the quaintly named Tickle Street in Shreveport. Thirty-eight years old. The wallet also contained Diner's Club and Texaco credit cards, and the business card of a men's clothing shop at Market and Stockton, near Union Square.

Nash tossed the wallet back to Crandall.

"He had a pistol in a real pretty calf's leather holster, strapped under his arm," Crandall said. He rolled the cigar around in his mouth, looking for a new spot to chew on. "The pistol is gone but the holster is still there, take my word. There's a throwing knife strapped to his ankle. I'm guessing Slocum wasn't a regular here."

Nash watched Crandall stare at the corpse for a while longer, then decided that Crandall could do his staring alone. Nash walked out to the long dining room full of wooden picnic tables. The heavy front door of the former restaurant was propped open.

Belcher stood just outside, right where Nash had left him when Nash arrived.

"Crandall looks like he's seeing ghosts," Nash said.

Belcher shrugged. "A guy without his noggin—it takes a little time to reconcile that with the big wide world."

Nash lit a gasper and smoked. A small crowd of locals had gathered across the street. Two bare-chested long-haired men squatted on the sidewalk, pounding out voodoo rhythms on bongo drums. The various police vehicles were parked helter-skelter in front of the restaurant, a disentangled traffic accident. Clouds congealed in the night sky. The stars disappeared.

Belcher removed his crumpled hat, smoothed his hair back. "A citizen heard a commotion and called it in. A prowl unit found what you just saw. The window was already open. No description of an assailant. No witnesses. Whatever the murder weapon is, it's big and sharp and has a lot of blood attached to it."

"The victim's pistol was taken."

"Yes, there is that angle." Belcher nodded sagely. "Looks like a problem for the police. Let's call them, so I can go back to bed."

"How did you wind up here?"

"Crandall called me. He wanted me to drop by and tell him what I thought. When I realized where the body was, I gave you a jingle. Since you know some of these jokers."

"I know bubkis about the dead man."

"It's a live one I'm thinking of."

Belcher paused, scratched his ear. Eyed the two bongo-playing men across the street. Nash wondered how many city ordinances could be broken by voodoo drums in the wee hours.

A man wearing a fisherman's cap with his black suit climbed out of one of the unmarked black Fords, where he'd been writing notes in a notebook. A Homicide Detail inspector, Buddy Arbogast. Nash didn't know him well but Belcher had worked with him in the past. Arbogast and Crandall had both been at the Hall of Justice when the call came in from the first patrol unit at the scene. They drove out to Haight Street together.

"Nothing much to go on," Arbogast said when he came over. Arbogast was a thin man with thick eyebrows, a chin sharpened to a point. The wrinkled black suit made him look like a shady undertaker, assuming there are other kinds.

Arbogast went on. "A fellow who lives across the alley from this joint reported hearing screams. He didn't see anything. I've got patrolmen beating the bushes. The blade work on the victim's neck isn't ragged, so the murder weapon was probably some type of sword. Nothing a person can drag behind him on the street without being noticed." Arbogast glanced at the bongo players. "Even on this street. The Crime Lab boys are on the way, and I've got an address for the fellow who runs this dump. He lives on Hayes, a few blocks from here. I sent a patrol unit to fetch him."

"Nash here knows him," Belcher said.

"I know who he is," Nash said.

"Nash is banging his sister," Belcher said.

"That's not a true statement," Nash said.

Arbogast, bemused, scratched his jaw and studied Nash's face like he'd never seen one before. Nash gave Arbogast the skinny on the occurrences of the previous night, first at Tina Gone's pad, then at Timothy Gone's Hayes Street residence.

Belcher had already told Arbogast some of it.

Nash was still talking when a prowl car pulled up behind the collection of other SFPD vehicles.

A patrolman jumped out of the car. Approached. He reported to Arbogast that he'd visited the residential address for Gone. The patrolman found no one at home, the house dark, no evidence of hasty egress.

"*Nada,*" the patrolman said, in summation.

"Call his sister," Arbogast said to Nash when the patrolman had returned to his car. "Maybe she's got a line on his whereabouts."

"Not in the middle of the night."

"We don't work banker's hours, Nash."

"I'll talk to her in the morning."

Arbogast nodded grimly to himself, as though he'd just learned an important truth. Nash considered the subject closed. He had no desire to question Tina Gone right now. Her brother's whereabouts could wait. He wasn't a suspect, at the moment.

Belcher studied his Timex wristwatch, announced that it was just past two o'clock, by the by. Arbogast disappeared into the building. When he returned he looked even more perturbed. "Ross, get Lou out of here. He's got a bee up his ass and it doesn't have much to do with my crime scene. Take him home, buy him a drink, whatever it takes. The Crime Lab will have enough to do without dealing with Lou the Sphinx."

There was a long silence. Belcher looked like he wanted to tell Arbogast all the reasons why Crandall was Belcher's good friend and Arbogast was just Arbogast, but he held his tongue.

CRANDALL AND Belcher drove out of Haight-Ashbury in Belcher's Pontiac Bonneville, heading toward Van Ness. Nash followed in the Plymouth. Belcher drove down to Hemlock, followed it a block and a half, then pulled the Bonneville onto a smooth patch of blacktop between two narrow buildings and parked. Nash parked behind Belcher's car and got out, still wondering where they were headed.

Nash followed the two full inspectors to a wooden door half-hidden by shadows and trash cans. A diamond-shaped window in the door was covered from the inside by a dark blue cloth.

Belcher knocked, then knocked again. A hand pushed the cloth in the window aside. A face peered out.

The door opened.

The three inspectors stepped inside. A short man with sad eyes closed the door quickly, checked to make sure the bar towel was back in place over the window.

Nash realized where they were.

They had come through the back door of the Golden Bubble. A fast and loose cocktail lounge that fronted on Post Street.

Like any decent watering hole, the Bubble had no front

windows, and right now the front door was locked tight. It was past the legal cutoff time for selling alcohol, but the Bubble still had numerous paying customers, and it was two bits a throw for beer on tap.

Nash had been to the Bubble for lunch with Belcher once or twice, but Belcher had never mentioned that the Bubble's owner, Chuck Roscoe, ran an after-hours hootch parlor.

The three inspectors took seats at a table in back. "Roscoe calls it a private club to keep PD and the Liquor Control Board off his back," Belcher said to Nash. "Since most of PD drinks here, I'd guess he doesn't have much to worry about."

Belcher, Crandall, and Nash finished one round of bourbon and sodas and were starting on the second round when Lou Crandall finally emerged from his thoughts.

"You know what I saw, don't you?" Crandall said to Belcher.

"I know what it might've looked like, Lou."

"Looked like? Hell."

"Don't jump to conclusions."

"It was a punch in the gut."

Nash had no idea what the other two were discussing.

Clearly they'd discussed it before.

The liquor slowly untied Crandall's tongue. Then Crandall told Nash a tale that Belcher was already familiar with, although he too seemed to be hearing some of the details for the first time.

"I was a gunner's mate," Crandall said. "The USS *Houston*, a cruiser, ninety-two hundred tons. I went aboard at Darwin in Australia. Valentine's Day, 'Forty-two. Two weeks later we duked it out with the Japs in the Sunda Strait, off Sumatra. The Japs kept coming at us—dive bombers and Zeros, one right after the other. We fired shells so fast the barrels on the twenty-eight millimeter ack-ack guns started to melt.

"There was an explosion, amidships. The fire spread and the

ship started to list badly. I grabbed a life preserver and went over the side, like everyone else who still could.

"We were in the water four days. We clung to pieces of wreckage, whatever would float. At first the screaming from the burn casualties kept up nonstop. Then it petered out. Some of the men died from injuries and some of them died from sharks. Some just gave up and drowned.

"I tied myself to two other men and we hung on to debris, kept our heads above water. We thought that three of us together, we'd be easier to spot by a rescue plane. But no one came looking for us. There was just water, all the way to the horizon, every direction.

"After four days a ship appeared. It was a little tub, an island steamer. When it got closer I saw two ack-ack guns, one fore, one aft. I saw the Rising Sun flag on the stern and knew we were cooked. The Japs had a reputation for shooting survivors in the water, just for the sport.

"But the Japs didn't shoot us. Maybe they were low on ammo. The three of us looked mostly dead anyway. The Japs pulled us out of the drink and gave us a ladle of fresh water to wet our throats. Then they threw us in the tub's hold and closed the hatch.

"We sat in darkness for days.

"When the Japs opened the hatch again they kicked and punched us off the boat and onto dry land. They didn't tell us where we were but it turned out to be Java. They took us to a POW camp in the center of the island. The prisoners there looked even worse than we three did. It was a camp full of skeletons that walked and talked.

"The prisoners were British, with some Australians and a couple of Dutch. There was only one other American in the camp, a Navy flier who was shot down. His name was Weber. He died a month later from a combination of beri-beri and tropical ulcers and no hope. Mostly it was the beri-beri. It caused fluid to build up in his lungs, until finally he drowned in it.

"Just before he passed over, Weber gave me a letter to deliver to his folks. He'd carefully written the name and address on the dirty envelope. I still remember it—Mr. and Mrs. Clarence T. Weber, One-twenty-seven Corral Street, Butte, Montana. Weber made me promise to get the letter to them. After Weber died I opened the envelope because I wanted to read the letter and learn something about this man who had just died, a long way from home. When I unfolded the sheets of paper I found they were blank."

Crandall's eyes were fixed on the ashtray in front of him. Nash watched Crandall's hand as the older man absently pushed the cigarette butts around in the ashtray with a wooden match stick until the smoked butts were neatly lined up, a row of orderly graves. "We lived on a handful of rice and a ladle of thin vegetable broth a day," Crandall said. "We were always hungry. I ate tree bark. I'd have eaten a shoe if I'd had a shoe. The British officers were at the top of the pecking order. They gave us jobs to do. A Limey major told me my job was fire detail.

"Fire detail was stacking up lengths of bamboo, then stacking the prisoners who had died that day onto the wood. Then we set fire to the bamboo, cremated the bodies. It was the only sanitary way.

"What I remember most is the way the legs and arms began to jump around as the bodies burned. Sometimes the contraction of the muscles would cause a corpse to sit right up in the fire with licks of flame shooting out of their empty eye sockets and their mouths. Like they wanted to have a quiet word with you, from Hell.

"The only news we got came from a radio an Australian put

together. Just bits of whatever he could get his hands on, and a whole bunch of nothing. When the weather was right he could pick up the BBC from New Delhi, even KGEI from San Francisco. Incredible.

"A radio was forbidden, of course. We kept the radio parts hidden, but the Jap guards got wind of it, they always did. They lined us up in formation in the yard. We stood out there in the sun all day while they ranted and raved at us to give up the man with the radio. Men keeled over, unconscious.

"Nobody squealed.

"So the Japs rearranged those of us still on our feet into eleven rows. They chalked one of the Japanese ideograms for the numbers two through twelve on each of our foreheads. No particular order. Then the Japs huddled together, rolled a pair of dice they had.

"The first roll came up nine.

"They rolled the dice again and it came up five. Two Jap guards walked to the eighth row of prisoners—there wasn't a row numbered 'one', you see—and they grabbed the first one in the row who had a five chalked on his forehead.

"They double-timed him up to the front of the formation, tied his hands together. Made him kneel, head down, in front of the Jap commander, dressed up, with his ceremonial sword. The commander grunted and growled. He wrestled his sword out of its scabbard. Waved it around with his short little Jap arms. Then he took aim. He brought the sword down and sliced off Number Five's head with one good whack.

"The severed head went into a wicker basket. There were three more heads in the basket before the Australian who'd put the radio together stepped forward and told the Japs where the parts were hidden.

"His head became the fifth one in the basket."

A puzzled expression crossed Crandall's face, as though he couldn't quite give credence to the memories he recounted. Nash finished his second bourbon and soda. The ice at the bottom of the highball glass rattled, a collection of broken teeth.

Crandall said, "That night when we burned the five bodies, there were no last words from flaming skulls. The five loose heads had been impaled on the posts of the camp fence. It didn't matter. We already had all the messages we needed from Hell."

In the long silence that followed Nash realized that the Golden Bubble had emptied out. Across the room sad-eyed Chuck Roscoe wiped the pitted wooden surface of the bar.

"One last one, Lou?" Belcher's voice was hoarse from drinking and smoking and not talking.

"Sure, Ross." Crandall's eyes remained fixed on the ashes in the ashtray.

Belcher stepped up to the bar, came back with a last round of drinks. Nash watched Crandall drain off half of his bourbon first thing, reach for a fresh cigarette. The pack was empty. Belcher shook one up from his own pack.

Crandall took the gasper and lit it and added the spent wooden match to the butts and burnt matches in the ashtray in front of him.

"What I don't understand," Crandall said. Nash watched the older man struggle with his thoughts. "When the Japs took over half the Pacific, they said they wanted to give the conquered people better lives. The Japs called their territory the Greater Asian Co-Prosperity Sphere. And now this fellow on Haight, he calls his soup kitchen the same kind of thing.

"Maybe it's only a joke. But then we find a headless corpse there, on its knees. Just like the Japs used to do."

Crandall turned to Nash like he wanted to ask a question, but instead he merely shook his head.

"You're right, Lou," Belcher said. He spoke quietly, not wanting to disturb the shadows. "It's a kooky thing."

Nineteen

BELCHER LOOKED WIDE awake when Nash arrived at the Hall of Justice at 1000 hours. Belcher smoked while Nash filled him in on the research Nash had done.

Nash found the confirmation he wanted in his set of Funk and Wagnalls encyclopedias. In June 1940, Japanese Emperor Hirohito, the divine "chrysanthemum warrior," and his government ministers created the Greater East Asia Co-Prosperity Sphere from the lands Japan had conquered in the Pacific. The brotherly label didn't hide Japan's imperial intentions.

Timothy Gone played on the name when he christened his Haight Street charity kitchen. It no doubt didn't occur to Gone that one day an unknown man would display the supreme discourtesy of getting himself beheaded in that same kitchen, in a manner that suggested a Japanese prisoner of war camp to Inspector Lou Crandall of the SFPD Homicide Detail.

Kooky, as Belcher had noted.

Belcher had been productive that morning too. He'd just gotten off the phone with the president of the San Francisco chapter of the Beatles International Fan Club—Miss Binky Schulman, of Menlo Park.

Schulman had assured Belcher that "Frank Barcelona" was not a name that figured in accepted Beatle lore.

Belcher had also spoken that morning to Dick Emory, the promoter of the Candlestick Park show.

Emory also had never heard of a Beatle named Frank Barcelona. He was, however, able to impart that the Beatles entourage would not stay overnight in San Francisco before or after the Candlestick Park engagement. They were staying in Los Angeles. Fly to San Francisco on the afternoon of the show, return to LA that night.

SFPD would be responsible for the Beatles' collective safety for no more than a few hours.

But it also meant that if SFPD wanted to interview the four Beatles about Barcelona, they'd have to do it at Candlestick, or at SFO, or en route between the two.

Another thing that Emory told Belcher: The Candlestick Park show wasn't close to sold out. Emory said he could offer tickets to SFPD at a discount, if the department bought in bulk.

Belcher saved the best for last.

"Dottie from Warrants ran down the number of a fellow in the Beatles camp, so I gave him a ring." Belcher read from the scribble on his yellow legal pad. "Desmond Smythe-Hodge—he's an assistant to a top banana named Taylor. The entire banana bunch is holed up in Vancouver right now. They're leaving for LA shortly. He never heard the name 'Barcelona' in connection with the Beatles or anything else, except maybe Spain."

"You didn't talk to a Beatle?"

"It seems only God talks to actual Beatles."

"Except when they're insulting him."

As for the decapitation case on Haight, Timothy Gone was still missing in action. A patrol unit had spoken to a Mexican female who had arrived for work at the kitchen that morning to find it shut down by SFPD.

The woman stated that not seeing Gone for a day or two wasn't unusual. She also said that there had been trespassers in the building before, sometimes they sleep there. She didn't consider that too unusual either. Given the clientele, the location.

As for the staff, the kitchen was open until nine o'clock at night, and the volunteers working there were sometimes present in the building until eleven.

The Mexican woman knew no one who answered to the name or fit the description of the victim.

NASH WAS reading the police blotter when Lieutenant Dark appeared in the Homicide bay. Dark directed Belcher and Nash to follow him upstairs.

"The big fellow wants to talk at us about every little thing," Dark said in the elevator.

In the upstairs conference room Nash was surprised to see Lou Crandall and Buddy Arbogast seated at the table, along with another homicide inspector named Vince Hillman. Across the room Miss Figgis, Chief Jellicoe's secretary, fussed with a coffee urn on a service table littered with cups and saucers.

The three inspectors seated at the table already had cups of coffee resting beside notebooks, pencils, ashtrays. Lieutenant Dark's eyebrows rose in appreciation as Miss Figgis poured a cup of coffee and handed it to him with a flash of her pearly whites.

Arbogast looked dog tired.

Lou Crandall looked like he'd woken from the dead.

Crandall still had the thousand-yard stare he'd had earlier that morning, at the Golden Bubble. So this meeting had to do with the headless Louisianan? Nash didn't know what Hillman's angle on this case was. When Nash took a seat next to Hillman and asked him, Hillman didn't know either.

The black telephone on the refreshment table rang. Miss Figgis picked up the receiver, spoke into it quietly, then hung up. The Hawaiian design on her tight-fitting dress involved big red flowers with big green leaves on a big yellow background. Everyone knew that Miss Figgis bought her clothes at I. Magnin and City of Paris, she left the receipts displayed casually on her desk.

Miss Figgis sashayed out.

"What are we in trouble for now?" Belcher said to no one in particular. He idly tapped his spoon against his coffee cup.

"Whatever it is, we're not doing it right," Hillman said. "How do I get a fat office with air conditioning and a secretary swishing her can in my face."

"The only can you yokels are getting is the shit can," Arbogast said. "Even your wives don't like you."

Hillman said, "What do you know about my wife?"

"Evidently, more than you do," Belcher said to Hillman.

"Put the kibosh on the wisecracks," Lieutenant Dark said from his chair near the head of the table. "This isn't monkey hour."

Chief of Inspectors Jellicoe arrived. His blue sharkskin suit, cut in the triangular Italian manner, seemed to reflect the ceiling lights. The deep lines on his flat face reflected the weight of his job as he saw it.

Two men followed Jellicoe into the room. Both men wore khaki Army-issue summer uniforms with short sleeves and squares of ribbons, and both men held the rank of lieutenant colonel. The legs of their uniform pants were bloused into the tops of heavy black paratrooper boots.

The beret caps the two officers carried were green.

The Army officers passed behind Nash's chair on their way to the head of the table with Jellicoe. Nash caught the odor of mothballs, as though the Army uniforms had just been pulled from a quartermaster's storeroom.

When Jellicoe reached the head of the table he called for silence.

"Gentlemen, let me introduce Colonel Kepler"—Jellicoe motioned toward the taller of the two officers, then the shorter one—"and Colonel Gorman. From the Presidio. They want to solicit our assistance in a certain matter. Give them your full attention."

Jellicoe rattled off the names of the gathered Homicide Detail personnel for the benefit of the two colonels.

Then Jellicoe and the officers took seats.

In the hush that followed, the tall colonel removed a buff-colored file folder from the leather briefcase he'd brought with him. He flipped quickly through the papers in the file, looking for something. He wore wire-framed eyeglasses with temples that pressed tightly against the skin.

The other officer was short, broad-shouldered, with a hook nose. His small sharp eyes surveyed the room quickly, as though searching for the immediate threat. Gray hair, not much longer than beard stubble. A patch of bare scalp apparent, a pink island on top of his otherwise bristly head.

Nash knew the berets both men had set on the table were the signature headgear of the Army's Special Forces units.

A few years back, Nash had watched a high-altitude parachuting demonstration that a squad of Green Berets put on at the Navy depot on Treasure Island, in San Francisco Bay. The parachutists had left for Vietnam the next morning, aboard the aircraft carrier USS *Yorktown*. The Green Berets were supposed to be the toughest of the tough nuts. There was even a song about them on the radio now: "The Ballad of the Green Berets." It wasn't tuneful, but it was good advertising.

Nash didn't know about Jellicoe, but Belcher, Crandall, and Arbogast were all Navy men back in the Deuce, and Dark had been a jarhead gunny. Hillman dropped bombs on Germany in a B-24 piloted by the Hollywood actor Jimmy Stewart. Nash had done time in the Air Force in the 50s. Nash guessed the two Army light colonels wouldn't get much sympathy in this room. Army dogfaces were a subject that could rightly be handled only in a Bill Mauldin cartoon.

The tall colonel—Kepler—cleared his throat.

"Gentlemen, maybe you've heard in the news recently, the United States Army took into custody a former soldier of the Japanese Imperial Army, a holdover from World War II, on the Pacific island of Morotai."

The colonel's voice sounded tight. His eyes didn't stray much from the onionskin briefing sheet in his hands. "The soldier's name is Haruto Shimatzu. He arrived on Morotai from Japan in 'Forty-three as a lieutenant in the Japanese Army's One-seventy-second Monsoon Brigade. As you may know, Morotai was part of the Dutch East Indies. It was taken by the Japanese in 'Forty-two, liberated by US and Australian forces in the autumn of 'Forty-four. At that time, Lieutenant Shimatzu and several others fled into the island's jungle. They awaited a Japanese re-invasion that would push the Allied forces back into the sea.

"That counterattack never came, of course. While they waited, Shimatzu and the others kept themselves alive by the most tenuous means."

It took Nash a moment to make the connection, but now he remembered. The article he had read in *Newsweek* the other day—Shimatzu had spent the twenty-one years since the end of the war hiding in the dense island rain forest, in the belief that the war was still on and reinforcements would eventually come to relieve him. The Japanese soldier had killed a US Army MP at the time of his capture.

Nash sat back, puzzled.

What did Shimatzu have to do with SFPD?

Nash saw that Lieutenant Dark also looked adrift. Buddy Arbogast, who had once shown Nash a snapshot of his younger self holding a burned Jap skull on Tarawa, looked interested but Lou Crandall looked ill, and Belcher's eyes stayed hooded. Hillman might've been daydreaming.

Colonel Kepler continued.

"The other Japanese soldiers who retreated into the jungle with Shimatzu either died there over the years or surrendered. Shimatzu was made of sterner stuff. He remained at his post." Kepler paused, as though giving the assembled cops a moment to appreciate Shimatzu's achievement. It was clear to Nash that the Army colonel held a certain regard for the Japanese lieutenant who had fought a one-man war on behalf of a country that had left him for dead.

"Army MPs and Navy Shore Patrol units caught up with Shimatzu two months ago," Colonel Kepler said. "Unfortunately, he was captured only after he'd killed a US Army soldier, near the village of Misio, on Morotai. We believe that Shimatzu may also be responsible for the killing of an American civilian two years ago near Pangeo, on the island's north coast."

The colonel cleared his throat. His voice rose.

"Gentlemen, to find a Jap soldier still active at this late a date is extraordinary. But it's not without precedent. There have been a fair number of holdout Japanese soldiers captured throughout the Far East since the end of the war.

"As for Lieutenant Shimatzu, he was taken into custody and shipped in leg irons to the Twenty-fifth Infantry Division headquarters at Schofield Barracks, in Honolulu. Not getting the news of Hirohito's ass kicking in 'Forty-five is not an acceptable excuse for the murder of an American serviceman."

Colonel Kepler paused to remove an olive-drab green handkerchief from his pants pocket and blow his nose. The other one—Gorman—watched Miss Figgis as she brought in a fresh bowl of sugar cubes.

The telephone on the refreshment table rang. Miss Figgis answered it. She gave the caller a whispered brush off, quietly set the receiver back on its cradle. Smoothed her dress, hustled back out of the room on teetering aubergine pumps.

Colonel Kepler stowed his handkerchief and circled the conference table distributing photostatted copies of a three-page brief.

Nash glanced at his copy.

The top sheet contained information on Lieutenant Shimatzu of His Imperial Majesty's Army of Japan. The second sheet referenced Shimatzu's activities on Morotai, and items of family history.

The third sheet appeared to discuss someone else entirely. It included a badly reproduced passport-sized photo that looked like an ink blot test.

Lieutenant Dark lit a gasper, pulled an ashtray closer. It was the signal for every inspector in the room to smoke. Colonel Kepler waited until everyone had lit up and was on the same puff before he went on.

"In Hono there were developments," Kepler said. "When the scuttlebutt got around that we'd captured a Jap soldier who killed a US serviceman because he believed the war was still on, the local population in Hono grew agitated. There were even calls to have Shimatzu shot, as a spy.

"For the sake of good relations with the community, and to keep the situation from coming to a boil, the Pentagon decided to transfer the prisoner to the mainland.

"Ten days ago we flew Lieutenant Shimatzu into Fort Ord on a C-130 from Hickam Air Field in Hawaii. At Fort Ord, he was put into the stockade. We kept his presence here in California as quiet as possible. The Pentagon didn't want a blow up like we had in Hono.

"Last Friday evening, Lieutenant Shimatzu complained of a stomach ailment. He was removed from his cell. As he was transported to the dispensary in a jeep, he overpowered his MP guard, took the guard's sidearm, and shot him with it. Shimatzu then held the pistol to the head of the driver and ordered him to drive off the post.

"The driver got Shimatzu out of the immediate Fort Ord area without further incident. In a wooded area north of Springtown, Shimatzu ordered the driver and the wounded MP out of the jeep and drove away.

"Outside of Gilroy, Shimatzu abandoned the jeep and stole a car from a motorist at a rest stop, by force. Shimatzu was last seen driving north on Highway 101, toward the San Francisco peninsula. We haven't as yet found the stolen car. We don't expect to find Shimatzu still using it, in any case.

"The guard Shimatzu shot at Fort Ord is in stable condition at a Monterey hospital."

Nash watched Lieutenant Dark nodding to himself. Dark saw the picture, or thought he did. Dark hit the surface of the table with a decisive fist.

"Count us in," Dark said. "We'll find him, if he's here to be found."

Kepler winced. His next statement seemed to cause him

physical pain. "As it happens, we know he's in San Francisco. We also know, at least to a degree, what he's been doing."

Kepler motioned to his colleague. Gorman stood up, just as the black telephone on the refreshment table began to ring again. Miss Figgis rushed in from the next room to quell the disturbance.

Lieutenant Dark jumped up and beat her to it.

Dark gripped the telephone wire in his good hand and, with a fair degree of composure, he pulled it out of the wiring box on the wall. Miss Figgis swished her caboose out of the room holding the now inoperative telephone at arm's length, like it carried a bad odor.

At the head of the table Colonel Gorman folded his hands tightly, an altar boy with an awkward bladder. "The top two sheets of the brief, as you see, include background information on Lieutenant Shimatzu. There is also a photograph that was taken upon his arrival at Schofield Barracks on Oahu, two months ago.

"The third sheet contains background information on a soldier named Chester A. Boggs. Boggs was a sergeant first class in an Army Special Operations Group team currently resident in Saigon. In recent months Boggs was TDY here in the States."

Nash studied the ink blot on the third page again. Slowly the smudge revealed its secret to him.

The secret dawned on Lou Crandall faster.

"This man is dead," Crandall said. He pointed the burning tip of his cigarette at the photograph of the man identified as Boggs. "We found his body in a storeroom up on Haight Street last night. He was murdered."

Lieutenant Dark looked surprised but Jellicoe appeared to know what the score was. The colonels had already briefed him. Now Colonel Gorman swung his gaze around the table, his head swiveling on his neck, a gun turret on a Sherman tank.

"Sergeant Boggs was assigned to Army SOG for several years," Colonel Gorman said. "In that time, he distinguished himself remarkably. When we realized it was likely that Lieutenant Shimatzu would hide in San Francisco, we brought in Sergeant Boggs to lead a team of military police specialists. Their objective was to pinpoint Shimatzu's location and recapture him.

"Quickly and quietly.

"It was important to us that Sergeant Boggs's team exercise a high degree of discretion. The Pentagon is worried that if news of Shimatzu's presence in San Francisco gets out, we might have even more of an outcry from the public than we did in Hono. Because of the tilt of the local community, we might also encounter anti-military sentiment that would impede our work. Innocent people might get hurt."

Colonel Gorman paused for emphasis. Then, "Sergeant First Class Boggs was killed in the line of duty, and he will be buried with the honor and respect a grateful country can bestow."

Belcher looked around the table like he'd just woken from a nap and wondered what these goofballs were doing in his house.

"How the hell do you expect to find this Jap in San Francisco?" Belcher said. "You could spend ten years looking for him. He'd be the mayor of Bolinas before you caught up with him."

"I'm glad you bring that up, Inspector," Gorman said. He didn't look glad. "Sergeant Boggs's team included three linguists from the Defense Language Institute, down the coast in Monterey. The three linguists are fluent in the common Japanese and Chinese dialects. Two of them have extensive Japanese ancestry.

"More importantly, we have a good lead on Shimatzu's possible whereabouts. From what we've learned from the Japanese consulate in Honolulu, Shimatzu's father and sister died during the war, but his mother survived. In the late Forties she immigrated to the United States.

"She settled here, in San Francisco.

"We don't know if she is still alive, or what name she might be using if she is. But we are making inroads. Boggs's team spotted Shimatzu on Fillmore Street yesterday. One of our men also spotted him in the Haight-Ashbury area. Shimatzu entered the soup kitchen where Boggs was murdered, looking for a free meal. At some point he must've hidden himself in the back of the building."

Gorman glanced at Chief Jellicoe, who shrugged and looked at Arbogast, who shook his head and turned to Crandall, who was lost in his own thoughts. A sour expression crossed Lieutenant Dark's face.

"The Crime Lab says the instrument used to murder the sergeant had a heavy cutting edge," Dark said. "Roughly the size of a machete blade. Of which there are probably a million in the Bay Area. Army surplus stores sell machetes by the crate. I've got one myself—it's handy for clearing underbrush and tall grass, if you sharpen it well. I used one in the islands during the war, but not for cutting grass."

Now Jellicoe took his turn.

"The Jap is armed and dangerous," Jellicoe said. "He killed Boggs and he'll kill again, mama-san or no mama-san. It's our job to find him before that happens."

Nash studied the faces of the inspectors assembled at the conference table. What he saw was a group of World War II veterans who were already licking their chops at the prospect of fighting the war again. This time they could shoot the enemy and still get home to their wives for dinner.

Twenty

THE SECOND PHOTOSTATTED page of the brief provided the details of Lieutenant Haruto Shimatzu's life in the Morotai jungle after the war ended, taken from statements the Japanese soldier had made to his captors while in Hawaii.

Based on what Nash read, the lieutenant had lived like a dog.

Shimatzu subsisted largely on insects and breadfruit, the occasional bird that he killed with a makeshift bow and arrow. He lived underground in a narrow tunnel that he dug in the center of a thick stand of ironwood trees and underbrush. He often passed the days lying on his back in his encampment.

Entirely alone.

Hearing only the sounds of the jungle.

But Shimatzu never gave up hope that the Japanese Imperial Army would return to Morotai to retake the island and rescue him.

The soldier's only companion in his final years on the island was a photograph of a Caucasian woman wearing a sarong. He'd torn the picture from a discarded magazine he found at the edge of a refuse dump.

Shimatzu talked to the woman in the picture. He made promises to her, planned a life with her. Over time the clipping became worn and discolored by the damp. Shimatzu's girlfriend and soul mate for life slowly faded away.

Shimatzu kept a diary of sorts, written with scraps of pencil lead on rolls of toilet paper he acquired in a night-time raid on a village storehouse. The soft strokes of his ideograms were written in a precise manner on the rolls of thin paper. They told his story as he lived it, against the possibility that he would die in the jungle alone.

At times, the only thing that kept him going was his unwavering belief in what he was told as a young soldier in Japan: To surrender to the Americans was to sign your own death warrant, because the Americans always kill their prisoners.

After Shimatzu was discovered and captured, the loyal soldier reportedly cried when he was told that Japan lost the war, and that his father and sister had died before the war ended. When Shimatzu was visited by a delegation from the Japanese consulate in Honolulu while he was incarcerated at Schofield Barracks, they showed him a photograph of a grave marker at a cemetery in his home village of Higashi-Naruse, in Japan's Akita prefecture.

The grave marker bore Shimatzu's name, recorded the year of his death as 1944. The year Morotai was re-taken by the Allies. When Shimatzu studied the photograph he remarked that he didn't know what to believe. His claim that he was alive, or the evidence that he was dead.

WITHIN AN hour after the conference with the Army colonels from the Presidio ended, Chief of Inspectors Jellicoe and Lieutenant Dark had put together a task force to locate and take into custody the last Japanese combatant from World War II.

It was decided to call it Task Force Z.

Meanwhile, the SFPD Crime Lab finished their work and confirmed what it had believed all along. A US Army standard issue machete, *circa* 1940, covered with blood that matched the blood type of the deceased Army sergeant, was found by a citizen in the back garden of a house on Baker Street. One city block from the Golden Gate Park panhandle, and six blocks from the Greater San Francisco Co-Prosperity Sphere free kitchen.

It was presumed that Shimatzu stole the machete from a garage or basement in the area, carried it with him, employed it when the need arose, then discarded it in favor of the deceased Boggs's .45 caliber automatic.

Based on the presumption that Shimatzu was still in the vicinity of the Haight-Ashbury neighborhood, the Task Force Z command post was set up at SFPD's Park Station, at the eastern edge of Golden Gate Park.

Three rooms were commandeered at the station, and Jellicoe and Dark handpicked Bureau of Inspectors personnel to serve on the task force. Most of the men selected were veterans of the Pacific Campaign during World War II.

Chief Jellicoe's boss, Chief of Police Thomas J. Cahill, quickly issued a gag order forbidding task force personnel from speaking about the search for Shimatzu to anyone outside of the task force. Most especially the press.

Initially both Belcher and Nash were assigned to Task Force Z. At Park Station they sat in on a briefing that outlined a proposed dragnet through the Golden Gate and Beuna Vista Park areas, including the Richmond District north to Geary

Boulevard, and Haight-Ashbury and environs south to Parnassus Avenue and the University of California Medical Center. Uniformed patrol officers had been placed at strategic bus stops and cable car hubs, although Nash encountered no one who truly believed that Shimatzu would be using public transportation.

Photostats of Shimatzu's Schofield Barracks mug shot were distributed to prowl car units and motorcycle patrols. Patrolmen in the field were told only that Shimatzu was wanted for questioning regarding an assault and battery in Haight-Ashbury. They were warned that Shimatzu was known to carry firearms and other weapons.

Approach with extreme caution.

As the search for Shimatzu's mother progressed, a team of US Army and SFPD personnel descended on the Japanese neighborhood along Geary Boulevard, as well as Chinatown and the area south of Market.

The Colonels Kepler and Gorman provided Chief Jellicoe with a photograph of the widow Shimatzu that was taken shortly after the end of the war, at a US Army internment facility outside of Osaka. The woman in the picture looked dazed and emaciated, a bandaged ear, a missing tooth.

Talks with the Japanese consulates in San Francisco and Honolulu continued. The dialogue was hobbled by a reluctance on the part of the federal government and the US Army to inform the Japanese diplomats of the situation unfolding in San Francisco. Shimatzu's transfer from Honolulu to the mainland for incarceration and trial was already causing ructions in the government's diplomatic relations with the sovereign state of Japan.

Or so the SFPD inspectors assigned to Task Force Z were told over hot coffee and Winchell's doughnuts at the Park Station command post. At 1600 hours a portable blackboard was rolled into the command post's main room. Chief Jellicoe used colored chalk to outline a plan of action for the task force that looked to Nash like a diagram of the chemical properties of bullshit.

After the briefing, Lieutenant Dark took Nash aside.

"I don't need every Tom, Dick, and Harry chasing Japs," Dark said. He poked the air with a bayonet thrust of his El Supremo cigar. "Nash, carry on with your current assignments. Let me know first thing if we need to put a halt to this Beatle escapade, before someone gets hurt."

Nash had his orders. He wasn't too disappointed. The Task Force Z command post had already turned into old home week for the Pacific Theater vets in the department. War fever had elbowed its way into Park Station with all the delicacy of bad personal hygiene.

AT THE Hall of Justice, Nash returned to his leads on the Gomez murder. Nash tried to reach Pearly Spence at the number he had for her, got no answer. He succeeded in reaching Stan Hotchkiss—one of the talent scouts Dorla Foote at the Kimono à Go-Go had spoken of—at his San Francisco telephone number.

Hotchkiss sounded groggy when he answered, like he'd just woken up.

Nash wanted to talk to him, in person.

Hotchkiss agreed.

"I want to see a fuzz buckle," Hotchkiss said. "On the phone, you could be anybody."

The building in the Marina District where Hotchkiss kept an apartment was three blocks north and two blocks east of Tina Gone's pad on Broderick. Nash hoped at least that Hotchkiss could identify known associates of Danilo Gomez. Hotchkiss might even point him in the direction of Frank Barcelona, who Nash assumed Hotchkiss had also talked to at the Kimono.

The middle-aged man who answered Nash's knock had combed the dyed hair on his head into an elaborate wave that washed over his right ear. The man's thinly mustachioed face was deeply lined, the sleeves of his white cotton shirt rolled up casually, revealing a carpet of gray arm hair.

The highball glass in Hotchkiss' hand contained ice and three fingers of an amber-colored liquid that Nash surmised had come from the bottle of scotch that rested on the bare wood floor, next to the telephone.

Nash produced his SFPD badge—the requisite fuzz buckle. Hotchkiss didn't give it a glance.

"Care for a snort?" Hotchkiss raised his glass.

"Thanks, but I'm on the clock."

"Nine-to-five gigs are tough."

"It's a living."

"I dig. The Man needs to eat too."

The walls and much of the floor space in the living room were taken up by painter's canvases, brushes, pots, tubes of paint. Many of the canvases contained only quick slashes of color. They didn't look unfinished so much as never started. As though the painter had entered into a battle of wits with the blank canvas and had lost, quickly and decisively.

"My *oeuvre*," Hotchkiss said.

Nash followed Hotchkiss out onto the balcony. Hotchkiss held his highball glass tightly. There was a slight tremor in Hotchkiss' other hand. The balcony looked out on the small craft docked in the marina slips. The sleepy movement of the boats, rising and falling, the softly rolling tide, matched the roll of Hotchkiss' boozy eyes.

Hotchkiss raised a confidential eyebrow.

"I began painting when I worked for Capitol Records in LA. It helped me keep my spiritual balance. Then I left Capitol. I couldn't in good conscience live in the white-collar conservative meat grinder any longer. But I'm still simpatico with the movers and shakers in LA. I make enough *do-re-mi* as a freelance talent scout to get by."

Nash spotted a tug boat in the distance, blunt prow elbowing the waves aside. On its way to Sausalito, points beyond. "Tell me about Danny Gomez."

Hotchkiss held the glass of scotch between the palms of his hands, rolled the glass forward and back, an incantation, as he thought about the question.

Hotchkiss said he'd known Gomez only as Danny O'Day.

"I scare up pop music talent," Hotchkiss said, after a sigh that was more complicated than it needed to be. "Pop music is where the action is. Next year it might be dancing poodles, but the happening scene right now is pop music, a hard backbeat.

"I spend most of my time in LA, but I'm here in Frisco a few days a month. New acts are sprouting from the cracks in the sidewalks here. I scout the talent, package them a little, then I present audition tapes to producers in LA. I get a cut off the top of the contract, and other emoluments. It's a good gig. Just what I want. I don't have business office bean counters telling me what to do. If I want to go to Acapulco tomorrow and paint, it's cool. I don't answer to clocks."

"That brings us back to Danny O'Day."

"Inspector, I didn't know Danny O'Day. Not a whole bunch. I spoke to him in passing, maybe a few times. I heard him gig at the Kimono, but he wasn't the kind of act that jazzes me. His songs were tight, but onstage he snored. He seemed like a 'with it' young man, serious about his craft, but I doubt I exchanged more than a words with him. It's too bad though, what happened. No one deserves to get the chop like that."

Nash wondered why Hotchkiss hadn't told him this on the

dozen telephone. Dorla Foote at the Kimono à Go-Go must've mixed up Hotchkiss with the other one—Turner.

"What about Frank Barcelona? He played saxophone at the Kimono, with O'Day. Does that name ring a bell?"

Hotchkiss shook his head. No bells. He studied his highball glass.

"From what little I saw, Danny O'Day had a spark, but his focus was wrong. He thought it was about writing songs and heartfelt emotions and artistry, but that's not it. It's about selling washing machines. It's about giving people what they want to hear. Whatever schtick it takes, a smile on your face.

"That's why I left Capitol. I'm a huckster, Inspector. That fact doesn't sit well with me. I drink to forget who I am, and I paint to remember who I wanted to be. I imagine that one day one half of the equation will win out over the other, but I don't know which half. Or maybe I do."

Hotchkiss rested his elbows on the balcony railing, still holding the highball glass in both hands. Hoping to catch drops of scotch from the sky.

"Talk to Jerry Turner, Inspector," Hotchkiss said. "Jerry's hideout is in Malibu, but he stays here when he's in town. We share the rent on this pad. He goes to the Kimono, and I seem to recall him talking about Danny O'Day. Jerry is close with that joker who runs the place."

"Jasper Rollo?"

"That very one."

Nash followed Hotchkiss back into the apartment. Hotchkiss jotted down Turner's Malibu address and home phone number on the back of a crumpled cocktail napkin, handed it to Nash. Nash already had one number for Turner, on the business card Foote had given him.

"One thing, Inspector," Hotchkiss said as Nash was on his

way out the door. Hotchkiss handed him a white envelope. "Can you help me out with a traffic ticket?"

Nash was so taken aback by the request that the apartment door was already closed before he could think of a response. Out front, he slipped the traffic ticket into Hotchkiss' mailbox. He wondered if getting the ticket fixed was the real reason why Hotchkiss agreed to talk to him.

NASH CALLED the Kimono à Go-Go from a pay phone in front of a Shell station on Cervantes Boulevard. When he asked for Jasper Rollo, Dorla Foote came on the line. She told Nash that Mister Rollo had called the club earlier that day. She didn't talk to him herself but, from what she'd heard, Rollo was back in town. Nash didn't bother to tell Foote that her information about Hotchkiss had been largely incorrect. Right idea, wrong clown.

Nash hung up and dialed Rollo's home phone number. No one answered.

It was 2012 hours. Dusk.

With nothing else pressing on his schedule Nash drove to Diamond Heights. Maybe he'd have better luck in person. It would be time well spent, if he could finally catch a further word with Rollo.

Rollo's residence at the end of the cul-de-sac looked dark. Nash heard music coming from the patio at the rear of the house. Rollo's neighbors must've loved him. Nash got no answer when he rang the front door bell. He walked around the side of the house, past the Japanese maple trees. Opened the gate in the wooden fence. The music Nash heard wasn't rock and roll. More like lukewarm jazz music, a clarinet out front. Like Acker Bilk, that English trad jazz virtuoso. Nash had heard of him, mostly how Bilk appealed to middle-aged spinsters and cats.

Two floodlights attached under the eaves at the rear of the house shone down on the patio and the swimming pool. As Nash approached, he saw someone floating at the shallow end of the pool. Jasper Rollo was conducting his sensory deprivation experiments again.

Nash stepped closer. Now he saw that the man in the pool was fully dressed. The man's body rested against the steps at the shallow end of the pool, his head face down in the water. His limbs had arranged themselves in awkward angles on the steps.

The surface of the water was still.

The man didn't move.

Nash jumped into the pool. He pulled the man's head out of the water. Dragged him up the steps. Nash laid the man out on the deck tiles, pressed his fingers against the man's neck, the man's wrist. No trace of a pulse. Timothy Gone's dead eyes stared up at the evening sky.

Twenty-one

IN THE BASEMENT room, Nash raised the phonograph arm off the LP record on the hi-fi. He was grateful for the silence when it came. SFPD patrol units from Ingleside Station arrived within ten minutes. Half an hour later, Inspector Fred Dempsey from the Homicide Detail drove up in his family station wagon.

Nash's clothes were wet. His feet were cold.

Patrolmen had already searched Rollo's house, downstairs and upstairs. They didn't find Jasper Rollo.

Or anyone else. Alive or dead.

Now Nash walked Dempsey through the crime scene.

Gone was shot in the rec room. Timothy Gone's chest had been punctured with two small-caliber bullets. The wounds had bled surprisingly little on his paisley-print shirt. Drops of blood left a trail that led from the edge of the pool to the closed patio door. Inside the basement rec room, the blood trail continued for a few feet, then stopped.

The sliding patio door had been open when he was shot. Then Gone stumbled outside, fell into the pool. Gone wasn't shot in the rec room and dragged outside because the trail of blood consisted of blood drops, not blood smears. The glass door must have been open at the time of the shooting—there was no obvious trace of Gone's blood anywhere on the glass or the door handle or the metal frame. Nor had the glass been shattered by a bullet.

The killer had politely pushed the patio door closed after Gone staggered out.

Inside the rec room, two throw pillows and a rumpled afghan blanket lay on the love seat. The two pillows were flattened. Someone had rested their head on them for an extended period of time. Beside the couch, an ashtray full of cigarette butts. Wadded hamburger wrappers and a paper sack from the Tic Tock Drive-In had been tossed into the brick fireplace. An empty bottle of rye whiskey lay on its side at one end of the hi-fi console. Next to a stack of 45 rpm records.

"Someone camped out here," Dempsey said.

Nash agreed.

Rollo had no reason to camp out in his own rec room. Which meant that Rollo had had a guest, or an unannounced visitor.

Had Rollo been here at all? Rollo seemed to be everywhere and nowhere, like a god or a lingering bad odor. Nash wondered what Timothy Gone's connection to Jasper Rollo was, had no luck with that question either. But Nash knew he'd be the one to tell Tina Gone that her brother was dead. He didn't trust anyone else to do it.

Nash and Dempsey, accompanied by Patrolmen J. Hewitt and G.B. Frost from Mission Station, searched the house again. No weapon was discovered. A search for shell casings in the rec room proved fruitless. Nash did find, inside the hi-fi console in the rec room, a reel of professional recording tape, in what appeared to be the original box. The tape was a half inch in width. The box it came in looked identical to the recording tape boxes found at Danilo Gomez's pad. Written on the outside of the box were the words BEATLES JUNE 61—27 MIN 16 SEC/15 IPS. There were further notations pertaining to individual songs. "The Sheik of Araby" was the only song title Nash recognized.

Someone had used a laundry marker to draw a picture of a Kilroy character on the front of the tape box. Big nose and fat fingers, the round-headed cartoon man peaking over a wall or fence.

Nash wished Kilroy could talk.

As the ranking inspector, it was Dempsey's case, for the time being. Dempsey scratched the stubble on his dimpled chin sadly, voiced the opinion that his Friday night with the missus had gone to pot. The Crime Lab team and a photographer had just arrived to begin their work with tweezers and brushes and flash bulbs when Dempsey called in a request for an all-points bulletin on *Rollo, Jasper Harold.*

Nash and three patrolmen canvassed the neighborhood. Nash talked to a man named Isaacs who hadn't heard a thing coming from Rollo's residence that evening. A woman name Eunice Golden said she thought she'd heard gunfire, with a Glenn Miller Orchestra tune mixed in. She'd assumed that Rollo was watching his television with the volume up again.

Nash returned to Rollo's residence. He was talking to a Crime Lab technician out front when Patrolman K. Lunsford appeared with a young woman in tow. He'd bumped into her on the sidewalk, down the street.

Patrolman Lunsford took Nash aside to explain.

The woman had been walking along the cross street. When she turned the corner into the cul-de-sac she paused at the sight of the police vehicles. When she turned to walk the other way she nearly walked right into the patrolman.

On instinct Lunsford asked her if she was going to Rollo's house. She denied that she was. When the patrolman asked her where she was in fact going, she stuttered and pointed vaguely, down the street. The patrolman was sure she wasn't being truthful. To prove it, he offered to walk her to the house she had pointed to. It was then that the woman admitted she had come to see Jasper Rollo.

The woman's face looked as plain as white bread. Her dishwater blonde hair lay flat and stringy. She wore a green shawl over a dark-colored shirt, a pair of oversized dungarees. She clutched a large sketchbook and a knitted handbag to her chest. The buttons attached to the bag shone when they caught the roof lights from the prowl cars.

Nash noticed that the woman wore white orthopedic shoes. The kind nurses wear. The heel of one shoe was higher than the heel of the other.

The woman gave her name as Bernice Scroggins. She had no driver's license but her California identification card carried a home address in Salinas. Scroggins said that she'd only recently moved to San Francisco. Her current residence was an apartment house on Telegraph Hill.

"I came on the bus," the woman said. "Mister Rollo has some bread for me. I stopped by earlier but there was someone here. I didn't want to barge in, so I left. I walked down to the boulevard, had a cup of coffee. It's a long walk. Longer than I thought."

Nash guessed that on mismatched legs it would indeed be a long walk downhill to Diamond Heights Boulevard, then back up the hill.

"I didn't expect to see police cars," the woman said. "It gave me a start. That's why I didn't want to say I was going to Mister

Rollo's house. Is he all right? Was there an accident?"

Nash assured the woman that Rollo was fine, although he wasn't certain of that himself. The fact that the young woman looked nervous didn't tell Nash much.

She struck Nash as a woman who might always look nervous.

Bernice Scroggins said that it was close to eight o'clock, the first time she dropped by. Rollo had told her a few days ago on the telephone to come by today to pick up the sixty dollars he owed her. She'd called Rollo's residence earlier that day. No one answered. But she badly needed the money, so she took a chance. Came out on the bus.

The money was payment for a sketch the woman had done. In charcoal. It wasn't the first sketch she'd done for him. Rollo had paid her to make sketches for him in the past.

Nash said, "When you got here earlier, how did you know that Mister Rollo had a guest?"

Bernice Scroggins nodded her head silently. Reviewing the question carefully in her mind before trying to answer. Nash caught himself wondering if she might be a bit deaf, and a lip reader.

The woman said, "I came up the street and got to that point over there"—she turned and pointed over the trunk of a patrol car to a spot on the far sidewalk, about thirty yards down the hill—"when a car pulled up here, in front of the house. A woman got out. She walked around the side of the house. Like she was going to the pool."

"What did the woman look like?"

"I couldn't see her too well."

"Fat, slim, short, tall?"

"It was getting dark."

"White, Negro, Oriental, Mex?"

"Average height."

"Blonde, brunette, redhead?"

"She was a white lady. Slim. Maybe brunette?"

"What did the car look like?"

Bernice Scroggins hummed and hawed. She didn't pay much attention to cars, didn't know the makes and models.

The conversation became more interesting when the woman showed Nash the sketch Jasper Rollo had asked for.

Bernice Scroggins set her knitted bag on the hood of the patrol car, opened the sketchpad she'd brought. She flipped a few pages over until she reached the one Rollo had commissioned.

She held it up for Nash to see.

Nash studied the thick dark lines.

The sketch depicted four figures wearing pith helmets. They were walking single file through thick leafy jungle vegetation. The man at the front of the line held a blunderbuss. A comical lion roared in the lower left corner of the sketch, as it prepared to take a rather large bite out of the man in the rear of the line. Off to the right, a cannibal appeared to be roasting another man clad in safari clothes over a flaming spit.

The cannibal, predictably, wore a bone through his nose. The safari hunter being roasted looked quite a lot like the washed-up actor who wanted to be governor, Ronald Reagan. The lettering at the top of the sketch was angular and misshapen. Nash had to study it for a moment before he could make it out: THE BEATLES ON SAFARI.

"What's it mean?" Nash said.

The woman shrugged. She looked embarrassed. "Mister Rollo told me to draw him a picture of the Beatles on a jungle safari. He wanted them to look scared. He told me to work in Ronald Reagan getting roasted by cannibals, if I could. I said, 'Sure.' I mean, he's paying, right?"

Nash left Bernice Scroggins in the care of the patrolman while he went to discuss this development with Dempsey. When he returned to the front of the house fifteen minutes later, Nash told Bernice Scroggins he had a few more questions. Then, "Are you hungry?"

AT HERBIE'S Skyline Diner on Gennessee Street, near City College, the only skyline visible was the one silhouetted on the front of the menu.

At a booth beside a window, Bernice Scroggins ordered a Green River soda, eggs scrambled with spinach and hamburger. A Joe's Special. The fry cook who stepped out of the kitchen for a glass of ice water from the beverage dispenser looked more like an Abdul, or a Gamal.

Nash ordered coffee and a cinnamon roll, heated.

While they waited for their food, Nash asked Bernice Scroggins to describe the other sketches she had done for Jasper Rollo.

There had been several, Scroggins said.

The last sketch also featured the Beatles—or at least the faces of the Beatles, torn from a teenybopper fan magazine.

She had drawn four skeletons wearing tuxedos, waving top hats in the air. She pasted the Beatle faces on the skeletons.

Nash said he might have seen that one. Around town.

"I only know Mister Rollo because I work with a girl who used to work at his club," Bernice Scroggins said. "She introduced me. I told him if he ever needed any art work done. You know, for his business. I don't know what he does with my sketches. They're all kind of music-related."

Nash suspected that Scroggins wasn't being forthright on that subject, but he let it go for the moment. When they had finished eating, Nash asked the woman to make a sketch for him.

The waitress picked up the empty plates, gave Nash a refill on his coffee, Nash listening to the soft brushing sound of charcoal on thick sketchbook paper as Bernice Scroggins set about filling his request. When the young woman finished the sketch, she added color from a colored pencil. She cocked her head, studied her work. She tore the sketch off the pad and handed it to Nash.

"That's what I recall," Bernice Scroggins said.

"It gives me something to work with."

"Sometimes my memory plays tricks."

"Join the club."

Nash paid the check, then drove Bernice Scroggins to the aging apartment building on Telegraph Hill where she lived. Then Nash stopped at a bar on Van Ness to call Tina Gone. He reached her answering service, left a message asking her to call him, as soon as possible.

It was two o'clock in the morning when Nash arrived back at his apartment. He tried calling Tina Gone again, without any luck. Nash tore two church key holes into the top of a Lucky Lager can and sat down at the kitchen table. He studied the sketch Bernice Scroggins had made for him while he finished the can of beer. As hard as he tried, he couldn't avoid the conclusion that the yellow sports car represented in the sketch bore a close resemblance to Tina Gone's Sunbeam Tiger.

Twenty-two

NASH FOUND A sheet of teletype waiting for him on his desk at the Hall of Justice the next morning. From the Marin County Sheriff's Office. The writer of the threatening letter regarding the upcoming visit to San Francisco by the Beatles musical group had been identified. *McGill, Lawrence Kenneth. Male Caucasian. DOB 2/17/42.*

McGill worked as a box boy at a Value Barn grocery market in San Rafael. He lived with his parents in Mill Valley. Among his favorite pastimes were drawing circles with crayons and crawling into bed between his mother and father in the middle of the night with a loaded 30.06 rifle and a fifth of vodka.

McGill's mother was sure he wasn't dangerous. His doctors at Napa State Mental Hospital made a similar judgment, during McGill's last stay there.

The teletype closed with a "please advise" from MCSO.

NASH CALLED Tina Gone's number several more times, left more messages with the answering service. The secretary who picked up the phone at the *Chronicle* offices couldn't help him either. Nash called the southern California phone number for Jerry Turner that Stan Hotchkiss had given him. The woman who answered said that Turner was out, but she'd take a message.

When Nash called the Kimono à Go-Go, the character who called himself Mister Enrique said that he had no knowledge of Mister Rollo's current whereabouts. "I wish you did not ask me," Mister Enrique said. He made a huffing noise on the other end of the line, as though Nash's questions had left him winded.

The SFPD and California Highway Patrol bulletins for Rollo hadn't as yet borne fruit. Fred Dempsey sent enquiries to the police departments in Eureka and Crescent City, and the sheriff's offices in Humboldt and Del Norte Counties. He made the enquiries on the basis that Dorla Foote believed Rollo had gone north to record music *al fresco,* in the redwoods. The two counties were home to all of the Redwood Forest National Park, the two towns the largest in the area.

A shot in the dark. Dorla Foote had been wrong about Rollo returning to the city, evidently. Was there any truth to the redwood forest angle at all? Nash had a bad feeling and tried to cover it up with a fried egg sandwich at the Swing-In Coffee Shop. He got indigestion for his trouble.

Nash drove to Tina Gone's place. The intercom remained silent when he pressed the buzzer. He didn't see the Sunbeam parked on the street or around back. The apartment manager appeared, picked at his stained teeth with a plastic swizzle stick. He hadn't seen Tina Gone, or her vehicle, in a few days.

Nash stopped at the Park Station command post on his way to the Haight-Ashbury neighborhood. He found Belcher barking into a Task Force Z telephone, in a room full of other barking SFPD inspectors. An office door on the far side of the room flew open and Lieutenant Dark stepped out, shouted at someone, retreated back into his office. Seconds later, Lieutenant Helstrom from the Hop Squad—a former Navy submariner, Nash recalled—stepped out of his office, shouted at someone, disappeared back inside. The two senior men operated like competing cuckoos on a Swiss clock.

Belcher slammed the telephone receiver onto its cradle.

He looked aggrieved.

"On Guadalcanal I could feel when a Jap was close," Belcher said. "It was a tingle at the back of my neck, except when it was an electrical shock to my balls. Let's get a bite."

Nash followed Belcher down a hallway to the Task Force Z break room. Tall urns of coffee had been set up, along with boxes of Winchell's doughnuts and a pineapple layer cake one of the steno ladies made. The Stars and Stripes hanging on the wall was the 48-star flag that existed during the war.

Belcher reached for a doughnut, talked while he chewed. "They tell me if a Jap dies without getting his prayers in order, his soul turns into a pile of shit on the steps of the Emperor's palace. But it's true, about him being close. I can feel his Nip vibrations. He's waiting patiently for me to put a bullet in his coconut."

Vibrations? Nash smiled. He recalled the *Newsweek* article, about the dogs picking up their master's happy vibrations in the air. Now Belcher claimed to be picking up vibrations from a Japanese soldier who forgot to surrender in 1945. Why not?

Belcher had stayed on duty at the Task Force Z command post until shortly before midnight the previous night. He'd gotten a few hours of sleep, returned at five o'clock that morning. He said that Task Force Z now had several squads of SFPD patrolmen and Army MPs from the Presidio doing the leg work.

Hunting the last Japanese soldier.

Settling an old score.

But Nash knew the score would never be settled. As an old Mexican gentleman once told Nash, spilled blood is never washed away.

The Mex ought to know. He was in San Quentin now, a double murder beef.

Belcher pushed his chair back. He got up and stepped over to a California Automobile Association road map taped to the wall, beside the refrigerator.

"We've got a skirmish line, moving in a westerly direction, right through the park," Belcher said. He described a loose circle on the map with his finger. "We'll move forward in a pincer formation until we hit the beach. Then we start working the surface streets. Radiate out from the park."

Nash thought of the one thousand acres of Golden Gate Park, full of trees and underbrush. The occasional ornamental garden or Japanese pagoda dotting the landscape. A person could disappear for days if they wanted to. Needed to.

"What about mama-san?" Nash said.

"Police informants with Japanese leanings recognized her from the photo. She's going by a different name than the one she used in 'Forty-seven, but we'll have our hands on her presently. If she's hiding her son, the weight of the department will come down on her, most chop-chop."

"She's just his mother."

"Hitler had a mother."

"So did you."

Belcher looked like he wanted to debate the point.

Nash recounted the highlights of the Timothy Gone murder in Diamond Heights, then unfolded the sketch that Bernice Scroggins made. The image of the sports car was clear enough. "A Caucasian female arrived in that car at Jasper Rollo's place last night. Maybe an hour before I got there. It could easily be a sketch of Tina Gone's vehicle."

"So find her." Belcher frowned. He dropped the sketch on the table. "Then read her the riot act. Or don't you want to?"

The idea that Tina Gone was a viable suspect disturbed Nash. But he wasn't aware that he didn't want to find her. He simply hadn't located her, as yet. But Tina Gone appearing at Rollo's pad certainly didn't mean she'd murdered her brother.

No, it was still Frank Barcelona who stood in the middle of this cheap Cracker Jack puzzle. Barcelona, who had a tape of the Beatles that he said proved his ownership of their songs. Nash couldn't confirm it yet, but he had a sneaking suspicion the tape found at Rollo's house last night was that same tape.

Belcher wasn't much help. Tracking down leads in a murder case was punch-the-clock work. Belcher had his hands full bringing World War II to a successful conclusion. Belcher reached into his pocket, removed what looked like the remains of a furry hand puppet. "I found this hairy turd on my desk this morning."

He tossed it to Nash.

It was a toupee of black hair, too long for a police inspector to wear. The tag on the inside identified it as an official Beatle wig.

"Marlene in the Property Room says these things sell for three-fifty, at Woolworth's," Belcher said. "We're in the wrong line of work, my young friend."

Nash tossed the wig back to Belcher. Belcher tossed it onto the remnants of the pineapple layer cake.

BENNY BENITEZ caught a ride with Nash when Nash left Park Station. Benitez needed to get back to the Hall, but he didn't mind making a stop first. Benitez was a Vice Detail inspector, but he wanted out.

"Vice is too soft," Benitez said in the car. "I like to get dirty. It keeps you young." Benitez raised his fists, took two shadow-boxing jabs at the windshield. The knuckles on his hands looked like sharp pieces of gravel. "Vice is dirty too, but not fistfight dirty. Just dirty."

Benitez had a badly reset nose, canting to the right. Four or five competing stories about how he'd acquired it. Benitez didn't serve in World War II though. For him, the search for the Japanese soldier was just another dragnet. When Nash gave Benitez a rough outline of the Gomez and Gone murders, Benitez wasn't too interested in the hows and whys of those cases either.

On Haight Street, Nash and Benitez found a dozen young men and women sitting at the bare wooden tables inside the Greater San Francisco Co-Prosperity Sphere.

It was 1035 hours.

The former Greek restaurant smelled of patchouli oil and wet dog fur. The free lunch wouldn't start for another forty-five minutes and the clientele, such as they were, looked morose. A young man with gaps between his teeth where other teeth had once been arpeggiated on a battered flamenco guitar while casting lonely glances around. Another boy wore a dirty blanket around his shoulders, pieces of tree leaves stuck in his thick hair. Sitting next to him, playing solitaire with a dog-eared card deck, was a blonde girl who scratched at the acne on her cheeks and moved her lips silently as she turned cards. Nash was sure that at least a few of them would match one of the two hundred or so photographs of runaways thumbtacked to Park Station's bulletin board.

An older man sat on a metal folding chair across the room. Twiddling his thumbs, staring resolutely out the front window. Looking down Haight, in the direction opposite the one Nash and Benitez had arrived from. Nash could only see the back of the man's round head. Then the man shifted his considerable weight in his chair, and Nash placed him.

He was Timothy Gone's friend. From the radio station. The one who fell on his face in Gone's kitchen on Wednesday night. The disc jockey Nash heard on the radio.

Riley Bardell.

The Emperor.

Nash hit Benitez's shoulder with the back of his hand, nodded toward Bardell. Benitez popped a fist into the palm of his other hand, nodded back. The linoleum floor was sticky, the soles of their shoes making soft peeling sounds as they crossed the room. A girl, sitting at a far table, asked in a loud voice if anyone smelled bacon. Nash knew it was a rhetorical question.

The pigs had arrived.

The Emperor turned his head. Stuck an unlit gasper in his mouth. Chewed the filter slowly. While he watched Nash and Benitez approach.

The Emperor's pale skin looked dull, like waxed paper.

"Can I help you, officers?" the Emperor said.

"You think we're officers?" Benitez said.

"You were at Timothy's place," the Emperor said to Nash.

"I'm surprised you remember," Nash said.

"I was tipsy."

"Face down on the floor, more like it."

"Not by half."

"And you were wearing a dress."

Benitez's eyebrows rose at the mention of the dress.

"It's called a kaftan," the Emperor said.

"Sure it is," Benitez said.

Nash let Bardell eyeball the SFPD star for a half-second. Benitez grunted. Nash hiked one foot on the seat of a nearby chair. He guessed the Emperor didn't know Timothy Gone was dead. His guess seemed to be confirmed when the Emperor said he was here to meet Gone.

"I need to pick something up," the Emperor said. "The old Mexican ladies in back haven't seen him."

"I'm here picking something up too," Nash said. He looked over his shoulder. The quiet inside the dining room hung thick in the air. Benitez took out a stick of gum, unwrapped it. Poked it into his mouth. Folded his thick arms as he studied the silent jury seated at the wooden picnic tables, watching. Sweat had made inroads on the collar of Benitez's light blue shirt.

The Emperor stretched his legs out.

"I help Timothy with his fundraising, for this dump," he said. "I've steered *mucho dinero* his way." The Emperor rubbed the tips of his thumb, index, and ring fingers together, emphasis on the notion of hard cash. "Now he's throwing some happiness my way. I'm the king of rock and roll radio, in this town. In a week I'll be king of rock and roll radio up and down the west coast. Across the nation. Baby, I'll be happening. I'll be the scene, Gene."

Benitez popped his gum. "Sure, *cabrone*," he said, wiseass. "I'm a celebrity too. Like Elvis." Benitez raised his arms, shook his hips back and forth, an arthritic man riding a surfboard. Then Benitez stopped abruptly, went back to chewing his gum.

"The Beatles are playing at Candlestick, right?" The Emperor nodded his head, agreeing with himself. "Well, Timothy got a line on a tape recording of the Beatles. It's never been heard, anywhere. The Beatles, playing in a German strip joint, for free beer. Colossal. Timothy's going to slip it to the Emperor.

"I'll give it some sell. I'll play it on my show, but not all at once. Little pieces of it. Let it ooze out, slow-like. I'll get ratings you've never seen."

"I've never seen ratings," Benitez said.

"Where did Gone get the tape?" Nash said.

The Emperor shook his head. He didn't know and didn't want to know. "Timothy pulled strings, I guess. So what?"

"Gone mentioned that tape to me," Nash said, not entirely truthful. "He said Rollo makes bootleg records. Gone thought Rollo might do it with the Beatles tape. Is Rollo a friend of yours?"

Nash wanted to see how the Emperor reacted.

It didn't take long.

The Emperor sat up straight in his chair. Like Nash had just jabbed him with a pointed stick. "I didn't know Gone talked to him."

Nash shrugged. Nash noticed that it was 'Gone' now—not 'Timothy'. "Talk to Rollo. Have you seen him lately?"

The Emperor unfolded his arms. He set his open hands firmly on his knees, fingers splayed, a man preparing to be electrocuted.

"Rollo is a pirate," the Emperor said. "He sells records that don't belong to him. I saw him the other day in Golden Gate Park. A folk gig. Rollo sat behind the bandstand with his tape recorder and his mike. No one okayed it. The musicians won't see any bread."

"What day was that?"

"Maybe Tuesday. Maybe not."

"Where does he get the records made?"

The Emperor scraped the sole of his shoe against the pitted surface of the linoleum floor. Back and forth. As nervous habits went, it was one. "San Jose," the Emperor said. "Rollo knows a gink who works at a pressing plant. They make educational records for schools. Gink goes in at night and cuts Rollo's discs. Rollo pays him beans. You didn't hear it from me though."

"I just did," Benitez said. "Gink."

Benitez squinted his eyes, like he was trying to make out tiny words written on Riley Bardell's forehead. When Nash mentioned Frank Barcelona's name, the Emperor looked befuddled. Nash gave the disc jockey a lot of silence to fill but the Emperor didn't fill it.

Nash changed the subject.

"Does Tina Gone see Rollo much?"

"I don't run with Gone's sister. You'll have to fish somewhere else. But you're asking a lot of questions about Rollo. What I know is, Gone was supposed to have the Beatles tape yesterday. I haven't heard from him, so I dropped by. I need that tape. Now. After the Candlestick gig, the kids won't be so interested."

"Let's stop playing," Nash said. He gave it enough twist to make it sound like the Emperor had just insulted him. "Timothy Gone is dead, Bardell. When did you find out, and how do you know?"

It was a leading question that didn't lead anywhere. Bardell looked blankly at Nash, waiting for a punch line. Benitez whistled tunelessly through his teeth.

"You're crazy," the Emperor said.

Benitez snorted. "Maybe, but Gone's still dead."

"If I knew Gone was dead, I wouldn't be sitting here. You can see that, right?"

Benitez gave the Emperor a chummy slap on the back, the Emperor looking even more uneasy. Nash didn't get much else out of the Emperor. But he was sure the Emperor wasn't acting. Riley Bardell hadn't known Gone was dead, until Nash told him.

When they finished with the Emperor, Nash and Benitez pushed through the swinging doors to the kitchen, full of feeble stainless steel equipment and noisy refrigerators.

An old Mexican woman stood beside a smoking flat grill.

The woman looked angry.

She shouted something in Spanish. Benitez picked it up and swatted it back to her in the same language. Benitez and the Mexican woman kept up their volleys of high-speed Spanish while the woman nervously wiped her hands on a dish towel. A white kid with hair like a patch of dry weeds, his arms elbow deep in a sink full of greasy dishwashing water, watched the exchange, like a tennis match.

Benitez turned to Nash.

"She runs the kitchen," Benitez said. He spoke quietly, out of the side of his mouth. "*El Jeffe* isn't here. He comes and goes. She says, last few days, Gone spent a lot of time on the telephone. Talking about someone named Ringo. Sometimes she doesn't see Gone for days, then he appears out of nowhere. She talks like he's a ghost, but she doesn't know he's dead."

When Benitez finished, he slapped Nash on the back. "That dishwasher isn't Mexican. Maybe you can communicate with him yourself."

Twenty-three

NASH FOUND HIMSELF at Coit Tower on Telegraph Hill, late in the afternoon. Tina Gone had told him that she went there, to be alone. To think. It was peaceful there, if the tourists weren't climbing over it.

Nash found several cars parked in the lot. None of them was a yellow Sunbeam Tiger.

Nash parked the Plymouth and got out. The air smelled like newly mown grass. On the observation deck, Nash lit a gasper and smoked as he studied the view of downtown, Nob and Russian Hills, Alcatraz. All of it, just empty buildings with dark windows. No life.

As he left, Nash saw a familiar-looking young woman across the parking lot. He opened his mouth to call to her, then stopped himself. The woman wasn't Tina Gone.

His mind was playing tricks.

Like the idea he'd had earlier, that he was getting Danilo

Gomez and Frank Barcelona mixed up. At times they seemed to be the two sides of one coin. All Nash knew about either of them were the stories people told him. When the stories changed, Gomez and Barcelona changed with them. Nash wondered when it would happen, all the people he needed to find becoming parts of the same person. Was the entire population of San Francisco made from different reflections of the same face?

Was this the road to madness?

Clouds raced across the sky. Nash watched shadows ripple across the square boxes covering Russian Hill. The suitcases in Tina Gone's apartment, the standby ticket to Ecuador—Nash had ignored them, willing to buy whatever story Tina Gone was selling.

Why? Perhaps it was only infatuation. Had Nash allowed himself to be hoodwinked, or had he hoodwinked himself?

Returning to the Hall, Nash found a copy of that day's San Francisco *Chronicle* lying on a bench. He took it with him to his desk, paged through it. He found Tina Gone's column, *The Gone Scene.* Written days or weeks ago, no doubt:

> *Rock and Roll music comes apart like an onion. The beat is up front, and when you peel it away you find the instrumentation, and the lyrics. Behind the lyrics you find ideas. Behind the ideas you find a pose, or a posture. And behind that there is fear, and isolation. Rock and Roll music is like whistling in the graveyard—we sing louder the more scared we are.*
>
> *It's human nature.*
>
> *And what happens when we peel away the fear?*
>
> *We come back to that beat again.*
>
> *It goes around and around.*
>
> *Rock and Roll music doesn't have any answers, but it*

allows us to dance all over the questions. And in doing so, push back the fear.

At least for a time...

Nash read the column twice. Tina Gone was writing about herself. The one thing Nash couldn't find when he read between the lines was a hint as to where she'd gone.

A SCRIBBLED phone message on Nash's desk.

Jerry Turner, returning Nash's call.

Nash poured a cup of coffee from the office pot and sat down. Placed a call to Malibu.

Malibu was a beach colony. Hollywood film people went there for naughty weekends, booze and pill-popping and free love. It was their respite from weekdays of booze and pill-popping and free love.

A woman answered the telephone. She said she'd get Turner. The rustle and shiver of Ma Bell's telephone lines sounded like the Malibu surf rolling in.

"It's terrible what happened," Turner said when he came to the phone. "Danny O'Day had talent. It should've made him piles of bread. I told him, 'Come to LA.' I'd help get his foot in the door. People respect bread in LA. It's the only thing they do respect."

"Hotchkiss said you might've signed O'Day to some kind of contract, Mister Turner. Is that right?"

A long sigh from Turner. "I offered Danny a contract. He didn't sign it because he couldn't. He was already tied up with that con artist, what's his name? Pinkrose.

"The contract Danny signed with Pinkrose was shit. It tied Danny to Pinkrose in perpetuity. It gave Pinkrose the right to claim a fifty percent songwriting credit on any song Danny released on the Hi-Tone label over the next five years, with an option to extend the contract after the initial period. And it gave Pinkrose seventy-five percent of the publishing. Kids like Danny, they'll sign anything. Just to see their name on a record.

"If Danny died or tried to break the contract in a manner that didn't conform to the stipulations contained therein, all rights to the songs reverted to Pinkrose, in full. That contract was a ball and chain. It even charged Danny a fee for the studio time he used at Pinkrose's studio, deducted from future earnings. Like making a condemned man pay for the noose that hangs him."

"Did you explain that to Danny?"

"I told him to hire a lawyer."

When Nash asked about Jasper Rollo, Turner told him the same sort of tale Hotchkiss had recounted. Rollo liked to find new talent for the Kimono à Go-Go, and Danny O'Day had played there, mostly as a solo folk act. That was where Turner ran into him.

Turner recalled speaking to Rollo on one occasion about Danny O'Day's legal hassle. "Rollo knows Pinkrose. He told me that short of a blizzard of cash or an atom bomb, Pinkrose wouldn't let go of Danny's contract."

"Mister Turner, what use would Jasper Rollo have for an old tape recording of the Beatles group?"

Turner hummed and hawed. Then, "Why do you ask?"

Nash lied, sort of. "I came across one. It belonged to someone at Rollo's club, who got it from Rollo. It purports to be a recording of the Beatles playing at a club in Germany a few years ago. I wondered where it came from."

Turner picked his words carefully. "Rollo collects recordings. I may have given him the one you're referring to. It's made the rounds down here for a couple of years, there are several copies floating around. It's a curiosity but that's about all. I warned Rollo when I gave it to him, it may or may not be the Beatles. If you got it from someone other than Rollo then maybe he passed it on, or made another copy. You'd have to ask him."

Nash guessed that Turner knew about Rollo's bootleg recording sideline, but Nash didn't press the issue.

He pursued other questions.

Turner said he'd never heard of Timothy Gone or Frank Barcelona. The name Tina Gone sounded familiar, but Turner couldn't place it, offhand. When Nash asked where Rollo went in Northern California to record music, Turner guffawed. "He goes into the redwoods with three electrical generators. He plugs the band into their amps and records them *en plein air* while he dances around naked. Kind of a flabby wood sprite scene. He says the sound vibrations traveling through his stinky body are a form of higher knowledge. Sounds nutty, but what do I know?"

Nash, disappointed, hung up the phone. Turner's comments about the recording contract Pinkrose had with Gomez didn't shed any light on a motive for murder. Gomez was more useful to Pinkrose alive, writing new songs.

Nash had just finished typing his notes on the Turner interview when Belcher called from Park Station.

"Get up here, college boy," Belcher said. "We found the Nip. He built himself a defensive position on the west side of the park. A hundred yards south of the Buffalo Paddock. He took a pot shot at a search team earlier but he's lying low now. I suggested we use a flamethrower to flush him out. Police work is muddy, but we're still God's soldiers."

Belcher also said that the lieutenant's mother had been located. "We're waiting for her to make an appearance. She's a seamstress in a tailor shop on Pine Street. New name and all of it. They told her that her son who died twenty years ago is back and preparing for combat in Golden Gate Park. She fainted, hit the deck like bricks. Shit, so would I."

Dusk. A light fog rolling in.

Two SFPD patrolmen positioned behind sawhorse barriers on the road leading into the park, and Park Station, stood by with riot guns.

A third patrolman shined a flashlight into Nash's car.

Nash waved his badge around. The patrolman with the flashlight said the park was surrounded by SFPD personnel, assisted now by SF County Sheriff's deputies, US Army MPs from the Presidio and Fort Ord, and patrolmen from San Rafael, Menlo Park, and Palo Alto. California Highway Patrol troopers were operating a line of defense along the coastal highway, at the west end of the park. Orders from Chief Cahill were to keep all civilians out of the park until further notice.

The patrolman with the flashlight claimed he'd heard shooting earlier, but he didn't know the circumstances.

Nash drove on.

In the distance portable field lights glowed among the trees.

The station house itself was strangely quiet. In the Task Force Z command post, bright parabolas of light hung above the receding hairlines of the three SFPD personnel present.

"The action has moved to the Buffalo Paddock," said the tired sergeant seated in front of a complicated field radio. "The Jap has a gun. He took a couple of potshots at the Army MPs, but he hasn't hit anyone yet."

The sergeant got up from his chair, used a wooden ruler to pinpoint the paddock on a map tacked to the wall. Then he moved the tip of the ruler to a point further east.

"A squad of patrolmen and MPs encountered the Jap in the

area of the Japanese Tea Garden—big surprise," the sergeant said. "That was seventeen-thirty hours. We'd already searched that area once, so he wasn't there long. From there he moved due west, across the park to the paddock—here. It took us a couple of hours to get a line on him again. Right now, he's probably found a defensive position in the area around the Chain of Lakes."

The sergeant made a wobbly circle with the ruler around the area of the park that contained the three small lakes. The ruler moved toward the western end of the park, where the park was separated from the ocean beach by the highway. "We've got CHP at the highway. Task Force Z and two platoons of Army MPs are running loose in the park, and we've got another MP platoon stationed at Kezar Stadium and the pavilion. Between you and me, someone is going to get shot by their own side before this is over."

The sergeant said a Task Force Z Forward Operating Base had been set up not far from the paddock. Everyone there was waiting for the Army to bring in the Japanese soldier's mother. It was hoped that she'd talk her son out of the trees. Without any further unpleasantness, and gunplay.

"What about the press?" Nash said.

The sergeant explained that the official line to the press was that a sizable bomb had been found in the park. Army explosive ordinance specialists were assisting SFPD. The criminal element that left the bomb might still be in the vicinity, and civilians—including the press—were barred from entering the park, for their own safety. The fog rolling in would keep news helicopters grounded.

The sergeant placed a finger to his mouth. "Loose lips sink ships."

Nash caught a ride to the Forward Operating Base with a

Robbery Detail inspector from Task Force Z who had come back to Park Station in a patrol car to pick up a case of flashlight batteries.

The inspector—Paulson—highballed his way along South Drive, talking nonstop. Nash couldn't make much of it, other than that there were thirty top brass from the Army and SFPD hunkered down in the trees, drawing up plans to capture the Jap.

Paulson shook his head, the wonder of it. "I wouldn't miss this for all the tea in Tijuana."

THE LONG olive-drab tent the Forward Operating Base was built around stood a hundred feet from the South Drive pavement. The area was well lit by field lights. Paulson parked the prowl car beside a row of Army jeeps. Outside the tent, SFPD and Army personnel congregated around a work table, studying survey maps. Boxes of radio equipment, SFPD riot helmets, Plexiglas shields, riot sticks, all of it neatly stacked beside the tent. In the shadows, soldiers and patrolmen gave orders to their men in the field over walkie-talkies and Army field radios. The US Army brought a whole new dimension to police dragnets, Nash mused.

Nearby, a single patrolman practiced the standard riot stick movements, like a new form of popular dance. The inside parry—*one-two*. The outside parry—*three-four*. The short swing—*one step to the right*. The back swing and jab—*twist and turn and repeat*. The patrolman was executing a side-on jab and thrust movement using a two-handed grip on the riot stick when the field generator behind the tent sputtered and died. For a minute the Forward Operating Base was thrown into darkness while several GIs worked on the machinery by flashlight.

The lights flickered back on. Nash found himself standing five feet from Belcher, just emerging from the tent, finishing a cup of coffee and a gasper. The disposable paper cup bore pictures of playing cards, for playing coffee cup poker.

"A straight," Belcher said. "Almost. Trey of diamonds to six. One jack of clubs to fuck it all up." Belcher held up the coffee cup, inviting Nash to study the cards himself. "Glad you could drop by, Nash."

Twenty-four

"THE HEAD SHED is pissed off about the fog," Belcher said. "The Army can't bring their choppers in and we can't either."

Belcher drank the last of his coffee.

Tossed his losing poker hand into a trash can already full of losing hands.

Belcher nodded toward the map table, where Chief Jellicoe and Lieutenant Dark discussed plans and operations with the Green Beret colonels—Gorman and Kepler—and several other Army and SFPD honchos. The frown lines on their foreheads ran deep as their fingers delineated flank defenses, tactical envelopment, and pincer movements on the map of the city park and the surrounding community.

After a few minutes the crowd at the map table thinned. Belcher approached the table, motioning to Nash to come along. Belcher pressed a fingertip against the clear plastic-covered map, traced an unsteady line from the park's South Drive to the

Buffalo Paddock, by way of Spreckels Lake and the Main Drive.

"Jellicoe and Dark believe the Jap is boxed in here." Belcher pointed to the eastern portion of the paddock, near the largest of the three lakes. "Our esteemed colleagues from the Army"—Belcher made a comical noise not unlike a raspberry—"believe that the Jap has already circumnavigated the big lake and is either making his way to the coastal highway to escape along the beach, or working his way north to break out of the park around Thirty-ninth and the Cabrillo Playground."

Belcher shook his head in stark disappointment. "I say 'nuts' to all that. I think the Jap will do just what Japs always did. He'll dig in right where he is, and fight until we kill him, or he kills himself." Belcher tapped the side of his head with his finger. "Inside the Jap mind the greatest glory he can achieve is to die for his Emperor. I believe we can assist him in reaching that goal."

They were spirited words, but Belcher looked troubled. Nash wondered if Belcher was thinking of his Seabee days, how it felt to charge forward on an earth mover on Guadalcanal, enemy bullets ricocheting off the steel blade. The Japanese soldier had his own troubles, of course. He'd lived like a dog in the jungle for twenty-two years, then travelled seven thousand miles across the Pacific Ocean and escaped the clutches of the US Army, only to face the distinct possibility that he would be torn to pieces in a blaze of gunfire in a city park on a foggy San Francisco night.

Surely there were easier ways to commit suicide.

The SFPD and Army officers milling around the Forward Operating Base tent paused in their conversations to watch two SFPD patrolmen wearing riot helmets approach on the road. The patrolmen pushed and prodded two prisoners forward with the tips of their regulation black truncheons.

"What is this shit?" one of the prisoners said, as he was pushed into the light around the map table. "We haven't done anything." He was a young man with an oddly-shaped head, and a goatee like a patch of mold. He wore a string of colored beads around his neck and, coincidentally, a well-worn olive-drab Army surplus field jacket.

The other prisoner was a pale young woman with lank brown hair. The ankle-length dress she wore hung off her narrow hips like a dishrag draped over a door nail.

One of the thick-necked patrolmen carried what appeared to be a badly rolled sleeping bag under his arm.

"We found them in the bushes, near the pagoda," the other patrolman said to Chief Jellicoe, who had stepped forward to ascertain what the matter was. "They refused to respond to our questions, or provide identification. I think they have knowledge of the suspect's whereabouts."

Right then the goateed man began shouting while he tried to wrench his arm free from the grip of the patrolman who held him. The man's outburst got him a clout on the head from the cop.

An Army officer wearing starched camouflage-pattern jungle fatigues stepped up to the detainees. The officer, a major, grabbed the beads hanging around the man's neck, twisted the string of beads around his hand until his fist rested tightly under the young man's chin.

The major said, "Son, what exactly did you speak about with the little Japanese man?"

"We didn't break the law," the young man said. The words sounded defiant but the hard look in the man's eyes wavered. "I'm an American citizen." The man glanced at his girlfriend. Her eyes remained downcast.

The major raised the man's chin with his fist until the man had no choice but to look at the major's face. The major noticed an

Army unit patch stitched to the shoulder of the man's fatigue jacket.

The patch gave him pause.

The major said, "Have you been to Vietnam, son?"

The young man swallowed hard. The young woman whimpered. The major smiled. He spoke carefully now, explaining long division to a slow child. "I didn't think so. You know why I didn't think so? Because you're soft. You're a soft little titty boy. I'd send you to Vietnam myself, but you'd curl up and die on me. Like a maggot in a campfire."

The major removed a folding buck knife from his jacket, slowly. Pulled the large blade out. "I'm going to ask you once more. What was the nature of your communications with the Japanese fellow?"

"Fuck you, man."

The major frowned deeply.

He directed the patrolman to take firm hold of the young man. When the man's arms were pinned tightly behind his back, the major raised the buck knife, used it to roughly cut the Army unit patch from the shoulder of the man's fatigue jacket.

When he finished, the major smoothed out the cloth patch, tucked it carefully away in his pocket, a sacred relic rescued from a heathen pygmy. The entire scene struck Nash as playacting on the part of the major, but well-done playacting.

Lieutenant Dark stepped forward. He directed the two patrolmen to take their prisoners up to Park Station, slap them with a vagrancy beef.

THREE SFPD prowl cars appeared out of the fog. They approached slowly on South Drive. They pulled off the road, came to a stop on the grass beside the operations tent.

"Mama-san's here," Belcher said, pointing a finger.

Jellicoe, Lieutenant Dark, Colonel Kepler of the Green Berets, and an interpreter approached the second of the three cars. The four men stood in a row beside the car, as stiff and officious as butlers in competition, while a patrolman opened the car's rear door.

A tiny Japanese woman in a darkly embroidered jacket climbed out of the rear seat, holding on to the patrolman's arm to keep her balance. A spindly Oriental man in a drooping baby blue sweater slid across the back seat, climbed out behind her.

A long discussion followed, the elderly couple and the top brass, the communication pushed along by the interpreter and lavish amounts of gesticulation. Finally, the colonel turned and gave an order to a nearby sergeant.

The sergeant disappeared into the command post tent. He returned with a white bullhorn. He handed it to the Japanese woman while the interpreter tried to explain how the device worked. The old woman stared at the apparatus in her hand as though the sergeant had just handed her a dead possum. Quickly she handed it back.

"She's in a quandary," Belcher said to Nash. "She doesn't want to appear uncooperative, but she doesn't want to help capture her own son. Oriental types stick together."

Soon it was settled. Mama-san got back into the prowl car, and the interpreter with the bullhorn followed. Before climbing into the car, the old man had his hand firmly shaken by a somber Lieutenant Dark. As though one of them would soon be entering a space capsule.

Chief Jellicoe issued stern orders. A dozen patrolmen wearing riot helmets and carrying Mossberg pump-action riot guns at port arms jogged off in squad formation down the concrete surface of South Drive, heading west. Their double-timed advance was quickly obscured by the fog. Nash watched as their outlines faded, tardy ghosts returning to the spirit world.

"Give them five minutes to get into position," Nash heard Dark tell the Green Beret colonel, while Jellicoe nodded his head sagely. "If our little friend is still where he was spotted earlier, we'll have a unit in front of him and a unit on either side of him. At his back is the lake. If he tries to escape, he'll have to walk on water."

Five minutes later, Kepler and an Army sharpshooter carrying an M21 sniper rifle climbed into a nearby jeep. Dark and Jellicoe moved toward the first patrol car in the line of three. Dark motioned toward Belcher and pointed at the third patrol car in the line, which three other Homicide Detail inspectors were at that moment climbing into.

"Break a leg," Nash said as Belcher departed.

The parade of vehicles on South Drive moved off slowly. It reminded Nash of a funeral procession. The Army jeep took the point position and the three patrol cars followed closely. The funeral's honoree wasn't quite dead yet, but the forecast leaned heavily in that direction.

The taillights of the vehicles wormed themselves into the fog.

NASH JOINED the remaining soldiers and policemen as they moved off on foot down the road leading to the Buffalo Paddock to watch the big show. Nash found himself walking beside an inspector from the Pawn Shop Detail. The inspector's eyes were focused upward, shifted back and forth. As though watching the tall trees close in on him. "This is a street rumble," the inspector said. "All we need are chains and knives. Maybe a hatchet or two."

The glow of portable field lights grew large as the green

expanse of the paddock slowly revealed itself in the fog. Nash had thought the field lights would reflect off the fog, throw odd shadows. But visibility was better than he'd expected. Nash wondered where the bison that normally inhabited the paddock were. Had the Army corralled them?

The crowd of stragglers drew up to the near side of the cover created by the four vehicles from the Forward Operating Base, now parked bumper to bumper. Jellicoe and Lieutenant Dark stood in the open, on the other side of the vehicles, studying the fog-draped landscape. Their hands raised to their brows, shielding their eyes from the glare of the field lights.

Nash, standing beside the front fender of the Army jeep, heard the ticking of the vehicle's warm engine in the chill air. He wondered how Jellicoe or his boss, Chief Cahill, was going to explain these events to the press. The press blackout had made sense earlier, when they were still looking for Shimatzu. Now that they had found him and he'd wounded one patrolman, it was a different story. What if a cop or a GI was killed? How would the City Hall mob soft pedal that?

An Army corporal standing near Nash passed around a pack of Mexican cigarettes while two military policemen loudly discussed the pros and cons of enfilade fire. Soon two of the three mobile searchlights in the paddock area were repositioned, the swathes of light meeting at the edge of the tree line. The Army interpreter who had travelled to the paddock with the old Japanese woman stepped past Jellicoe and Dark, moved out into the open field.

Mama-san followed. Teetering, the ground uneven.

The harsh manufactured light of the field lights was rendered softly focused by the fingers of fog. The interpreter carried the white bullhorn cradled infant-like in his arms.

The mother's arms were folded tight across the front of her

dragon-themed housecoat, probably to help keep her nerves from shaking her to pieces. She walked with head bowed. Slowly her back-leaning shadow slipped past her to lead the way.

The interpreter and the old woman had walked thirty feet when two Army MPs and Belcher stepped away from the vehicles and followed them. Belcher walked stiffly, hands out at his sides. A Wild West gunfighter. Nash wasn't surprised to see the .38 caliber snub-nosed revolver tucked into the waist of Belcher's trousers, behind his back.

After another thirty feet, one of the MPs directed the interpreter and the old woman to hold up. The group came to a halt in the center of the field, the two MPs and Belcher now standing twenty feet behind the two huddled figures they had followed.

The MPs looked left and right, as though expecting cross traffic. Belcher scratched the back of his head. The interpreter raised the bullhorn. A short metallic screech tore through the quiet as the interpreter tried to position the bullhorn so that mama-san could speak into it easily.

The interpreter held the bullhorn while the tiny woman began her plea.

Her soft voice cracked. The bullhorn gave her demur Japanese syllables a sharp edge. The woman hadn't seen her son since World War II. She had believed he was long dead in a forgotten battle on a lonely Pacific island. But her son was alive, in San Francisco. He'd killed a man, in the Haight-Ashbury neighborhood. Just the night before.

The old woman stopped speaking. A squeal from the bullhorn followed, a punctuation mark. As the squeal died out the sound of the woman's congested breathing, amplified by the bullhorn, carried across the paddock. The old Japanese woman took a step back just as a noise came from the tree line.

The noise grew louder.

The noise became a high-pitched burst of Japanese.

Belcher and the two MPs craned their necks, looking in every direction. There was no movement in the darkness at the edge of the paddock. The clamations in Japanese from the cover of the trees continued.

The Army interpreter handed the bullhorn to the old woman. She held it tentatively in both hands. The interpreter again showed her how to operate the grip switch. She nodded along elaborately, like she was getting detailed directions to a supermarket across town.

The interpreter retreated to where Belcher and the two MPs stood. The voice from the trees had fallen silent. The old woman now stood alone, in the center of the paddock. She raised the bullhorn to her mouth. She spoke again. There was strong emotion in her voice. Then the old woman paused. The silence that followed was complete. Nash thought he could hear the fog thickening.

A figure appeared in the fog.

The figure skirted the edge of the paddock, with deliberation.

Like a forest animal, wary of open spaces.

The figure paused.

It was the soldier.

The dark jacket the soldier wore looked vastly too large for him. His trousers appeared to be tied around his waist with a length of cord that hung down his leg. Then Nash saw the automatic pistol the soldier held, close to his side. Quite probably the pistol he'd taken from the dead US Army sergeant, Boggs. At the soup kitchen on Haight. Nash wondered how many cartridges the soldier had expended.

The Japanese soldier stepped forward a few feet. Under the field lights he looked pale. His face had the stark frozen aspect of a Noh mask from Japanese theater, or so Nash thought. The mother, for her part, seemed to display the darkly furrowed brow and crooked gesticulation of the Kabuki tradition.

The Japanese soldier paused in the middle of the paddock.

Twenty feet away from his mother.

He studied her, in silence.

He straightened his shoulders.

Raised his chin.

He continued to hold his arms pressed close to his sides. The barrel of the automatic in his right hand rested against the side of his knee. He didn't look alarmed by the array of pistols, rifles, and riot guns zeroed in on him from the far edge of the paddock. Where the vehicles were parked, and Nash and the others stood.

The Japanese soldier named Shimatzu began talking. Nash stood close enough to Chief Jellicoe and Lieutenant Dark to hear what one of the DLI linguists translated for them.

The gist of it was, Shimatzu wondered if he was already dead. Was he now meeting deceased ancestors, and deceased enemies?

Nash didn't think Shimatzu was much taller than his tiny mother. The stoop in the lieutenant's shoulders made him look defeated. Nash thought of photographs he'd seen, not so long ago. In *Look* magazine. Broken outlines of half-sunken ships and invasion boats, still resting on island beachheads, throughout the South Pacific. Rusting combat machinery, littering the surf.

Nothing but riveted tombstones now.

And this Japanese soldier—servant of the Emperor, Hirohito, son of God and the Rising Sun—wasn't he himself a piece of discarded war materiel, left behind to rot?

Lieutenant Shimatzu took a step forward. Careful. As though pushing the limits of a private dare.

The lieutenant bowed deeply to his mother.

The old woman raised the bullhorn to her mouth, spoke through it, even though her son stood only a dozen or so feet in front of her. When the old woman finished her tirade she dropped the bullhorn at her feet, in disgust. Belcher and the two MPs—still twenty feet behind mama-san—looked at each other, alarmed. How close should they let Shimatzu get before they pounced, wrestled him to the ground, the final rodeo trick?

According to the DLI interpreter, Shimatzu then told his mother that he had dishonored his family and his country. He'd failed to fight hard enough to win the war and vanquish the heathen murderers from America and the other Godless round-eye countries.

The lieutenant dropped to his knees, sat back on his heels.

Shimatzu asked his mother for forgiveness.

The old Japanese woman stared in silence at her son.

As Shimatzu spoke further, Nash studied the shadowy faces of the men gathered around the vehicles. The captive audience. Watching the surrender play out on a flickering movie screen.

Nash was still looking elsewhere when the night air was torn by a gunshot.

The old Japanese woman shrieked.

The first gunshot was followed quickly by three more shots. The line of spectators from around the parked vehicles surged forward into the paddock, weapons drawn. Lieutenant Dark and one of the Green Beret colonels got out ahead of crowd and ordered them back. Two Army medics rushed into the field carrying camouflage-patterned medical kit bags. Ducking their heads as they ran, as though expecting more enemy fire.

Belcher fired the first shot. Two of the three remaining shots had come from the Jap soldier. An Army MP had fired the fourth shot. Now Belcher lay on the ground, one of the MPs crouching over his motionless form. The other MP in the paddock moved cautiously toward the prostrate form of Lieutenant Shimatzu.

The old Japanese woman collapsed in a faint.

The Japanese soldier was a lost cause. The medic who checked on him left his side quickly, went to assist the other medic with Belcher. The elderly Oriental man in the baggy blue sweater reached the old woman. He revived her, helped her to her feet. When she regained her senses the old woman crept forward, knelt softly, beside the body of her son. Quietly stroking the hair on his head. No one had noticed the automatic pistol still clutched in the soldier's hand. The elderly man finally pulled it free of the soldier's dead fingers. He held it carefully between his thumb and forefinger until an MP relieved him of the burden.

Two ambulances that had been stationed along the road now drove forward into the paddock. Nash watched Lieutenant Dark and the two medics bundle Belcher onto a stretcher, slide him into the back of an ambulance.

There was no rush to move Lieutenant Shimatzu. One of the ambulance attendants removed the oversized leather jacket the dead Japanese soldier had worn, then assisted in shifting the small corpse to the stretcher. Nash, standing nearby, noticed with a degree of professional interest that the back of the soldier's leather jacket was covered by a cloth patch. It identified the wearer as a member of the Coffin Cheaters Motorcycle Club, Frisco.

Twenty-five

BELCHER WAS TAKEN to San Francisco General, *pronto.* Chief Jellicoe departed while Lieutenant Dark barked orders under the Army field lights. Every minute that Task Force Z stayed in Golden Gate Park increased the chances of tripping over news reporters, with their notepads, cameras, impertinences.

The crime scene needed to be tossed for facts and cleaned up. Most *pronto.*

Lieutenant Shimatzu's mother and the old man, her escort, were bundled off to the Hall of Justice. Shimatzu's corpse had a date with a refrigerated compartment at the morgue.

Shimatzu's war had begun twenty-three years ago, when he shipped out, Japan to the Moluccas.

It ended in Golden Gate Park.

But the lieutenant hadn't surrendered. He'd upheld his oath to Emperor Hirohito, to die for the cause. Maybe even regained honor for his family, by dying in the service of the Emperor. It was small comfort, but Nash was certain that comfort had never been the issue.

The Crime Lab eggheads stepped in and got to work.

Sifting dirt, scraping up blood.

There wasn't much to investigate. The identity of the dead man was not in question, nor was the fact that he shot an SFPD inspector before he committed suicide—neither Belcher's shot nor the shot from the MP hit Shimatzu.

The single gunshot wound Shimatzu suffered was the one to the side of his head that he inflicted on himself.

The angle that got the Crime Lab up on its hind legs was the question of whether or not the Jap soldier had murdered Staff Sergeant Chester A. Boggs at the free kitchen on Haight. Nash didn't understand their consternation. SFPD now possessed the machete used in the killing, the fingerprints attached to the machete, and the dead Japanese soldier attached to the fingerprints.

It ought to be a cinch.

Except for the Coffin Cheaters patch.

Shimatzu wasn't a motorcycle-based social deviant, so he hadn't acquired the leather jacket by the usual methods. Nash was still pondering the question of the jacket when Lieutenant Dark climbed out of the back of the patrol car he was using as an office, stepped over to where Nash was holding the end of a long piece of string. A Crime Lab technician held the other end. The taut string represented the angle of one of the gunshots. Wooden stakes pounded into the ground represented Belcher, the soldier, and the MPs.

Dark had just spoken with San Francisco General.

The bullet that hit Belcher had gone into his side, deflected off a rib bone. Came to rest in his right lung.

He'd just come out of surgery.

"He's knocked out on dope, but out of danger," Dark said. The lieutenant frowned at the string and the flat-faced man holding the other end of it. "Make some time tomorrow to visit your partner, Nash. If you're done flying your kite by then."

THE PRESS blackout was still holding at 1000 hours the next morning. The statement issued by City Hall related that the unusual type of bomb discovered in Golden Gate Park the night before had been disarmed, at the scene, by Army bomb disposal experts. The search for evidence and the culprits was, of course, ongoing.

End of statement.

When a television crew tried to interview Army soldiers leaving the Presidio about the events in the park, the station owner was quickly advised by SFPD and the US Army that what had happened in the park had a national security angle. Any efforts by the press to report unsubstantiated rumors would have "consequences."

The strong-arm tactics worked, for the moment.

At noon on Sunday, the black leather motorcycle jacket Shimatzu had worn was identified as belonging to Frank Barcelona. The identification was made primarily on the basis of several loose business cards found in a jacket pocket. The cards carried Barcelona's name. On the back: YOU HAVE BEEN ASSISTED BY A MEMBER OF THE COFFIN CHEATERS MOTORCYCLE CLUB, SAN FRANCISCO CHAPTER.

At 1320 hours on Sunday, SFPD Patrolman G. Fenwick of Company F, Park Station discovered a disused drainage pipe not far from the Japanese Tea Garden, on the eastern side of Golden Gate Park. The concrete pipe measured four feet in diameter and forty feet long. The foliage growing at either end of the pipe had been disrupted recently.

The body of Frank Barcelona was found ten feet inside the northern end of the pipe. A single knife wound to Barcelona's neck had sliced the carotid artery.

Barcelona had quickly bled to death.

The corpse had been in the drainage pipe for four or five days, according to the medical examiner. There was no indication the body had been dragged there, and Barcelona was too big to be easily carried. It was reasonable to assume he was murdered near the pipe.

If Barcelona had carried a wallet, it was gone now. A Spanish-style goatskin bag half full of red wine lay beside him inside the pipe.

There was no evidence of defensive wounds on Barcelona's hands or arms, and neither the leather jacket nor the goatskin had blood on them. Which suggested that Barcelona or someone else was carrying the two items when Barcelona was killed. The two items were thrown into the pipe after the body was deposited there.

Had the Japanese soldier holed up in the park for several days, knifing Barcelona in the process? Nash didn't think it played out that way. Much more likely that the soldier discovered the corpse, and took the leather coat for himself.

For one thing, the truck Barcelona drove to the park had been parked illegally on the street along the Panhandle, where it received a parking citation. Before it was moved to the yard behind Eddie Euclid's pad. According to the Traffic Bureau, the date of the ticket was August 23rd—last Tuesday. Barcelona was last seen on that same date, in that same location. The truck had been dusted for prints but the results were still pending.

Someone murdered Barcelona, then moved the truck to muddy the waters. The fact that the truck landed in Euclid's backyard, a spot where the truck was a sure bet to be dismantled and sold piecemeal, suggested that whoever ditched the truck there knew the inhabitants of the house well, or well enough.

The case had circled back on itself in important ways. The skinny kid at the Celestial Eyeball store had ID'ed Frank Barcelona as the man he saw at the free concert in the park the previous Tuesday. Standing beside an older man. Drinking wine from a goatskin bag. But the answers Nash wanted continued to evade his grasp.

IN BELCHER'S absence, Lieutenant Dark assigned Lou Crandall to work with Nash on the Gomez/Gone case. Crandall sounded punchy when Nash met him at the Hall. Crandall's bloodshot eyes made Nash wonder if Crandall had spent the previous night with his face back in the trough, at the Golden Bubble.

"Lou, have you been home, at all?" Nash said.

"Since when?"

"Since yesterday."

"What day was yesterday?"

The first order of business, locate Pearly Spence. But the woman had already moved out of her Richmond District pad, and her former landlady didn't know where to. Rollo must've had a good idea where Spence was right now, but where was he?

Next was Max Pinkrose. Nash was sure Pinkrose had information that he wasn't sharing with SFPD. Not wanting to forewarn Pinkrose with a telephone call, Nash and Crandall dropped by the Hi-Tone office in North Beach, and struck out. The office was locked up tight.

They stopped at the *Chronicle* offices on Mission, not finding a trace of Tina Gone but taking a look around, the other business at hand. Then they headed further south, to Pinkrose's listed home address.

In the car, Crandall's fingers didn't stop fidgeting with the brim of his chocolate brown Trilby hat. Nash's own nerves didn't feel any calmer. He hadn't slept much. His reactions seemed wrapped too tight. He saw tiny flashes of light that sparkled at the edge of his vision. At times he felt like he was falling, even when he was sitting down.

Nash's thoughts kept returning to Tina Gone. He wasn't sure what he owed her, or why. But he felt, in some inchoate way, responsible for her safety. As though this murder investigation belonged to him alone, and now he needed to pull her out from under it. Pull her free, before it rolled over her.

Nash had a bad feeling about Tina Gone's disappearance. When he mentioned this to Dark, the lieutenant told Nash to get used to it, bad feelings.

Pinkrose's residence was two blocks south of Ocean, on the corner of Plymouth and Grafton. It was a two-story cracker box with red roof tiles. Out front, a plastic flamingo had toppled into the boxwood shrubs. Nash had expected a bit more from the owner of a record company, an *impresario*.

Was Pinkrose married? Kids? No one answered Nash's knock. The house was quiet. Nash walked around to the back door and knocked some more and got the same goose egg.

"Our bird has flown," Crandall said, back in the car. His fingers repeated the comment in Morse code on the brim of his hat.

Nash recalled that Pinkrose's secretary sang in a restaurant lounge, on the weekends. He checked his notebook. Miss Amador. Raylene Amador. He hadn't written down the name of the restaurant though.

Nash searched his memory. The Captain's Table? The Oak Table?

The Round Table was located on Leavenworth Street. The billboard outside the club advertised Miss Raylene Amador, of

"Chuck and Mookie" fame. Saturdays and Sundays, until ten o'clock. Fridays were reserved for an act from Reno, Gorgeous George Salazar and his Tinkling Spoons.

The dressing room behind the club's stage was narrow and tight. A round man wearing a yellow and brown plaid sport coat made noises like a low-rent boyfriend when Nash and Crandall pushed their way in.

Raylene Amador sat on a folding chair in front of a vanity table. The lighted mirror she used to put her make up on had five working bulbs, six others that had given up the ghost. The boyfriend stank of garlic and objected loudly to the presence of SFPD in Miss Amador's dressing room.

"We want to talk to the lady," Crandall said to the boyfriend. Crandall took hold of the man's coat collar and shoved him toward the door. "You're sucking up all the air."

The man slammed the door closed behind him when he left. The door latch didn't catch and the door swung back open and the man slammed it closed again. Nash smiled.

Chuck and Mookie.

"Was that Chuck?" Nash said.

Raylene Amador studied her grimace in the mirror. The thick eyeliner gave her a raccoon aspect. "Chuck runs a junkyard in Pinole," she said. "That fine hunk of half a man who just stepped out is Leon, who fell out of love with his last wife because she hates him and beat him up. He manages this joint while he searches for a spine."

"Where do we find Pinkrose?" Crandall said.

Raylene Amador sat back. Folded her arms across her chest, a sudden sharp chill. Nash was pretty sure the only sharp chill was in her brown eyes.

"You think he killed that Gone fellow?" Miss Amador said.

"Why do you say that?" Crandall said.

The Department hadn't issued a press release on Frank Barcelona's murder, but the death of Timothy Gone had been widely reported.

Miss Amador unfolded her arms again. With the back of her hand she brushed at a patch of her evening gown that had shed most of its sequins in the distant past. There was a shout outside in the hallway—a waitress needed placemats.

"Max thought Danny broke into the studio and stole the tapes of his songs," Amador said. "Max sent Miss Gone over to Danny's to get them back, but she didn't get them. Maybe Max sent the brother too. Max knew him, the brother was always scrounging money, his Mother Theresa gig. So maybe the brother gets the tapes, but decides to hold out for more money. Who knows?"

"Where did you hear this?" Nash said.

"A little bit here, a little there. I can read between the lines."

"Did Pinkrose tell you this?"

Raylene Amador studied her reflection while she shook her head to get her hair to lay right. The tiny glittering balls of her earrings danced under her ear lobes. "I don't recall, not exactly."

Crandall said, "What else did you hear?"

"Not a thing. But when I heard about Gone getting killed, I started thinking. I don't owe Max anything. It was time to say something."

Crandall grunted. "So you waited for us to turn up."

"I would've called."

Amador's gut feelings didn't seem to be worth much. But after several more questions, Nash and Crandall established that Amador had heard the name Jasper Rollo once or twice around the Hi-Tone office. She didn't recall ever meeting the man, and she wasn't sure what connection Pinkrose had with him.

Amador also didn't know if Pinkrose owned a rifle, but she

knew that his wife and kids lived in Bakersfield, and Pinkrose wasn't bothered about it. Pinkrose spent a lot of time at the bar inside Corsetti's Crab Pot Restaurant, on Fisherman's Wharf. "He's tight with one of the bartenders. I think they know each other from the war."

As he and Nash departed, Crandall advised the woman that she'd be getting herself into a spot if she warned Pinkrose that SFPD wanted to have another chat with him. Raylene Amador shrugged. She went back to painting over the blemishes on her chin, while Nash and Crandall hit the bricks again.

Twenty-six

NASH'S SENSE THAT he was falling grew stronger. It wasn't dizziness. He felt like he'd become unmoored from the world around him.

Maybe the weather had something to do with it.

The day had turned cloudy and gray. At Fisherman's Wharf, tourists priced bric-a-brac while squirrely children waved plastic pirate swords at each other. Further along Jefferson Street, two dozen teenage girls were staging a go-go dancing marathon on the sidewalk. A countermeasure, aimed at the anti-Beatles picketers congregating on the next block.

Meanwhile, toward the east end of Jefferson, students from the

San Francisco College of Art had erected scaffolding and were busy painting a mural on a long brick wall. One hundred years of wharf history rendered in stick figures, or so it looked to Nash when he and Crandall drove past.

Nash parked in the fire lane outside of Corsetti's. As he and Crandall got out of the car Nash glanced in the direction of the go-go dancing girls. He wondered if a permit was needed to dance, en masse, on public sidewalks. What would the newspapers say, SFPD carting off a truckload of frugging high school girls in cheerleader skirts to the hoosegow? Pointed questions would be asked, and pointed editorials written, without a doubt.

Some things exist beyond the reach of the law.

"I've never eaten here," Crandall said, as they entered the restaurant. "My wife doesn't like seafood. She says it tastes fishy. There isn't an answer to that."

Conch cells attached to *faux* fishing nets hung on the walls of the softly lit bar that adjoined the restaurant's main dining room. The bar area also had dining tables, small and round. Light chatter wafted through the bar like chiffon curtains in a gentle breeze.

Crandall and Nash spotted Max Pinkrose sitting at a table across the room. A polystyrene seagull suspended from the ceiling above Pinkrose's head seemed to point him out. Pinkrose, plastic bib tied around his neck, looking speculatively at the bowl of cioppino in front of him. Across the table sat Stan Hotchkiss, the independent talent scout that Nash talked to on Friday. Hotchkiss' dinner was a Bloody Mary in a large Polynesian-themed goblet.

Pinkrose dropped the crab claw he was trying to break open with a nutcracker when he saw Nash and Crandall approach. Several more crab claws littered the surface of the cold red stew, making a break for freedom.

"Sorry to interrupt your date," Crandall said. He took hold of

Pinkrose's shoulder, dug his fingers in hard. "We need to talk."

"I'm eating," Pinkrose said.

"I'm not," Crandall said.

"Hello, officers," Hotchkiss said. The smile on Hotchkiss' face was elastic. His eyes seemed to move in competing directions. Hotchkiss was soused. Nash stood beside Hotchkiss' chair while Crandall studied the contents of Pinkrose's bowl of cioppino like it was something Pinkrose had just coughed up.

The tomato-based stew was splattered down Pinkrose's front and across his face and all over the sleeves of his shirt.

Pinkrose said, "I'm not going to be pushed around."

"Think again," Crandall said.

Nash said, "We found Frank Barcelona."

"Tell him I said 'hello,'" Pinkrose said.

"He's dead," Crandall said. "Your name pops up. Go figure."

Pinkrose raised his hand, catching the attention of a passing waiter. Crandall raised his SFPD joy buzzer, motioned for the waiter to get lost. The waiter made a bee line for the swinging doors leading into the kitchen, no doubt to tell his boss about the two cops who were killing his tip.

"His throat was cut," Nash said. "A good-sized knife, serrated edge. Maybe a fish knife. His body was discovered in Golden Gate Park. His neck looks like what you've got in that bowl, except for the claws."

"What do you want from me?"

"People saw you with Barcelona at the Panhandle the other day," Crandall said. "There are photographs. We're wondering what you two beauties talked about."

So far it was mostly a fabrication, about the witnesses. But Nash and Crandall could thank the *Chronicle* newspaper for the photos. From the same negatives as the stack of photos Tina Gone had in her apartment, the night Nash first interviewed her.

Nash had remembered the photos when he and Crandall stopped by the *Chronicle* newsroom earlier, to inquire about Tina Gone. The one photograph Nash found useful depicted the same scene the record store clerk had described to Nash and Belcher on Thursday—the older Pinkrose talking to the younger Barcelona. Barcelona wearing his leather jacket, a goatskin wine bag hanging on a strap from his shoulder. The two men stood in the background, at the edge of the Panhandle crowd, partly obscured but identifiable.

Pinkrose studied a crab claw with a level of deliberation the claw didn't deserve. Pinkrose didn't appear concerned about photographs, or witnesses. He cracked the crab claw into pieces, taking his time. Extracting the meat and chewing it. Then, "I told you myself, I saw Barcelona at the park that day. What are you trying to pull, Inspector?"

Nash didn't recall Pinkrose making such a statement. "Let's go talk about what you told us. And some other things."

"Are you arresting me?"

"Don't get your hackles up," Crandall said to Pinkrose.

"Or what?" Pinkrose said.

"I'll muzzle you," Crandall said.

Crandall was aching for a fight. Ready to jump in the middle of Pinkrose's chest, tap dance on his ribs. The older couple at the next table gaped at the two police inspectors. Crandall stared them down. Hotchkiss stirred what was left of his drink with a dinner fork. Maybe he was listening to the conversation or maybe he was just imagining a better cocktail lounge, with no static from policemen to disrupt his imbibing.

Nash had a number of questions for Pinkrose when they reached the Hall.

There was one subject Nash wanted to broach right now, couldn't help himself.

"Barcelona didn't steal anything from you," Nash said. "It was Gomez. Gomez told you he'd gotten his draft notice. When he stole the tapes of his recordings, you knew what the score was. You wouldn't give them back, so he broke in and took them. Then you asked Tina Gone to get the tapes back from Gomez. They were the only recordings of some of those songs, and you thought they belonged to you. But Gomez was out of his gourd that night. Miss Gone got spooked. Then, when I called her because her name was written on a note we found in Gomez's pocket, she got scared. She wondered how I knew she'd been there, and what I might accuse her of. It was you who dragged her into this mess, and she called you and asked for help. That's when you grabbed a rifle and drove across town. I don't think you meant to shoot me, Pinkrose. You just wanted to point me in the wrong direction."

Nash studied Pinkrose's face as the older man looked up at him. Pinkrose's glare was sharp and narrow, a razor blade.

For a moment Nash thought the entire room had fallen into a bottomless silence. Crandall massaged the back of his hand, limbering up knuckles.

A curious momentum had taken hold of the discussion. Nash couldn't reign it in. "You want to know what's funnier?" Nash said. "The name on the note we found in Gone's pocket wasn't 'Tina Gone.' It was 'Tim Gone.' Tina and her brother used the same answering service, and the two names look similar, scribbled on a note. I misread the note but it put me on the right track anyway. Except I didn't know it. But I know it now.

"A real scream, right?"

Nash had only just found out that curious fact. He'd called Tina Gone's service that morning, and the woman who took the call asked him if he meant Timothy Gone. The woman's comment had opened up an entirely new area of speculation.

Now Crandall raised a pudgy finger. He pointed it at Pinkrose. Before Crandall could speak, Pinkrose ripped the plastic bib from around his neck and threw it aside. He pushed his chair back, shot to his feet.

Crandall stepped in close, keeping Pinkrose from throwing a swing. Pinkrose was three or four inches taller than Crandall, but the two men stood nose to nose. Crandall looking up, chin raised.

Nash leaned in. "Where's Tina Gone, Pinkrose? Her brother is dead. She's disappeared."

Pinkrose's voice sounded like water gurgling in a drain. "I don't have a crystal ball."

The diners in the room had stopped eating. The bartender paused behind the bar, watching the confrontation. His hands flat on the bar, his head cocked to one side. Two waiters and a bow-tied busboy watched from the swinging kitchen doors. Crandall raised his hands, punched the palm of one hand with the fist of the other. The point of impact occurred an inch from Pinkrose's chin. Crandall wanted to make sure he had the taller man's undivided attention.

"Let's go outside," Crandall said to Pinkrose.

Crandall nodded toward the hallway leading out to the dining room, and the street entrance beyond. He took a firm hold on Pinkrose's arm. Pinkrose roughly pulled his arm free of Crandall's grasp.

Crandall turned fast, grabbed Pinkrose's shirt front with both hands. "I'll drag you out by your goddamn ear."

Pinkrose started to reply. He thought better of it.

Crandall had removed his set of handcuffs from the back of his belt. Pinkrose's face turned as red as the bowl of cioppino. Hotchkiss became deeply engaged in inspecting his fingernails. Nash watched a manager in a rumpled gray suit approach the table. He asked Nash in a stage whisper if SFPD could please handle this elsewhere.

Crandall nodded, handcuffs dangling from his hand.

"Outside," Crandall said to Pinkrose.

Crandall gave Pinkrose a push to get him moving. Pinkrose didn't fight. He strode purposefully through the bar room, out into the hallway, Crandall marching right behind him. School kids going to the alley, a tussle in the dirt.

Nash stayed behind for a moment.

"Hotchkiss, you knew Danny Gomez better than you said." It was an open-ended remark. Nash wasn't sure what he'd get out of it.

Hotchkiss blinked elaborately, as though he'd just stepped into the sunlight from the basement. "I didn't know him. But I know Pinkrose. I know about his songs." Hotchkiss shook his head to deny whatever it was he thought Nash had just accused him of.

"I didn't know Pinkrose wrote songs."

"He doesn't."

"He steals them."

"Songs belong to the world, Inspector. When all is said and done."

"Sounds like theft to me."

"It's the practical view."

"It's a view."

Hotchkiss shrugged.

"Tell me, Hotchkiss, what was your cut?"

Hotchkiss studied his now empty glass, then looked around once again for a waiter. Nash noticed the careful part in Hotchkiss' hair, the dandruff on the shoulders of Hotchkiss' yacht club sport coat. Confetti for mice, or rats.

When it became clear that Hotchkiss didn't intend to answer the last question, Nash let it go, walked out of the bar room.

He'd said too much as it was.

Nash walked through the main dining room, toward the front doors. The dining room stank of fried fish. Maybe Mrs. Crandall was right.

When fish tastes fishy that's all there is to say.

Like a lot of things.

The maitre'd at his podium pointedly looked elsewhere as Nash walked past. Nash was in the short entrance hallway when he heard the sharp report of a pistol, close by.

Nash pulled the .38 revolver out of the holster under his jacket. He pushed through the front doors of the restaurant.

Raced down the steps.

Nash saw pedestrians running along the sidewalk, away from the restaurant. Others had ducked behind a tourist bus parked across the street. A man in a workman's shirt and dungarees knelt beside a man on the ground, near the front steps.

The man on the ground was Crandall.

He'd been shot.

Nash pushed the workman aside.

He knelt beside Crandall. Crandall's hand clutched his chest but it didn't hide the flowing blood, or the froth from the air bubbles the blood contained. The bright red blood slipping out of Crandall's mouth was also full of air bubbles.

Crandall's unfocused eyes looked adrift in the paleness of Crandall's face. He lay entirely still. A low moan that came from someplace deeper than pain passed Crandall's lips.

Crandall's waistband holster was empty.

Pinkrose had somehow taken Crandall's weapon from him. Then he'd shot Crandall with it, point-blank.

A patrolman who'd been monitoring the go-go dancing exhibition down the street came running. Nash shouted to the patrolman to radio for an ambulance. Nash tossed his car keys to the patrolman, pointed to the unmarked Ford he and Crandall had arrived in.

When Nash looked in the other direction, he thought he spotted Pinkrose, running beside the line of parked cars on the south side of the street. Moving east, in the direction of Pier 43.

Nash turned back to Crandall.

Time had slowed. Blood continued to rise from between Crandall's fingers. A thin trail of blood led across Crandall's cheek from the corner of his mouth. Nash stood frozen. He knew he couldn't help Crandall. He also knew that he needed to, more than anything. Nash struggled to recall how to apply pressure to an open chest wound, without endangering the victim further.

A breeze picked up a crumpled sheet of newspaper from the nearby gutter, sent it tumbling off. Nash realized his questions were academic.

Nash checked for a pulse.

Crandall was dead.

Nash got to his feet.

Pedestrians pointed to the east end of Jefferson as Nash broke into a run. Pinkrose had a good head start but Nash was fifteen or twenty years younger. A truck turned off Jefferson Street onto Mason, and Nash darted around the back of the truck, ran on. He again caught sight of Pinkrose, a block ahead.

Moving down the sidewalk now.

Almost staggering.

Pinkrose was winded. Or injured.

Pinkrose stopped to lean against the brick wall of a building, catch his breath. He looked back. Saw Nash running toward him. Pinkrose raised the pistol in his hand. Pedestrians scattered. Citizens hid in doorways, or crouched low behind parked cars. Nash shouted "police," just in case someone thought he was the villain and tried to tackle him.

As Nash ran closer, he shouted for Pinkrose to drop his pistol. Pinkrose pushed himself off the wall.

He raised the gun higher, extended his arm.

Nash ducked behind a postal service mailbox as Pinkrose fired. The pistol's report sounded too loud. It echoed against the buildings like surf against rocks.

Nash heard the sharp clang of a cable car bell in the distance. He looked around the side of the mailbox. He was sure the round Pinkrose fired hadn't come close to him. Maybe Pinkrose hoped the wild shot would convince Nash to stay where he was.

Nash jumped out from behind the mailbox and ran on.

Later Nash would recall the tread of his feet on the concrete, the ache in his lungs, gulping air, the beads of sweat on his forehead. But the only picture in Nash's mind as he ran on was Lou Crandall, dead on the pavement.

Ahead Pinkrose stumbled, regained his balance.

Pinkrose ducked into a shadowy doorway, then reappeared on the sidewalk. Then darted into a small parking lot, beyond a row of shops. Disappearing again.

Nash stopped at the edge of the building next to the empty, roped-off lot. He tried to catch his breath. On the far side of the lot stood the scaffolding used by the art students, who had run off at the sound of gunfire. At the back of the lot stood a chain link fence that Pinkrose was, at that moment, attempting to climb.

Nash stepped around the corner of the building.

He raised his revolver.

"Pinkrose—drop your weapon."

It did no good. Nash hadn't expected it to. Pinkrose turned quickly, jumped off the fence. He fired one wild shot as he ran along the base of the scaffolding, toward the street.

Nash again ordered Pinkrose to stop and drop his weapon.

Pinkrose turned. Pinkrose raised Crandall's revolver.

Nash fired.

Nash thought he'd hit Pinkrose in the shoulder. The impact spun Pinkrose around. Pinkrose grabbed one of the scaffolding supports and hung on to it. He started to fall backwards.

The scaffolding teetered.

Pinkrose clung harder to it.

Pinkrose landed flat on the asphalt surface of the parking lot. The steel supports of the scaffolding remained standing, but several planks that made up the wooden catwalk, and the paint brushes and cans of paint on the catwalk, crashed to the ground.

Pinkrose was still alive when Nash reached him.

Pinkrose lay spread-eagled. Two planks from the catwalk had landed on his chest. Nash's shot hadn't hit Pinkrose in the shoulder after all. The round had torn into Pinkrose's neck. The bib that Pinkrose wore in the restaurant was gone, but the red spatters of cioppino on his clothes and face mixed rather well with the darker red of the blood soaking into the collar of Pinkrose's shirt, and forming a halo on the ground around his head. The cans of blue and red and green and yellow paint the art students had left behind on the catwalk had spattered Pinkrose's clothes and his face when they fell.

Pinkrose looked like a Pop Art masterpiece. The art students could hang Pinkrose on the wall, pressed between two sheets of glass. Like people with microscopes and glass slides did, with other dead things.

When the ambulance arrived, Pinkrose was just a mess that needed scraping up.

Twenty-seven

NASH SPENT THE night at the Hall of Justice with typewriter keys pounding in his ears. The report Nash wrote discussed in minute detail the incidents at Fisherman's Wharf leading to the deaths of SFPD Inspector Louis T. Crandall, 49, and Maxwell W. Pinkrose, 46, a local businessman. By 0700 hours Nash's throat was raw from cigarettes. His eyes felt gritty when he closed them, grittier when he didn't.

Nash made it back to his apartment for an hour or two of sleep.

He dreamed he could hear dust settling on his grave.

That afternoon there was another question and answer fistfight with Lieutenant Dark and Chief of Inspectors Jellicoe at the Hall. A police shooting at Fisherman's Wharf—it was bad for business, and Dark made sure Nash knew it.

Dark took Nash's revolver so that the Firearm Discharge

Review Board could examine it, every which way. Nash was supposed to be placed on administrative leave, but Dark didn't press the point. He assigned Nash a sidearm from the armory, believing that no police inspector should go unarmed.

Later Nash stopped in at San Francisco General. A patrolman was stationed outside of Belcher's private room, ready to give press magpies the bum's rush, if any turned up.

Belcher was laid out on his hospital bed. Motionless, a log wrapped in bandages. Bleary-eyed from sedatives, or from the black and white gunk blaring out of the television set bolted high on the wall opposite the bed.

A whiplash brace was fitted around his neck for reasons that even Belcher couldn't explain.

"How do you feel?" Nash said.

"I need a quart of bourbon."

"Try again."

"I need walking shoes."

"No sale."

Estelle, Belcher's wife, had just popped down to the cafeteria for coffee and pie. She'd left her purse and a movie magazine behind. An ashtray rested on Belcher's chest. His cigarettes and lighter lay on the nightstand, next to a bouquet of dissolute flowers.

Nash gave Belcher a light, then lit a gasper for himself. He opened the window a crack to let out the smoke and let in the automobile exhaust from the parking lot.

Nash had to broach the subject of Crandall's death but, unaccountably, he didn't know where to start. How much had Belcher heard?

"Tell me about my friend," Belcher said.

Nash's sympathetic phrases rang hollow in his own ears. Crandall was dead and Belcher wanted facts. Belcher listened closely as Nash explained the sequence of events at Fisherman's Wharf. Belcher didn't ask questions, merely nodded when Nash was done. As though Belcher had filed the information word for word in a locked cabinet in a dark corner of his mind, where he planned to sift through it again and again, when he was alone.

The one-sided conversation turned to Golden Gate Park and what occurred after Belcher became *hors de combat*.

"The theory now is that the Jap hid near the tea garden at first, but didn't get tagged the first time the dragnet came through," Nash said. "When the dragnet passed, he went looking for a better bolt hole. He discovered the drainage pipe and the body inside. He took Barcelona's jacket."

Nash explained that the Japanese lieutenant's shirt, blood-spattered from his exertions with the machete, was found in the pipe where he discarded it. There was evidence that Shimatzu had also tried on Frank Barcelona's boots.

"So much wasted time," Belcher said to himself. Nash couldn't guess what Belcher meant, and he didn't ask.

Belcher and the other veterans of the war had entered into the hunt for the Japanese soldier to get a few last punches in for their side. In the end, it was Shimatzu, afraid of the future and ashamed for having given up, who delivered the final reckoning. Shimatzu had gone from a hole in the ground on an equatorial spice island to the skyscrapers of San Francisco. The city must've looked like a shiny chrome nightmare to him.

Belcher blew a smoke ring at the ceiling. On the television screen a woman in an apron displayed a can of green beans that shimmered, a religious vision for the modern housewife.

"The last ID on Barcelona was at the park on Tuesday," Belcher said. "You sure it was Pinkrose who eighty-sixed him? You told me Rollo was there too."

Belcher was right. Nash hadn't found a picture of Rollo tucked in with the other *Chronicle* photographs of the Tuesday jam session at the panhandle, but Riley Bardell had said Rollo was there.

Nash didn't see a strong motive for Rollo murdering Barcelona. The theft of the Beatles tape didn't seem enough, since Rollo reportedly gave Barcelona a chance to return the tape, after the dust up in the alley behind the Kimono à Go-Go. But Pinkrose might've killed Barcelona, if Barcelona was trying to blackmail him. Maybe about the murder of Gomez, maybe about something else. He'd have to ask Rollo. If Rollo ever surfaced.

But how did Timothy Gone fit into it?

And Tina?

As Nash got ready to leave, Belcher offered him a piece of fruit from one of the fruit baskets sent by well-wishers. Nash took an apple from a basket on the window sill.

Lying next to the basket, and still attached to the colorful cardboard backing, was a plastic ukulele, the faces of the four Beatles painted on the surface of the instrument. An official Beatles souvenir ukulele, according to the packaging blurb. Nash wondered which wag in Homicide sent the gag gift.

AT THE Hall, Nash telephoned the sheriff's offices in Humboldt and Del Norte counties, trying to step up the search for Jasper Rollo. Meanwhile the news blackout on the Golden Gate Park incident was still holding.

A platoon of Pentagon top brass on a Military Airlift Command C-124 Globemaster flight from Andrews Air Force Base to San Francisco were coming to take charge of the blowback, when and if the dam broke, the truth rushing out.

Shortly before 1500 hours, Lieutenant Dark cornered Nash in the hallway. The Crime Lab eggheads had a few last rites to perform at Danny Gomez's Clipper Street apartment before SFPD could release it back to the manager.

Dark asked Nash to go with them. Provide his expertise on the case, if it was needed.

Nash met the lab men at the Clipper Street address. Nash recalled his first visit to the apartment. Racing up the steps, a moment of real fear at the thought of a patrolman being shot. But recalling the sequence of events on that day also jogged something else, somewhere in the back of Nash's memory.

On a hunch Nash went downstairs to talk to the manager.

She wasn't wearing a housecoat this time, but the harlequin-style glasses and the tuxedo cat in her arms were the same. Nash asked her about the wicker basket full of ribbon he'd seen on the second-floor landing, five days ago. The woman said that she often put the basket there for her cat to sleep in. The cat appreciated the sunlight from the stairwell window. The cat also liked sleeping on wadded gift box ribbon.

The woman disappeared into her apartment, came back a moment later with the basket, still full of gift box ribbon. Mixed in with the ribbon were pieces of half-inch recording tape, neatly cut into strips of roughly a foot each.

The manager explained that she'd found a grocery store bag full of those strips of tape. Beside one of the garbage cans behind the building. It might have been a few days before she discovered the body of Danny Gomez in his apartment, now that she thought of it.

She'd added the shiny tape to the cat's gift box ribbon.

There was still some tape left, in the grocery sack she'd found it in.

The manager handed the sack over, and Nash added the tape he extracted from two cat beds to the contents of the sack. When Nash showed the lengths of tape to the Crime Lab technicians and disclosed what he suspected, they shook their pointy heads.

Nash left it with them all the same.

IT WAS 2000 hours and change, according to the dashboard clock. Dusk had arrived. Nash shook the last gasper out of a flattened Chesterfield pack as he drove southbound on Van Ness. He opened the Plymouth's wing window. The evening air carried the dull odor of engine oil drying on concrete.

Nash lit the gasper.

Dragged on it.

Waited for a green traffic light, at the intersection of Van Ness and Pacific.

Nash had called Tina Gone's number four times that day. He'd stopped at her apartment twice. He'd left messages for her with her answering service, the manager of her apartment building, her colleagues at the *Chronicle* offices. He told himself it was par for an investigation, the muddled communications, but he knew it wasn't, not entirely.

Nash had also called SFO. The Pan Am clerk told him that Tina Gone's name didn't appear on the manifests of any recent Ecuador-bound flights.

An hour ago, he'd initiated an APB.

Tina Gone was here, in town.

Nash was sure of it.

The green glow from the Plymouth's dashboard lights was an eerie counterpoint to the half-light of dusk. The fog horn on Angel Island bellowed in the distance.

The report from KGO on the car radio was that a fog bank was filtering in on the marine layer through the Golden Gate. It would grow heavier over the city through the night. Just as it had the night before last.

The city looked deserted. Nash was reminded of a movie he'd once seen, at the Spruce Drive-In in South San Francisco. *Panic in The Year Zero.* Ray Milland was a father driving his family in a station wagon through the desolate aftermath of atomic warfare. Nash tried to imagine who or what would take over San Francisco, after the atom bomb fell. The North Beach Italians? The beatniks? The merchant seamen? The Chinese on Grant? The blue-haired society ladies who brunched at the Mark Hopkins? Junkies, juicers, pill poppers, draft dodgers, fry cooks, bottle washers? What beastly child of dead flowers and bad poetry and existential *malaise* would crawl from the atomic rubble to take control of the city?

Nash flicked the butt end of the gasper out the car window as he crossed Divisadero on Lombard. He turned left on Broderick. He'd just crossed Bay when he spotted Tina Gone's yellow Sunbeam Tiger.

Parked in front of the Tahitian Breeze Apartments.

It was some sort of relief.

But Nash felt nervous.

Nash drove past the apartment house to the next corner, turned around. Pulled up in front of a cramped storefront called the Liberty Market. Painted on the white stucco wall outside, a cartoonish dairy cow holding the Golden Gate Bridge in its front hooves.

Inside, Nash bought a pack of Chesterfield king size. He tore the cellophane off the pack as he emerged from the market. He was back behind the wheel of the Plymouth, reaching for the ignition key, when he saw a woman approach the yellow sports car parked down the street.

In the fading light of dusk Nash could just make out that the woman wore tight black pants and a dark bulky sweater, blue or gray.

A bright green scarf over her hair, worn peasant style, tied under her chin.

The woman climbed in behind the wheel of the sports car.

The red taillights came on.

The yellow sports car jerked forward, pulled away from the curb. It accelerated through the intersection of Bay and Broderick, heading south.

Nash started the Plymouth and followed.

The Sunbeam Tiger turned left onto Lombard, heading east. Over the Plymouth's dashboard radio Nash heard a jingle for Alka-Seltzer fade into radio static. Ahead the yellow sports car seemed to glide through the night, a predatory fish, while undersea streetlights slid past. The world had fragmented into unfocused colors. For a moment Nash's entire existence was reduced to the steering wheel in his hand, the steady rumble of the engine.

Nash followed the Tiger southbound for sixteen blocks. The sports car turned onto the Geary Expressway, heading east. Tina Gone changed lanes, veered right at Steiner.

Nash was caught in the wrong lane.

He couldn't reach the Steiner egress in time.

Nash continued on to Webster, then backtracked to the corner of Geary and Fillmore, where knots of people milled on the street corners, spilling into the street.

Nash took a chance, headed southbound on Fillmore. He spotted Tina Gone's sports car halfway down the block. Nash drove a block further up, made a U-turn, parked on the opposite side of Fillmore Street.

Nash locked up the Plymouth and walked down the street to the Fillmore Auditorium. Passing the Tiger he heard the metallic ticks of the warm engine in the cool night air. Nash reached the intersection of Geary and Fillmore, stepped into the crowd in front of the auditorium.

The Fillmore was hosting a pop music dance concert, the so-called "Beatles Go Home" event that Nash had seen advertised on flyers around town. Young citizens in exotic accoutrement loitered on the sidewalk. Folk songs strummed on out of tune guitars erupted from dark corners. Near the front doors a long-haired boy sat against the wall holding an open cigar box full of colorful military medals. The cardboard sign hanging from his neck on a string: WHO WILL BUY MY EVIL?

Nash searched the faces in the crowd. He saw no sign of Tina Gone. He spotted a pair of SFPD patrolmen further along the sidewalk and approached them. Had they seen a young woman in a bulky dark sweater with a bright green scarf over her head enter the auditorium in the last few minutes? Nash knew it was a long shot.

One of the patrolmen shook his head. "There's a thousand kids here. They come, they go."

Nash recognized the name of one of the bands listed on the handbills outside, suddenly recalled Tina Gone telling him the Medicine Hat Blues Band was playing at the "Beatles Go Home" dance. It might explain why Tina Gone had come here. Nash pushed through the crowd toward the entrance, brushing past three Negro men decked out in black berets, eyeglasses with tiny dark lenses. The men studied Nash, expressions of disgust on their faces.

One of the men said, "Hello, pig."

Nash moved on.

The girl collecting tickets at the top of the entrance stairway wore bracelets of small bells that rang together, a Tibetan alarm clock. Nash flashed his SFPD buzzer to gain admission. A second girl tried to hand him a red apple.

"The Fillmore loves you," she said.

The house lights were on inside the crowded auditorium.

Recorded music pounded out of the public address speakers. The music was full of complicated rhythms that grew shrill as they wound tighter. It occurred to Nash suddenly that there were too many people here.

Too many people, packed in too tight.

Costumes were the order of the night. Nash noticed several Halloween-style Beatles masks. The same kind of mask he'd found covering the dead face of Danny Gomez.

Other patrons hadn't bothered with store bought masks or Beatles references. They'd settled for splashes of dayglo paint on their faces or costume glitter in their hair. The crowd didn't look much like a God-fearing bunch. Nash felt sure they weren't here to protest the Beatles' "more popular than Jesus" wisecrack. Maybe they were just plain tired of the whole Beatle gag—the records and movies and wigs.

The ukuleles.

The ice cream bars.

Every dog has his day. Then it gets a swift kick on its way out the door. And who would be the next big dog? That Herman fellow, and his Hermits?

Nash stepped past several dancers in the crowd. They moved sluggishly, off-kilter. How much reefer and pills and LSD circulated in the auditorium? Nash wondered if this was what the newspapers called a "happening," people gathering to stretch their minds into new directions, like salt water taffy.

Nash raised his eyes, studied the arches of the gallery above the auditorium floor. The gallery looked dark and cluttered, old stage equipment and boxes. A few gasper-smoking employees leaning on balcony railings, watching the crowd below. One arched opening was curtained off with a canvas tarp. Nash was studying the three electrical cables snaking from under the tarp, descending the wall to the main floor, when, out of the corner of his eye, he caught a glimpse of the correct shade of green.

Tina Gone's scarf?

The flash of green disappeared back into the crowd before Nash could be sure. Nash pushed through the crowd, toward what he thought he'd seen.

He glanced up at the gallery again.

It would give him the height to see over the crowd.

Nash changed course, heading now for the rear of the hall, where the stairs were. He'd made it halfway across the dance floor when the auditorium suddenly went dark. Colored spotlights appeared, illuminating six young men standing on the stage. Three of the men held guitars tightly to their chests. Five of them wore Nehru jackets, strings of beads. The singer's goatee was waxed into a defiant point.

A stray guitar note joined another.

Sticks hit drum heads tentatively.

Shouts arose from the crowd.

The sixth man stood to one side of the stage. He wore a thin tie, a white shirt that changed color with the changing hues of the lights, a turban perched on his head. The two heavily amplified conga drums in front of him had been refashioned to look like elongated human skulls, a startling effect.

A disembodied voice introduced the band over the public address system. The Immaculate Teapot Conspiracy, from New Jersey. The disparate noises coming from the stage grew louder, more cohesive. In the darkness of the crowd there wasn't much Nash could do, Tina Gone could walk right past him and he wouldn't see her.

The music cracked through the auditorium like a bullwhip. The singer might've been good or he might be stinking up the place, Nash couldn't tell. Nash felt pinpricks up and down his arms and along his spine.

The pinpricks spread to his scalp.

Nash began to see the colors on the stage melding together into a sharp bright red that grew and breathed, of its own volition.

Nash knew it was all in his head.

His synesthesia was reacting to the loud music.

Nash pushed on through the crowd, toward the rear of the auditorium. The faces in the darkness looked contorted in pain. Mouths grimaced. Screamed. Claw-like hands reached out to him. The smells inside the auditorium had changed, from incense and perfume to an acrid stench of uncertain origin. Nash was close to the wall. His peripheral vision registered a blur of movement that seemed different than the blurriness he already saw.

A fist appeared from nowhere.

The punch landed on Nash's jaw.

Nash's knees buckled. He reached out.

His hand found the wall in the same instant that his forehead did. Somehow Nash managed to keep his feet under him. He looked dazedly around. A flutter of lights framed his vision. Nash saw the three Negro men he'd passed earlier, outside. The cartoon French existentialists, in their turtleneck sweaters and black pants and berets.

The three men stared at Nash with expressions of stone. One of them had punched him. Nash started to reach under his coat for his joy buzzer before he realized it wouldn't help him. His status with SFPD probably wasn't a point these men were overly concerned with. Perhaps hitting a police inspector with a sucker punch was their idea of a successful night out.

The lights in Nash's eyes popped and sizzled.

The Negro men stepped forward.

More punches came, hard and fast, Nash throwing a few of his own. Nash took two hard punches in the ribs, one in the stomach, one haymaker on the jaw. The cacophony coming from the public address system sliced through his consciousness, a meat cleaver.

His head throbbed.

His breath came in gasps.

For a moment a larger commotion grew, surrounding Nash. Then the Negro existentialists faded back into the crowd.

Two men stood beside Nash now.

One of them asking if Nash was all right.

Nash's stomach seemed to be in his throat. He shook his head to clear it. One of the men beside him wore a football helmet painted in fluorescent orange paint. The other wore a tight-fitting vest over an old-timey striped shirt with a celluloid collar. An Edwardian bank clerk, except for the high-top sneakers on his feet.

Nash pulled out the SFPD star.

Told the two men the situation was under control.

After a minute the two men moved off.

Nash took shallow breaths, then deeper ones. The music sliced and tore at the public address speakers, an orchestra of buzz saws. It sounded blood red in Nash's ears.

The needle-like pinpricks he'd felt on his arms and legs earlier were now the prodding of knife tips.

Nash began to move again. Toward the rear of the auditorium. Keeping close to the wall.

Now the auditorium filled with white hot strobe lights. Nash had made it ten feet when he saw a green scarf. Tied around the head of a woman in a bulky sweater. The triangular tail of the scarf waved lightly in the air as the woman moved through the crowd.

The patch of green disappeared, then reappeared. Nash caught one last glimpse of the woman as she entered a stairway leading to the gallery.

Nash reached the foot of the stairway. A tall man wearing and Indian headdress stood nearby. The man tried to stop Nash from climbing the stairs and Nash pushed him aside. The tall man appeared to be intoxicated, and one push was enough. The man opened his mouth to shout as he stumbled backwards but Nash didn't hear anything come out.

Nash climbed the stairs quickly. To his right at the top of the stairs was what appeared to be a shadowy walkway leading through a substantial collection of old furniture piled together, dusty theater equipment, poorly stacked cardboard boxes. The gallery arches Nash had seen from the dance floor were on the other side of the clutter. Aside from the dull glow of the stage lights from the dance floor below, filtering through the storage area, the only light along the walkway came from two exit signs.

Nash paused, watching Tina Gone's silhouette move slowly toward the far end of the gallery. He shouted her name, to no purpose. His voice was lost in the noise from the stage below. Nash's vision was interrupted by tiny flashes of light that glowed and bright patches that didn't. Through the muddle that existed in his mind Nash sensed that there was someone behind him.

He turned.

Nash expected to see the tall man with the headdress.

Instead, he saw the dark outline of a much larger man.

Standing at the top of the stairs.

Where Nash had stood, a moment ago.

Nash turned back around in time to see, dimly, Tina Gone step out of the walkway at the far end of the gallery. An explosion tore the air. The sound of the gunshot was sharp and palpable inside the larger roar of the music from below. Nash reached the spot where Tina Gone had disappeared, found a single burning candle inside an enclosed space. The candle rested on a console board that looked like a smaller version of the recording console

Nash had seen at the Hi-Tone recording studio. There was also a tape recorder with two large tape reels fitted onto the face of the machine. The reels revolved slowly. On the far side of the enclosure, curtaining off the balcony space, was the heavy tarp that Nash had seen from the dance floor.

The young woman with the green scarf on her head stood three feet from the tape machine. She stood over a body lying on the floor in the center of the enclosure.

She held a small automatic pistol. Loosely, in one hand.

The candle flame guttered. The woman looked up to see Nash standing there, his eyes fixed on her. Nash saw her face clearly. Her slack features and agape mouth, like a fractured children's doll. The man she had just shot lay with one hand resting flat on his chest, the other arm stretched out on the floor.

She moved her pistol hand. Raising the barrel.

Nash reached for his police revolver. He was too slow.

She fired.

Something hit Nash hard. Exploded into him like shrapnel. Nash spun. Fell. Heard the second gunshot before he hit the floor. His last thought before he slipped into a long black elevator shaft that pulled him down into the bowels of the earth was that the woman was not a good shot.

She was also not Tina Gone.

Twenty-eight

LATER NASH WOULD hazily recall someone pulling him to his feet while someone else stepped on him to keep him on the floor. His limbs felt encased in concrete. An SFPD harness bull Nash didn't know helped him stumble outside.

Nash gulped the cool night air. The back of his head felt like the shit end of a freshly-swatted baseball.

Fog had settled over the city. The drone of traffic on the Geary Expressway mixed with the crackle of police radios. The sounds reminded Nash of watching stock car races from the grandstand at Sears Point.

Five SFPD prowl cars and an unmarked SFPD Ford were parked outside the front entrance to the Fillmore Auditorium. More prowl units were en route. A GMC ambulance truck was just pulling up and another one had just left the scene, on its way to San Francisco General.

The "Beatles Go Home" dance concert was over.

A stream of concertgoers in their anti-Beatle finery were herded out the front doors by SFPD patrolmen gripping their nightsticks in both hands, horizontal, just high enough to catch the necks of slow-moving young citizens. The youths, and the youthful with them, spilled into the street. The patrolmen watched the growing crowd warily. An angry shout from the crowd was punctuated by a lobbed glass bottle that shattered inside the patch of sidewalk and street cordoned off by the prowl cars.

A police bullhorn broadcasted the order to disburse. A man waving a clipboard appeared in the doorway of the auditorium. He shouted to the crowd that the intervention of SFPD was largely no different than an act of God and, therefore, no refunds would be issued.

The street lights glowed dully in the fog. Nash leaned against the rear of a patrol car with his legs braced. He felt the blood on his arm under his clothing. He saw the blood that covered the back of his hand and his fingers.

An ambulance attendant appeared. The attendant apologized for any discomfort as he helped Nash out of the sport coat, cut away the left sleeve of Nash's shirt. The attendant assured Nash that he'd be driven to SF General shortly.

Nash said there was no rush.

When the arm was properly bandaged, a patrolman from Northern Station helped Nash slide his coat back on. He handed Nash a gasper, gave him a light. The damage to Nash's arm was minor. The bullet from the woman's small caliber pistol had gone through muscle tissue. The wound truly looked worse than it was.

Nash closed his eyes. Puffed on the gasper.

It was one of the patrolmen Nash had talked to outside the

auditorium when Nash first arrived who had appeared behind Nash in the gallery. The patrolman was told by the man in the fluorescent orange football helmet that a policeman was in trouble inside the auditorium. The patrolman knocked Nash to the floor to get him out of the line of fire, while at the same time firing his own weapon at the pistol-waving woman standing over the body on the floor.

The patrolman's prowess as a marksman was better than the woman's. She was already on her way to San Francisco General with a gunshot wound to the abdomen.

The image of the man on the floor of the gallery came back to Nash. A dark trail of blood ran from the entrance wound under the dead man's jaw. The exit wound was hidden from view, but in the dim light the pool of blood on the floor around the man's head looked like a black dinner plate halo of unholy design. The walrus moustache under the dead man's nose looked like a bristly rag that he'd been busy swallowing at the time of his death.

His identity came to Nash as a dull fact.

Jasper Rollo.

Rollo had returned to the city from Humboldt County to record tonight's concert. Perhaps one of the groups appearing tonight was the one he'd taken to the redwoods to record, but what did it matter? The woman in the green scarf who had emerged from Tina Gone's apartment and driven Tina Gone's car to the auditorium had murdered Rollo.

Suddenly Nash had no difficulty recalling her name.

Pearly Spence.

Frank Barcelona's squeeze.

Spence had worked for Jasper Rollo, off and on. They'd lived together. If the stories Nash had heard were true, there was a child. Spence must've known that Barcelona was dead.

Perhaps she blamed Rollo for his death.

Decided to settle the score.

Nash tried to rearrange the pieces of the puzzle in his head so they fit together better than they had previously. It was clear that Barcelona stole the Beatles tape from Rollo, tried to sell it to Max Pinkrose. Somehow Timothy Gone stepped in and acquired the Beatles tape from Barcelona. It was the tape that he'd promised to the Emperor, Riley Bardell. But in the end, he took it to Rollo's pad, and was murdered for his trouble. Why?

The negotiation must've turned sour indeed.

Meanwhile, Barcelona showed up at Golden Gate Park, meeting Pinkrose there, intentionally or unintentionally. Tina Gone said she thought someone else was in the apartment the night she visited Danny Gomez—could that someone have been Frank Barcelona? Or did Barcelona somehow guess that Pinkrose murdered Gomez in a fight over Gomez's tapes. Maybe Barcelona tried to blackmail Pinkrose with that knowledge. Or maybe Pinkrose just wanted Barcelona out of the way, he knew too much.

But killing Barcelona at Golden Gate Park was a rash act. Pinkrose was deeply scared if he'd felt a need to get rid of Barcelona then and there. People see things and hear things, even after sundown, in Golden Gate Park.

Then there was Barcelona's plea. *Don't make Ringo suffer.* A wild threat from an addled mind? Had Barcelona truly said it, or was it part of Pinkrose's alibi? Send the line of inquiry spinning off on useless tangents.

Nash dropped the cigarette butt. Crushed it out under the sole of his wingtip. He overheard two patrolmen talking nearby. One of them had just come from Candlestick Park, where the Beatles had finished their concert and were already on a plane back to Los Angeles. The English pop group had arrived in a bus and departed in an armored car, with an SFPD motorcycle escort.

It seemed demonstrably odd to Nash that four young men with musical instruments had to be protected from their fans by steel plating and heavily-armed outriders. Nash recalled what Tina Gone had said, how the Beatles lived inside the cage of their own success. Like circus animals.

The words lingered in his mind but the face Nash saw inside the cage didn't belong to a Beatle. Unaccountably, it belonged to Lieutenant Shimatzu. The cage wasn't Candlestick Park or a suite at the Beverly Wilshire Hotel in LA, but a hole in the ground in the center of a remote tropical jungle.

Maybe everyone lived in a prison of their own design. It was a thought worth considering. Nash resolved to consider it, sometime. Along with every other little thing, and the price of eggs.

Nash took a deep breath.

His thoughts had carried him out on a limb.

The crowd of disenchanted citizens had grown into a mob. Police bullhorns continued to growl but it did no good. The mob rallied in the fog. More glass bottles smashed against the sidewalk, the façade of the auditorium, the parked SFPD vehicles.

Police riot helmets pulled from the trunks of prowl cars had appeared in the hands of the watchful patrolmen. A sergeant from Richmond Station quietly mentioned tear gas canisters to a colleague, who nodded sagely and used a prowl car radio to contact the station.

A sharp voice from within the mob called for more kindness and less war. A voice from elsewhere in the crowd called for more music and less bullshit. Nash had seen all of this too many times in recent months. The citizens were angry and fearful, and they wanted to take it out on the police, who were also angry and fearful, but well-armed. The veneer of civilization was cracking like cheap linoleum. But what did anyone expect, in a city built on ever-shifting tectonic rock?

Nash wiped at the dried blood crusted on the back of his left hand. He looked up to see a woman arguing with two patrolmen on the sidewalk. One of the patrolmen turned to look in Nash's direction, then allowed the woman to pass. The staccato heels of go-go boots hit the concrete hard as she approached. A leather pocketbook hung at her side from a long shoulder strap. Tina Gone kept one hand on the pocketbook, as though holding the butt end of a pistol that was holstered at her waist.

Nash saw the look of dread on her face.

"I'm looking for my sister," Tina Gone said.

THE WOMAN who shot Jasper Rollo dead tonight had once claimed that she made drunken phone calls to the police because she was lonely. Nash saw now that it had been a lie, or partly a lie. She'd called the police that night because she was afraid for Frank Barcelona. Because of the tape Barcelona stole from her ex-boyfriend Rollo. And sold to her brother, Timothy Gone.

Nash studied the softness of Tina Gone's face. When he spoke, his throat felt dry and raw. He ought to cut down on the smokes. "Your sister is at San Francisco General. She was shot by a patrolman but she'll pull through. Jasper Rollo won't. He's dead. Your sister shot him. More than once, from what I gather."

Tina Gone's gaze moved from Nash's face to a point on the sidewalk ten feet away. Now that she knew the worst, she didn't look shocked. She didn't look angry or saddened. Maybe it was only defeat that Nash saw in her expression.

"I'm guessing your sister hasn't been well for a long time," Nash said. "So spare me a minute and tell me what happened tonight, and all the other nights. Do you know that your brother was shot and killed?"

Tina Gone covered her mouth with her hand. She nodded her

head. There was a silence while she composed herself.

"Pearly is staying with me," Tina Gone said. "She was in trouble in LA, so she came up here to ditch it. A few months ago. Make a clean break. But she tried to go back to LA Friday night on the bus. She ran out of bread in Paso Robles and called me. I had to drive down to get her. We just got back, this morning. I know she shot Timothy. She told me. She's got her head together, most of the time."

Just then another glass bottle shattered against the side of a nearby prowl car. A patrolman chased a long-haired shirtless boy down the sidewalk, tackled him hard. Tina Gone looked east down the Geary Expressway, then west. There was no escape, for anyone.

She folded her arms tightly.

Tina Gone said that her sister had gone to LA from San Francisco a couple of years ago. With a man named Richard Spence. "Before she ran off with Spence, she played house up here with Rollo. They had a child—a boy. Two years old now. She was flipped out when she dumped Rollo and ran off with Spence, so Rollo took custody of the boy."

Nash thought of the child and the reefer-smoking babysitter in Jasper Rollo's living room, the first time he'd visited the Rollo residence. Rollo had been a big bull-headed man with big bull-headed ideas. No doubt he'd believed he knew what was best for young children.

Tina Gone's sister and Richard Spence got married in LA. "Then Pearly spent six months in the LA County jail for kiting personal checks. When she got out she found that her husband was a secret square. He'd returned to Oklahoma, to sell tractors.

"Pearly didn't want to go to Oklahoma.

"When Pearly came back to Frisco, she went straight to Jasper. He gave her a job at his club so she could earn her keep. He didn't trust her with the baby. She put up with that arrangement to buy time. She waited for a chance to heist the baby, and run.

"In the meantime, she hit the sauce again. Hard. Who knows what else. She shacked up with Frank. I think she really loved him but Frank had his own demons. I guess their demons ganged up on them. But she didn't stop trying to get her baby back. Frank wanted to help her."

Nash didn't mention that it was he and Belcher who had gone to Pearly Spence's Richmond District apartment to question her about the drunken report of a murder. He let Tina Gone explain her sister, however she wanted.

"That's why Frank stole the Beatles tape," Tina Gone said. "Frank met the Beatles once and it short-circuited his mind. He felt the tape was rightfully his, so he stole it from Rollo's office at the Kimono. He wanted to sell it, hard cash. Frank and Pearly wanted to disappear with the baby. Down to Mexico. But even life in Mexico requires scratch.

"Pearly went to Timothy for help. That was Sunday. Then Pearly got mad at Timothy. She thought he was working against her too."

Nash watched Tina Gone's eyes suddenly go narrow. As though she saw the source of her troubles in Nash's face, but distrusted her vision.

"How did Danny Gomez fit into this?"

"I went to see Danny because Pinkrose asked me to." Tina Gone paused, pressed the palm of her hand against her forehead. Then, "Pinkrose knew it was Danny who broke into the studio. Pinkrose wanted those tapes back. As far as Pinkrose was concerned, those songs were his."

Nash saw clearly the intersection of two corrupt ideas, two wrongheaded men. "Just like Barcelona and the Beatles tape."

Tina Gone shook her head, not in denial but in disbelief. The whole story, unfolding into sharp-edged angles, a bouquet of knife blades. "I went to Danny's pad on Sunday. He was boiled. He said he didn't have the tapes. But he mentioned the Beatles tape that his friend Barcelona wanted to sell. I didn't know where the tape came from, but I was sure it would interest Timothy—he was always looking for ways to ingratiate himself with Riley Bardell. I gave Danny the answering service number, to give to Barcelona when he turned up. Barcelona could call Timothy."

Nash didn't need to ask Tina Gone what happened next.

He thought he already knew.

"Before your brother got involved, Barcelona tried to sell the tape to Pinkrose," Nash said. "He showed Pinkrose an old tourist snapshot, from his Army days. Him with the Beatles, in Hamburg. He also spun the wild idea that he wrote Beatles songs. Pinkrose told us that Barcelona seemed high on something that night. It explains some of his craziness. Maybe not all of it.

"But Pinkrose wasn't interested in Barcelona. He must've known the Beatles tape wasn't on the up and up. What he wanted were the Gomez tapes. After you came back, without the tapes, he realized he'd have to get them from Gomez himself. Is that the way it was, the hard way?"

"I don't know." Tina Gone frowned, considering what Nash had just said. Her eyes looked distant and tearful. As though she'd gotten lost in her thoughts, couldn't find her way out. "You called me. You wanted to talk about Danny. I couldn't understand how you got my name. I called Pinkrose, I was afraid. He told me not to worry. He said he'd lay down a smokescreen. I didn't know what he meant. He told me not to get too frosted, whatever happens. When you showed up, he shot my windows out."

"He wanted me to believe it was Barcelona?"

"He didn't say."

"You're an accessory."
"You're a cop. I couldn't tell you."

NASH PONDERED the baroque tale. Rollo got the tape from Jerry Turner, intending to sell bootleg recordings of it. Barcelona stole the tape from Rollo, and tried to sell it to raise the jack he and Pearly Spence needed to disappear with the child that Rollo had fathered with her, and that they intended to kidnap—if "kidnap" was the right word. Rollo found out about the theft of the tape and beat some sense into Barcelona behind the Kimono à Go-Go. The beating in the alley prompted Pearly Spence's drunken phone calls to SFPD.

It was a complicated circle of life. It got more complicated when Pinkrose got rid of Barcelona at Golden Gate Park, then ditched Rollo's truck behind Eddie Euclid's pad.

Pinkrose knew the carnivores who shared the house with Euclid would tear the truck to pieces. They'd derail the search for Barcelona.

Tina Gone cast her eyes downward. "Pearly said that Timothy attacked her. That's why she shot him. But I don't know what to believe. Timothy always went to bat for Pearly, she's never understood that. He went to Rollo's to help her. I think Timothy found out where the tape came from. Rather than give it to the Emperor, I think Timothy changed his mind, decided to return it to Rollo. He wanted to use the return of the tape to influence Rollo into giving Pearly some time with her son."

Nash could see it made some kind of sense. Pearly Spence at Rollo's pad, waiting with the pistol in her hand for Rollo to return from up north. But it was Timothy who turned up.

Spence argued with him.

The argument got wild. Spence got wilder.

Nash's mental picture of the scene at the Rollo house was suddenly punctuated by a shout that rose to a scream. Half a dozen young men had just attempted to toss a bicycle off the Fillmore overpass. A trio of patrolmen armed with night sticks chased them across the overpass, into the darkness beyond. Whatever was at stake for this mob, it was more substantial than a curtailed evening of music and dancing at $2.50 a throw.

"Pearly knew Jasper would be here tonight," Tina Gone said. "The Teapots—Jasper had recorded them before. He thought they were the living end."

There was another pause that drifted into the fog. Then Nash watched an expression of alarm grow on Tina Gone's face.

"You've found him, of course?" she said.

Nash had to ask her what she meant. Tina Gone said that her sister's young son must be here too, somewhere. Rollo always kept the boy close by. Tina Gone glanced around at the knots of policemen and police vehicles. She saw nothing that assuaged her concerns.

Without another word, Tina Gone started to walk hastily toward the street corner.

Nash couldn't let her run off. Where did she think she was going? The situation on the streets around the Fillmore was too fluid for standard police work. SFPD was bracing for a riot. It was anyone's guess what dangers lay ahead, and where.

Nash broke into an awkward jog to catch up with Tina Gone. A patrolman stepped out from behind a prowl car on Fillmore, tried to block their path. The patrolman advised them to stay behind the police line. Fillmore Street, right now, was a threat to a citizen's welfare.

Shop windows had been broken. Parked cars had been vandalized. An ugly crowd of hotheads and looters was converging, two blocks south.

The intersection of Fillmore and Eddy Streets.

The patrolman shook his head gravely.

Tina Gone was having none of it.

She pushed past the patrolman and broke into a run. Nash told himself that he had no choice, he couldn't let Tina Gone go alone. If things got out of hand, he'd carry her out bodily. *Bodily?* If the situation had been less grim Nash would've laughed out loud. He couldn't move his right arm. Could he even protect himself?

He had a firearm, at least.

Tina Gone jogged in her boots down the middle of Fillmore Street, looking left and right. She knew what she was looking for. Nash followed behind, his injured arm throbbing with every footfall. Nash saw figures huddled in dark doorways, the glow of cigarette hot ash, the clatter of empty beer cans kicked lazily into the street. Nash studied the street lights in the distance, the corner of Fillmore and Eddy. The gathering crowd, shapeless in the fog. Nash knew what the mob could do if it chose to. He was sure the wrong choice had already been made.

Maybe it was time to retreat.

Maybe it was too late.

The tension in the air only grew tighter, a knot in Nash's stomach. Nash thought of a photograph he'd seen in the *Chronicle* that morning. Two Negro men, fearful and weary, escaping from a cloud of police tear gas during a race riot in Cleveland. On the same newspaper page, a photograph of American forces in battle in Quang Tri Province, South Vietnam. The weary, fearful look on the faces of the two US Army soldiers, one Negro and one white, framed by twisting trails of smoke from exploding mortar rounds. Maybe the steel helmets that kept the rain of shit off the soldiers' necks were the only significant difference between the two fights. For all of them, every day was a battle. Against people they didn't know, and for reasons that shouldn't have existed.

Tina Gone slowed down and Nash fell in beside her as shadowy figures moved, from doorways into the street. Tina Gone studied the rows of parked cars. She explained again that Rollo hadn't liked to be away from his son for long. "Rollo took him everywhere, he found young girls to babysit. Girls he picked up in Haight-Ashbury."

The fog seemed to congeal ahead of Nash and Tina Gone as they turned into O'Farrell Street. Halfway down the block she pointed to a red and white Volkswagen microbus with skylight windows. The vehicle was parked on the north side of O'Farrell, under the glow of a street light.

A softer light glowed inside the vehicle.

Nash studied the shadows on the street for signs of an immediate threat while Tina Gone knocked hard on the sliding door at the side of the vehicle. A young woman, sitting on a bench seat inside the Volkswagen, looked up with a start. The girl's expression changed when Tina Gone mentioned Jasper Rollo. Nash wasn't sure, but the girl might have been the same one Nash had seen at Rollo's pad on Wednesday, painting her toenails.

The girl leaned over, unlocked the side door. Nash slid the door open. The interior of the microbus smelled of cigarette smoke and pistachio nuts. A two-year-old boy climbed around the girl's legs. He pointed and squealed in delight at the two figures standing in the vehicle's doorway.

Gently the girl took hold of the boy's arm to keep him from stumbling forward, falling out of the microbus.

The boy's name was Ringo.

From Fillmore Street came the sounds of breaking glass. The city was dark and in motion, the shadows on the street moving crabwise. Nash heard a sharp explosive noise and turned to look. The police were arrayed against their own children now, and the path to victory was skewed, a fun house mirror. Nash wondered when the mirror would shatter under its own weight, or the weight of pounding fists. To reveal another warped mirror, and another. And all the others, further still.

ROY CHANEY'S FIRST novel, *The Ragged End of Nowhere*, won the Tony Hillerman Prize for best debut mystery set in the American Southwest. He has worked as a military journalist, photographer, newspaper editor, investigator, and auditor. A native of Seattle, Washington, he currently resides in Kansas City, Missouri.